"GET IN!"

It was one too many shocks and I couldn't think. Frozen with one leg in the car, my hand on the door, and my butt almost on the seat, I said, "Is that pepper spray?" I accidentally sprayed my boyfriend in the eyes once. I didn't want to experience that myself.

"Oven cleaner. It was all I could think of to make you listen to me."

I blinked, getting a cramp from my position. "You bought that oven cleaner just now?"

"Do you have any idea the damage this stuff would do to your eyes, nose, and mouth? You'd be screaming in agony. Then there's the permanent damage it could do to your respiratory system and your lungs."

I held up my hand, stopping him. "Will you really spray that at me if I don't get in the car?"

His blue eyes blinked behind the wire-framed glasses. He wasn't clinking his keys or his change now. "I'm desperate."

I could see that. I got in the car. It seemed a better choice than a face full of oven cleaner. Closing the door, I looked at him and realized the truth of the situation.

Damn it, I was being kidnapped by a geek.

<u>BOOK YOUR PLACE ON OUR WEBSITE</u>
<u>AND MAKE THE</u>
<u>READING CONNECTION!</u>

We've created a customized website just for our very special readers, where you can get the inside scoop on everything that's going on with Zebra, Pinnacle and Kensington books.

When you come online, you'll have the exciting opportunity to:

- View covers of upcoming books
- Read sample chapters
- Learn about our future publishing schedule (listed by publication month *and author*)
- Find out when your favorite authors will be visiting a city near you
- Search for and order backlist books from our online catalog
- Check out author bios and background information
- Send e-mail to your favorite authors
- Meet the Kensington staff online
- Join us in weekly chats with authors, readers and other guests
- Get writing guidelines
- AND MUCH MORE!

Visit our website at
http://www.kensingtonbooks.com

A Samantha Shaw Mystery

DYING TO MEET YOU

Jennifer Apodaca

KENSINGTON BOOKS
Kensington Publishing Corp.
http://www.kensingtonbooks.com

To my husband, Dan Apodaca:

For making my dream our dream.
For all the work and talent that you generously pour
into these books.
For being my true Heart Mate.

I love you.

ACKNOWLEDGMENTS

I'd like to thank the Lake Elsinore Police and Sheriff Department for graciously showing me around the facility and answering all my questions. And for their good-natured acceptance that The Samantha Shaw Mystery Series is not meant to reflect the excellent work the police and sheriff's department does in "real life."

I'd like to thank my sister, Carol Raney. An avid reader practically from the day she was born, I rely on her finely honed instincts and gentle honesty to help shape each book. I wish to thank my brother-in-law, Steve Raney, for being my appointed weapon's expert and classic muscle-car guru.

Finally and with great gratitude, I'd like to thank my editor, Amy Garvey, for her support and vision of this series. I couldn't have done it without you, Amy!

1

My idea of a breakfast meeting sat on the red vinyl passenger seat of my 1957 classic Thunderbird as I drove through the small Southern California town of Lake Elsinore. The smell of the cream cheese–filled muffins made my stomach growl. I tried not to think about what those muffins would do to my thighs. The memory of my years as a soccer mom in stretch shorts and tent dresses momentarily killed my hunger. But I'm no longer that woman. Besides, the workout of driving my T-bird without power steering or brakes would make up for the muffin calories.

In my new role as a mentor, I was helping Faye Miller to launch her business, *Faye's Printing and Design,* by having her design and print advertising brochures for my dating service. I had a cool slogan—*Get Hot With Heart Mates.* I'd bought Heart Mates after my husband died of a peanut allergy as a tribute to our love since we had met there. Then I discovered that I had been married for thirteen years to a panty-collecting drug dealer who got himself murdered by one of his mistresses. Oh, and he'd planned to run out on our two sons and me with a half-million dollars of stolen drug money.

That's when I turned my back on happily-ever-afters for myself and instead concentrated on finding happiness for my clients.

Love was my business, and I meant to make Heart Mates into the most successful dating service in Southern California. Which was why I hoped the brochure Faye designed would bring me new clients. Right now, Heart Mates was a small, two-person operation. Actually, coming up with the money to pay the phone bill and the lease on my office suite was a monthly adventure.

Pulling the T-bird into the Night Haven Motel, I longed for a cup of the hot coffee Faye had promised to have ready in her room. Having left her husband a while back, Faye lived in the motel but planned to move to an apartment soon. I passed by the small rental office and strained to see the numbers on the bright teal doors set into textured terra-cotta walls. They began with 100. I spotted Faye's room, 120, at the end of the row and closest to the Fifteen Freeway. The tightly closed, heavy blackout drapes probably helped to block out the constant roar from the freeway traffic. The Night Haven Motel was situated in the south end of Lake Elsinore, close to the upscale gated community of Canyon Lake and surrounded by fast food, car dealers and other assorted businesses.

Parking the car next to Faye's eye-catching purple Volkswagen Beetle, I grabbed the bag of muffins and my purse. The foggy morning air instantly undid the twenty minutes I'd spent with anti-frizz gel and a blow dryer this morning. I could almost feel my blond-streaked hair going into frizz spasms, but for once I didn't care. Excitement danced in my stomach. Today was another step in the road to my dream. Turning Heart Mates into a success. Despite a few setbacks, my determination to succeed never wavered.

I looked down to double-check my mentor outfit, brown leather pants topped by a white stretchy silk shirt that crisscrossed over my breasts. I'd had my breasts enhanced after my husband died, shocking the entire world of PTA and soccer moms that I had once belonged to. But one thing I'd learned, I would rather have them talking about the choices I'd made than the stuff my panty-chasing husband did behind my back. Satisfied with my choice, I walked on my sling-back heels to knock on Faye's door.

I hoped she had the coffee brewed and ready. My stomach growled impatiently. I knocked again, listening. I thought I heard the voices of one of those network morning news shows over the constant reverberation of the traffic. If Faye was in the bathroom and listening to the TV, she might not hear me.

I could go back to my car, scarf down both muffins and then come back to knock when Faye could hear me. My mouth liked that idea, but I had promised Faye I'd bring breakfast.

I knocked again, pounding harder on the door. There were few cars in the parking lot, so bothering others didn't worry me. The sound of cars whipping by on the freeway muffled noises inside the room, but I knew I heard faint TV voices. Shifting the muffin bag, I reached out and turned the knob.

Locked. Motels had those automatic door locks that engaged when the door closed and required a key card. Chewing on my lip, I debated my options. Would she hear the phone over the noise? Shifting my big leather purse, I dug inside for my cell phone.

"Locked out?"

Surprised, I looked up at a woman in a pink maid uniform. "Uh, yes, can you open the door for me?" It was only a little lie since Faye expected me, and besides, I was hungry.

The maid smiled and pulled a master key card out of her pink pocket—the card was attached to one of those phone cord things. A silver clip kept it latched firmly on her pocket. "It happens all the time," she said as she slipped the card into the lock unit. She turned the knob and the door opened. "You probably didn't even realize you'd forgotten your card when you ran out to grab some breakfast." She dropped her eyes to the white bag in my hand.

"Thanks." Giving her what I thought passed for an embarrassed smile, I fled inside the door and quickly closed it, then leaned back on the cool wood.

Guilt and pride had me breathing hard. Dang, that was pretty cool and I didn't even need those slick tools that my private-eye boyfriend had. Of course, I wasn't really breaking in.

The roar of the freeway was muffled now, and I could clearly hear the TV. "Faye?" With only the light from the flickering TV screen, I looked around the standard room. On my left was a dresser holding the TV and empty coffee-maker.

Damn, no coffee. That was a disappointment.

Gazing over the small dressing area, closed bathroom door, double bed covered in a green spread, small nightstand with a lamp, clock radio, phone and paperback book, I looked to my far right and yelped in surprise.

In the shadowy light from the TV, I stared at Faye slumped over a small round table in the middle of computer equipment. In her outstretched hand, I caught sight of the bright blue-and-poppy brochure. It took me a second to realize that Faye was sound asleep. She must have worked a good part of the night on the brochure and fallen asleep.

Obviously exhausted, and with the background noise of the freeway traffic and TV, it was easy to understand why she didn't hear me knocking. I didn't want to scare her. Going a couple steps to the coffeemaker, I looked up into the mirror. "Faye, wake up. You must have worked all night." I dropped my gaze to look for a can of coffee. I didn't see one.

"Faye, where's your coffee grounds? I'll get some started . . ." I lifted my gaze to the mirror and froze.

Faye hadn't moved.

"Oh, God." Turning around from the mirror, I looked at Faye's still form. Her thick chestnut hair fell in straight, layered clumps to cover her face. The glossy brochure stuck up like a flag in her loose fingers. "Faye? Wake up!"

Asleep. She had to be asleep. I've done a little private detective work, so I knew these things. "Please, God, let her be asleep." My heart whacked unevenly against my rib cage as a bunch of thoughts slammed into my brain. Pushing my purse back behind my right hip, I walked a couple of steps back to the door and flipped the light switch.

The overhead light flooded the room. I couldn't see her face beneath her hair. "Faye? It's Sam." I had to force my feet, stuffed into high heels, to walk around the table toward her. Part of my mind detached and measured the steps I took. Three small steps from the light switch to the edge of the bed. "Remember, Faye, I'm here to look at the brochure you are making for Heart Mates?"

Two more steps. I could touch her. I had to touch her. Wake her up. "Faye?" I stuck out my hand and touched her hair.

She didn't move. *Oh, God.* Wait, I had seen dead people before. She didn't look dead. Not that I could see her face covered in all that hair. Normally, I envied Faye her Jennifer Aniston hair, but now it looked limp and tangled. She wore blue checked sweatpants and a matching crop top. Had she been exercising? Faye was into jump rope to try and slim down what she called her big-boned frame. What if she overdid the exercise and passed out? I looked at her back covered in the blue checks for any signs of respiration.

No movement.

Was she holding her breath? That didn't make sense. What should I do? Closing my eyes, I desperately wished I were anywhere but here. "Please, God, let her be all right. Just asleep. Even a little bit sick. Sick's okay. I know how to do sick, God. You remember how many times my two boys got sick, right, God? I did okay with that, so I can deal with sick."

I opened my eyes. She still wasn't moving. Taking one more step, I crouched down beside the chair. Faye's stomach rested against the edge of the table with her head lying on her sprawled arms. If she was asleep, she was going to have a sore neck and a backache.

I had to know. I had to. The fear seeped out as the need to help Faye took over. Considering myself her mentor meant I had to help her. Carefully, I reached up from my crouching position and put my hand around her bare upper right arm.

It felt like the cool plastic arm of a doll. Not real. Yanking my hand back, I clamped my jaw together on a panicked scream. My thighs quivered in my crouched position, and I tried to get my balance on my sling-back heels. At the same time, Faye must have woken up because she moved.

Startled, I jerked and fell backward. Instinctively flinging my hands out behind me, I got my wrists entangled in the strap of my purse. My back hit the carpet just as Faye slid off the chair and fell on top of me. Hard.

My chest hollowed. I couldn't breathe. I stretched my mouth wide, desperately trying to suck in air. A chunk of chestnut hair fell into my mouth while my paralyzed lungs refused to work. Faye was a dead weight on top of me.

Dead! I knew she was dead.

Suddenly my chest unlocked and I could breathe. Gulping a lungful of air, the horrible panic swelled as my brain regained enough oxygen to realize that Faye was not breathing, had not taken a single breath since I'd been in the room. She was dead and sprawled on top of me. Taller and heavier, Faye had landed on me slightly crossways, so that her head lodged under the bed frame, and jammed her right shoulder up beneath my chin.

I tried slipping out from under her but there was no room to escape. With the bed on my right and the legs from the table and chairs on my left, plus assorted computer equipment, I was trapped.

Trapped beneath a dead woman. Panting in fear, my ears rang and black spots danced in front of my eyes. I did manage to get my left hand free to reach up over Faye's shoulder and yank the hair out of my mouth.

A dead woman's hair. Almost gagging, I wondered why these things don't happen to other people. I had to calm down. *Had to.* I had two sons to think of. I could not die of fright beneath a body. Maybe I should scream? But the TV was still on, and the freeway traffic—

My cell phone! It was in my purse. My purse was stretched from my right shoulder, beneath my back to my left side. Using that hand, I dug around to get out the cell phone.

"Don't think about Faye." I talked out loud, trying to

keep calm. My hand closed around the cool plastic phone. I had to yank my shoulder far up into the socket to pull the phone out of my purse. Bending my elbow, I pushed my chin down into Faye's shoulder to see the numbers on the phone.

So far so good. I could dial, then get the phone close enough to my mouth to yell. But whom did I call? What choice did I have? I dialed 911.

Hearing a ringing, I bent my arm to get the phone as close to my mouth as I could. My breathing sounded like a woman in the throes of childbirth. Hysteria crawled around in my head, chanting—*you're trapped beneath a dead woman.*

A voice came out of the phone. "911. What's your emergency?"

I stared at the black phone, took a breath and told them. "Help! A dead body's fallen on me and I can't get up!"

Someone had ushered me into the empty motel room next door to Faye's room. A cup of cold coffee sat in front of me on the round table. Perched on a copy of the chair I'd found Faye in, I tore my gaze away from the window framing the flashing red-and-blue lights in the parking lot to look at the man who stood in the doorway.

He stepped inside. "You must be Samantha Shaw."

Except for the suit and tie, the man looked like he belonged in a lifeguard tower on the nearest beach. Close-cropped blond hair, square face with a strong chin, Ray-Ban sunglasses and a set of powerful swimmer shoulders beneath the jacket. "Who are you?"

Pulling out the chair opposite me, he swung it around to straddle it. "Detective Logan Vance." Sliding off his sunglasses, he fixed his light-brown eyes on me. "I re-placed Detective Rossi."

Uh-oh. I had a little history with the Lake Elsinore po-lice and sheriff's department. One of their detectives, who had been investigating some missing drug money connected to my dead husband and my dating service, ended up dead. Actually, I sort of set him on fire. I still had nightmares about it. The police in Lake Elsinore were a good sort for the most part, but having one of their own exposed as corrupt by me was a sore point. But that wasn't important right now. "What happened to Faye?" I still couldn't believe she was dead.

"She was murdered. What I want to know from you is what you were doing here this morning?"

I blinked, trying to order my thoughts. "Faye was start-ing a business doing some advertising brochures and other printing services. She had a sample brochure for my dating service, Heart Mates, and we were going to review it over breakfast before I went to work." God, I had thought of her as my protégée and now she was dead. I just couldn't accept it.

"I see. So that was the brochure she had in her hand?"

My throat ached. It was hard to force the words out. "I didn't actually read it, but I assume it was. I was Faye's first client. She considered me kind of a mentor."

He took out a small spiral notebook and flipped pages with concentration. "So you knew her well?"

It was hard to think. "Not real well. More like I was getting to know her."

Looking up from the pages of his notebook, he fixed a hard stare on me. "You just said you were her mentor. That implies a certain closeness, doesn't it?"

I squeezed my eyes shut. Why did it feel like he was attacking me? "All I can tell you is that Faye and I were becoming friends and that she told me she was trying to fix her life. She knew about me from the newspapers, which is what brought her to my dating service in the first place."

"Ah, yes. I've read all about you in the papers, Ms. Shaw. And then, not six weeks on the job here in Lake Elsinore, I find you trapped beneath a dead body. Sort of makes me wonder how it is you keep finding yourself involved with murders."

I snapped my eyes open. My heart rate picked up, creating a hum in my ears. "You can't think I had anything to do with Faye's murder! Her body was cold when I . . ." The words died in my throat. I couldn't say it.

Watching me closely, he said, "As a matter of fact, we believe she's been dead for hours, probably since last night or early this morning."

Today was Tuesday, so Faye died on either Monday night or early this morning. She had been here, living her life, then just . . . gone. "Oh, God, poor Faye." Turning the paper cup of room-temperature coffee around and around on the table, I swallowed before asking the next question. "How? How did she die?"

"There'll be an autopsy, but it looks like strangulation."

I had wondered if Faye had been exercising—her hair had that sweaty, tangled look—but more than likely, she'd been trying to fight off her murderer. Tears filled my eyes and I looked away, back out the window to the parking lot filled with police cars and a coroner's van. The fire trucks and ambulance had already left. Using the back of my hand, I wiped the tears off my face.

"I have a few more questions, Ms. Shaw."

"Sam. Call me Sam." Cops and other people were moving back and forth across the parking lot, looking purposeful.

"Okay, Sam, where were you last night and this morning? Please just walk me through getting home last night from work until you arrived here this morning."

Details. I could think about details. Staring out the window, I ran it down for him. "I got home about five last night. My two boys were home and so was Grandpa. We live with Grandpa."

"Their names and ages?"

"Grandpa's name is Barney Webb and he's about seventy-two. My oldest son is TJ for Trent Junior Shaw; he's just turned fourteen. My youngest son, Joel Shaw, is twelve. Once I got home, we all cooked dinner, then did homework and watched TV. After the kids went to bed, I did some work, then went to bed about eleven."

"What kind of work? For your dating service?"

His tone had gone back to hard suspicion. What was wrong with this guy? I turned to look at him. Not many people knew about this part of my life, but I saw no reason not to tell him. "Actually, I write critiques on romance novels for a monthly magazine."

"Romances? Like bodice rippers?" Disdain rolled through each word.

So he was one of those. The kind of man threatened by romances. Afraid he couldn't live up to the heroes in the books. These guys just didn't get it—the books were simply fantasy. I was too tired and sick about Faye to deal with his insecurities. "Tell it to your shrink, Detective. I'm not going to defend what I do to you or your fragile ego."

To my surprise, a wicked smile curved his full mouth. His flat cheeks dimpled, and suddenly I could see him out on the beach, or maybe on a boat. Possibly even as a hero-hunk on a book cover. "Remind me not to criticize your reading choices."

"Count on it." I was more bluff than substance now. I couldn't pin this guy down.

He bent his head and wrote in his notebook. "So after you finished working on your"—he looked up at me—"critique, you went to bed? Did anyone see you when you got up this morning?"

"My kids and Grandpa. I made the kids breakfast, packed their lunches and Grandpa took them to school about seven-twenty. I left about ten minutes after that and went by the donut shop, then arrived here."

"Which donut shop? Will anyone there remember you?"

I had the weird feeling that I was stuck in one of those TV detective shows. "Donut Bliss on Lakeshore Drive. Ling is the owner and will probably remember me. Our kids played soccer together."

"Then you brought the white bag on the dresser in Ms. Miller's room?"

My stomach clenched and rolled over queasily at the thought of those cream cheese–filled muffins. "Yeah, Faye was supposed to have the coffee ready."

"Faye went to your dating service, is that correct?"

"Yes, like I already said, she read about me in the newspaper when she split up with her husband. She dated a couple of men we set her up with. Her ex-husband made it hard to find a date for her at first."

"Her ex-husband?" He referred to his notebook again, flipping pages until he found the one he wanted. "That would be Adam Miller? What did he do?"

It looked like Detective Vance wasted no time getting his facts on Faye. "That's him. He didn't like her dating at Heart Mates. Faye's profile on our computer system was tampered with. She was convinced Adam did it."

"Tampered with how?" His brown eyes narrowed as he listened and wrote notes.

"He changed her into a fat woman with gray hair, yellow teeth, and a hobby of growing a cockroach colony.

My assistant probably kept a copy of the changed profile in our files."

"And why did she think her ex-husband did that?"

I shrugged. "Well, you know, divorces are like that. Plus
he's supposed to be some kind of computer genius. From
what Faye said, he's a real nerd."

"How did he get into your computer files? Was there
a break-in? Did you report it?"

I shook my head. "We never really knew how it was
done. I can't even say for sure that Faye's ex-husband did
it. Only her files were tampered with. We changed them
back and never had another problem, so we let it go."

"Okay." Tapping his pen on the notebook, Detective
Vance fixed his full attention on me. "I'm going to need
the names and addresses of the men Ms. Miller dated, the
information you have on her files that were tampered
with and any information you have on her ex-husband.
I'll come by your office to pick those up as soon as I'm
done here."

I briefly considered my obligations to Faye, and to my
clients. Faye was dead, but the men she dated were alive.
Didn't I owe them privacy?

Vance leaned across the table, his light-brown gaze
fixed on me. "I can get a court order for your records,
Sam."

He had a point. "I'll get you the information."

Nodding as if this were no more than he expected,
he sat back in his chair. "One more question. Why did
you trick the maid into letting you into Faye's room?"

Under the circumstances, I now saw how unwise that
had been. "I didn't trick her. Faye wasn't answering her
door and I was standing there thinking about calling
her on my cell phone when the maid came by and assumed I had locked myself out." Shrugging, I said, "I let
her believe that."

"Convenient." He wrote in his spiral notebook.

I began to hate that little book. "Look, Detective, I thought Faye couldn't hear me. From outside her door, I heard her TV, and then there's the freeway traffic. I had no idea that she was dead." I couldn't get used to the idea.

He closed his notebook and slipped it into the breast pocket of his shirt. Leaning forward, he studied me. "Thing is, Sam, I know about you. You have a tendency to stick your nose where it doesn't belong, and you have an uncommon knack for trouble."

Those things might be true. "So?"

"I'm warning you, Sam Shaw. Stay out of my way and out of my investigation. I'm not Detective Rossi and likely to be swayed by your"—his gaze rolled down to my chest—"charms."

Was this a cop thing? Did Detective Logan Vance hate me because I'd exposed Rossi as a bad cop, then killed him in self-defense? Drawing myself up in my chair, I stiffened my backbone against the memories. I intended to set the record straight. "Rossi was going to kill me, Detective."

His face relaxed as he brought his gaze back up to my face. "Yes, I think maybe you could bring that out in a man."

2

Heart Mates was in a suite carved out of a run-down strip mall sitting on Mission Trail Drive in Lake Elsinore, California. It wasn't much, but it was mine. A solid comfort to me and proof that life goes on. After leaving the motel, I drove straight to work. Parking the car, I got out feeling ten years older than my thirty-some years and dragged myself inside.

"You're late, Boss."

Blaine, my scolding assistant, sat behind his desk and munched on some sort of greasy breakfast burrito while tapping the keys of the computer. When I didn't answer, Blaine looked up over the monitor at me. "Boss? What's the matter?"

I set my purse down and walked two steps to the coffee-maker resting on a TV tray at the edge of Blaine's desk. I picked up my white mug stamped with pink hearts and peered inside it. Had I cleaned it out last night? Shrugging, I poured coffee into it, then looked at Blaine. "Faye's dead."

Blaine dropped his burrito on the white bag spread

out on his desk. He brushed a thick hand through his brown, feathered hair and automatically checked the ponytail at the back of his neck. His chest expanded beneath his blue work shirt—Blaine always wore Levi's and a blue work shirt reminiscent of his days as a mechanic. "Faye Miller? The Faye you had a meeting with this morning about the advertising brochures?"

"That's the one." I took a sip of the strong black coffee and looked up at the water-stained ceiling tiles. The need to cry ambushed me. I fought it. I had to gather the information that Detective Vance wanted. Looking around the small reception area that consisted of a few folding chairs with another TV tray holding magazines, I tried to organize my head. "The detective will be here soon. He wants a list of the men Faye dated through Heart Mates and a copy of her files. He also wants anything we have from when Faye's profile on the computer was changed."

"I can get all that, Boss, but what happened? How did Faye die? If a detective is involved, they must suspect murder."

"She was murdered. Strangled. I found her this morning at her motel." Gritting my teeth, I willed away the memory of Faye slumped over the table.

"You found her? Inside her room?"

"Actually, she fell on me."

Blaine's face shifted, his brown eyes narrowing. "Fell on you? Boss, what did you do?"

"What's that supposed to mean?" I grabbed my purse off the corner of his desk. "It was an accident. It could have happened to anyone!"

Blaine regarded me calmly. "Could have, but it usually happens to you."

"I'll be in my office when the detective shows up!" I turned around and stormed across the threadbare carpet to the cubicle that divided the front of the suite in half, giving me the illusion of an office. Going inside, I slammed the door, went around my desk and dumped my purse into the bottom drawer of the oak desk that used to be in my house. The house was gone and the oak desk barely fit into the small office. Sinking down into my chair, I picked up my mug of coffee.

The phone rang, startling me into sloshing coffee down the front of my white shirt. "Shit." Grabbing the shirt on either side of the deep V, I yanked the hot fabric away from my skin.

"Line one for you, Boss!"

That was the trouble with cubicles—since the walls did not go all the way up to the ceiling, Blaine and I just hollered back and forth over the blue-specked divider. Letting go of my shirt, I took a handful of tissues from the box on my desk and dabbed at my cleavage and shirt. "Who is it?"

"Your mom."

"Oh, hell, what next?" I stared down at my chest. It was hopeless. It looked like I had dipped both my breasts into a vat of coffee. "Tell her I'm out of the office."

"Sure thing, Boss."

I held my breath and stared at the light on the phone indicating a line was in use. I heaved a big sigh when the light went out. I picked up the phone and dialed my best friend, Angel. She would understand how terrible this was. Angel and I had been friends since high school. We'd made a pact after my husband had died—since we'd both picked losers in men, we were going to focus on our careers. We were going to find the one thing we'd wanted to do most in the world. I'd found mine in Heart Mates. Angel was still looking for hers. Holding a job wasn't one of Angel's strong points.

I hung up when her answering machine came on. A

murder wasn't exactly the kind of thing I wanted to talk over with a machine. Nor did I want to call her cell phone. I didn't want to talk about this while Angel was getting a pedicure. Better to wait.

"Boss." Blaine opened my office door and came in holding a stack of papers. He stopped in the doorway. "Did you have that big stain all over your shirt when you came in?"

I ignored the question. "Those the files on Faye? That was fast."

"We're in the computer age, Sam. All you do is pull up the file and print it. It's not difficult. Oh, by the way, your mother said that news of Faye's murder is all over town."

That didn't surprise me. Small-town news traveled fast though a gossip vine that would impress the hell out of the FBI and the CIA. "She say anything else?"

"We're talking about your mother."

"Sorry, what else did she say?"

"That Faye's ex-husband killed her because she came to Heart Mates. Oh, and your mom will be here in half an hour."

I leaped up from my desk. "Here? She's coming *here*?"

Amusement twinkled in his brown eyes. "Yes, right after she talks to her boss about getting you a temporary job answering phones at her real estate office while you work on getting your real estate license."

Yanking open my desk drawer, I leaned down and snatched up my purse. I needed to change out of my coffee-stained shirt, and more importantly, I needed to avoid my mother. Priorities were everything. "Tell her that I'm going to be out of the office all day. Tell her anything!" I went around the desk. "Oh, and give those copies to the detective when he gets here." I pointed at the papers in Blaine's hand, then went to the front door.

When I turned around to ask if there was anything else before I left, Blaine held out the top half of the stack of papers he'd copied.

Baffled, I took the papers. "What are these for?"

He grinned. "Copies. A lot of people in town are under the impression that you do private investigating on the side. Little things like not having a license doesn't change their opinion."

Flushing, I remembered Detective Vance's odd warning about staying out of his investigation. Although it was true that I had gotten involved in some private investigations, I didn't think Vance would tolerate me getting involved in this. I held the papers away from my wet chest. "I'm not getting involved. I'll leave these on your desk."

The front door opened before I set the papers down. Turning, I saw Detective Vance walk in. "Going someplace, Sam?"

Hugging the papers to my chest to cover the stain, I tried to look confident. "I'm going home. My assistant has the information you requested." Still hoping to avoid my mother, as well as not letting Vance see that I had spilled coffee all over myself, I tried to slip out the door.

A strong hand caught my arm. I glanced down to see long, tanned fingers curled around my biceps. "You wouldn't be thinking of getting involved and mucking up my investigation, would you?"

I glared into his brown eyes. What did he see when he looked at me? What exactly did he know about me? He was intense, and damn it, good-looking. Good-looking men were always trouble. Fixing a smile on my face, I asked, "Why? Do you need my help to do your job?"

His firm mouth fell open, the grip on my arm loosened and I made my escape.

* * *

I got in my car, started it and wondered what would go wrong next. Turning left on Mission Trail, I was heading home to change my coffee-stained shirt when I remembered dog food.

Dang, I smacked my hand on the steering wheel of my T-bird. The echo of my son's voice rambled in my head. *"Mom, we're out of dog food! I'm giving Ali Shredded Wheat instead!"*

Once upon a time, I would not have run out of dog food. Of course, we hadn't had a dog. My husband, Trent, wouldn't hear of a dog messing up our house.

Breezing down Lakeshore Drive, past the lake famous for spawning algae and fish kills during the hot summer months, I made a mental list. Dog food and, hmm, whatever else I remembered when I got in the store.

With my shopping list firmly in my head, I turned right into the supermarket parking lot. We now had two supermarkets on the north side of the lake. I still shopped at the original one, a Stater Bros. Old habits die hard, I supposed. Parking my car, I got out and remembered the coffee stain on my chest.

Okay, it's noon on Tuesday, a workday. I'm not likely to run into anyone I know. Grabbing a cart, I headed into the store and right down the pet aisle to stare at the array of pet items.

What did I need again? I was having trouble focusing. Getting trapped beneath a dead friend was hell on my concentration.

The metallic click of jangling keys caught my attention. I turned from the selection of gerbil food and toys to see a tall, thin man standing next to me. His bony shoulders were hunched beneath a plaid shirt and he had both hands stuffed in the pockets of his baggy tan Dockers. He was fidgeting either with his keys or with the loose change in his pockets.

Feeling his stare, I looked up. His hair stood on end like a porcupine dipped in coppery red paint. Deep blue eyes contrasted sharply in his pale, freckled face. He angled his head down to stare over his wire-rimmed glasses. "Are you Samantha Shaw?"

The keys or change in his pocket kept up a steady clatter.

"Uh, yes." Who was he? Maybe a potential client who was afraid to come to the office? I ran my professional gaze over him. His plaid shirt was wrinkled with the last button undone. Pants were in same condition. Shoes—oh, my God—were those Velcro tennis shoes? Did they sell Velcro shoes for anyone over six? This poor guy screamed geek. I fixed a smile on my face. "Can I help you?" I didn't normally conduct business in the pet-supply section of the grocery store, but hey, I needed clients.

He used a hand to push his glasses back up his nose. "I hope so. You're the only person I could think of."

The continuous clanking in his pocket hurt my teeth. I forced the smile to stay on my face. "I see. Perhaps you are interested in my dating service, Heart Mates?"

"No. I—" He looked away. His Adam's apple bobbed up and down in his throat. "I want to hire you."

"Hire? Do you mean hire my dating service?" I couldn't quite understand what he wanted. He appeared distraught. Possibly he was lacking in social skills. That jangling alone would deter women from getting to know him. And those Velcro shoes!

"No, hire *you*. I know you know how to find out stuff. Your boyfriend's a private investigator."

This guy knew way too much about me. Alarm traveled up my spine and tightened my shoulders. I glanced around the store. We were alone in the pet-food aisle. I could hear the squeaky sounds of a few carts mixed with the piped-in music. Clutching my purse tighter, I stuck my hand in to search for my keys. I had a little can of defense spray on the key ring. Unable to find the key chain quickly, I stalled. "Who are you? What exactly do you want?"

"It's all over town." He looked at his shoes and I could barely hear him over the jingling of his change or keys. "That you found her."

I shivered. "Who are you?" It was hard to force the words out.

He looked up. "I'm Adam Miller, Faye's husband. I didn't kill her, Samantha, and I need you to help me find out who did."

The tension in my shoulders shot up into my jaw, clenching my teeth. Forgetting about my key-chain defense spray, I stepped back and stared at him. Adam Miller? Faye's ex-husband? I read the newspapers, so I knew that when a woman is murdered, it's usually the boyfriend or husband.

Run! Escape! The two thoughts bounced around in my head like rubber balls. "Look, Mr. Miller, I'm sorry about your ex-wife, but . . ."

"Wife."

"Huh?"

"The divorce wasn't final. I was willing to give her what she wanted." His mouth trembled for a second. "I took her the divorce papers, but Faye didn't sign them."

"She didn't? But I thought—" My mind tried to sort it out, but suddenly all I could think about was Faye dead. This man might have killed her. "It doesn't matter, Mr. Miller. I can't help you. This is a matter for the police. If you didn't kill her, they will find out who did."

The jingling stopped and he pulled his hands out of his pockets. Stepping closer to me, he said, "No, they won't, because they're not going to look any further."

He stabbed his fingers through his spiky hair. "The police have already been looking for me."

Hot fear raced through me. Taking a deep breath, I tried to think. I had to calm him down, at least until I could get help. I tried to watch him while looking for another customer, checker or someone I could signal for help. "Okay, Mr. Miller, I see your point. But what you need is a real private detective, not me. I just do little things to help out friends. I can give you the names of a few people—"

"No! Faye told me all about you. She looked up to you and was trying to emulate you. She told me how you figured out who was behind the scheme to get the drug money your husband had stolen. You dealt with a bad cop. I need you to help me find who killed her." He stopped dragging his hand through his hair and looked at me. "You knew her, and you knew who she was dating."

Oh, God. What if Adam wanted the names of the guys Faye dated to kill them?

Or what if he didn't kill Faye? I did feel a responsibility to Faye. Mostly, I felt sick that she was dead.

I didn't know what to do. *Think!* "Umm, Mr. Miller, you see, I, that is, why don't you let me look into this and get back to you?" Yes! That could work. Convince him I would help and send him on his way. Then call the police on my cell phone.

He jerked his head, apparently looking around the grocery store. "That's not going to work. You have to help me. I—" His voice filled with frustration. "Faye was so good at the people stuff. She could read them, understand them." His gaze returned to my face. "Why don't you believe me?"

He sounded like one of my kids. "Look, Mr. Miller—Adam—I want to believe you. That's why I'm going to look into this and get back to you."

His thin shoulders slumped. Without a word, he turned and left.

I stared after him. Should I call the police? Detective Vance's warning to stay out of it came back to me. Chewing on my bottom lip, I struggled with what to do.

Dog food! That's what I came here to buy. It was not the answer that I was looking for, but it gave me something to do. I found a ten-pound bag of chow and hefted it into the shopping cart.

Nothing like a little weight lifting to help me think. I decided that I'd wait until I paid for the dog food and got out to my car, then I'd phone Detective Vance and let him know I had run into Adam Miller.

But what had Adam meant that the police were looking for him? Had they gone to his house? Had Adam been at his house when they got there? Or had he been somewhere else, like in hiding after murdering Faye? His clothes did look rumpled—maybe slept in?

The squeaky wheels of a shopping cart made me look up from the dog food I'd been staring at in my cart.

"Sam?"

Great. Jan Flynn. The perky town librarian. Her standard uniform consisted of soft pink jackets worn over long skirts, pearls around her neck. She always smelled like Jergens hand lotion. She read stories to the town children with hand puppets. She had a treasure chest by her desk for children to pick a toy out of for every five books they read.

Dead bodies did not fall on her.

"Hi, Jan. On your lunch break?"

"Oh, yes. I'm restocking my treasure chest. We've had a lot of readers this month."

I couldn't resist. "From the pet food aisle?"

She smiled. "Of course not! I'm getting some fish food while I'm out. Two birds with one stone and all that."

She rolled her cart down to the fish food. "Gotta run, Sam. Need to get back to the library. Oh, try some vinegar on that stain, unless it's blood, then you might want to try baking soda. . . ." Her voice faded away as she turned the corner.

I wondered if I had vinegar at home. Thank God it was only coffee and not blood on my shirt. I needed to get home. Heading for the checkout stand, I endured weird looks at my coffee-stained chest by a gum-chewing clerk, then left the cart and carried the dog food to my car. Deep in thought about calling Detective Vance, I stored the bag of food in the trunk.

Going around the car to my door, I stopped by the rear porthole in the hardtop of my T-bird. How had Adam Miller known I'd be at the store? I hadn't known I would be at the store until I remembered the dog food.

I shivered and searched the parking lot. It was pretty empty, revealing lots of potholes and oil stains. If he had been following me, he must be gone. Trying to shed my uneasiness, I opened my door and started to slide into the car when I saw Adam Miller sitting in the passenger seat. He had a can of something pointed at me. Pepper spray?

"Get in."

It was one too many shocks and I couldn't think. Frozen with one leg in the car, my hand on the door and my butt almost on the seat, I said, "Is that pepper spray?" I accidentally sprayed my boyfriend in the eyes once. I didn't think I wanted to experience that myself.

"Oven cleaner. It was all I could think of to make you listen to me."

I blinked, getting a cramp from my position. "You bought that oven cleaner just now?"

"Do you have any idea the damage this stuff would

do to your eyes, nose and mouth? You'd be screaming in agony. Then there's the permanent damage it could do to your respiratory system and your lungs."

I held up my hand, stopping him. "Will you really spray that at me if I don't get in the car?"

His blue eyes blinked behind the wire-framed glasses. He wasn't clinking his keys or change now. "I'm desperate."

I could see that. He twitched in the seat, sweat dotted his hairless lip and the hand holding the can of oven cleaner shook. But the finger on the spray nozzle of the cleaner was firm.

I got in the car. It seemed a better choice than a face full of oven cleaner. Closing the door, I looked at him and realized the truth of the situation.

Damn it, I was being kidnapped by a geek.

Gripping my keys in my hand, I wondered about my chances of squirting the small can of defense spray in Adam Miller's eyes before he doused me with the oven cleaner. It occurred to me that spraying the defense spray in the small space of the car might be risky.

Mixing it with Adam's oven cleaner sounded like a phone call to the poison-control center.

I didn't seem to have any other choice. Looking at Adam, I asked, "What now?"

His eyes, magnified behind his glasses, stared at me. "Drive. I want to show you something. Then you'll listen to me. You'll believe me."

I stuck the key in the ignition, started the car and backed it out of the space. "Adam." I kept my voice calm. "I'm not clear on what you want from me."

"I want you to find out who killed Faye. I'll pay you. Something was wrong in the last few days. She wouldn't tell me what, but she—"

He stopped talking, but the anger in his voice resonated through my chilled blood.

"Turn right on Lake Street."

I did that, then risked a glance at him. "Adam, are you blaming me for Faye's death? She had already left you when she came to my dating service." You never knew with some people.

"Blaming you?" His deep blue eyes furrowed in bewilderment. "I don't know what happened! She was thinking of coming back to me and now she's dead!"

Stopping at a red light, I realized I was holding my breath. "I'm sorry, Adam. It must be awful for you. But kidnapping me isn't—"

His head snapped up off the headrest and he waved the can at me. "The police think I did it. They were at my house this morning. I spent the night at a friend's. We heard about Faye, so I drove home and the police were there. I left before they saw me."

The light turned green, and I started across the intersection. "They probably just wanted to ask you some questions." Like why he had tampered with Faye's file at Heart Mates. I didn't think now was the time to mention that I'd told the police about that.

"I can't talk to the police. Not yet. I'm not good at talking. I won't be able to make them believe me. You won't even believe me and you knew Faye."

I glanced at the oven cleaner. He wasn't real adept at getting his point across. Part of me was starting to feel sorry for him. He had seemed distraught and upset in the grocery store. And when he couldn't make me understand what he wanted, he used oven cleaner to kidnap me. "Look, Adam, the police just want to ask you questions. You just tell them where you were—"

"You don't understand! I was there last night, at Faye's motel room. The police are going to think I did it."

Oh, God. Cold heat burst out of my pores. My heart raced in my chest and a low roar started in my ears. He could be the murderer. And I had stupidly gotten into the car with him.

"There. Turn right on that street."

I needed time to think and make a plan. I turned on the street. It was a low-income residential area that didn't have sidewalks. Some of the houses had fresh paint and nice lawns, while others boasted graffiti and weeds.

"Stop here."

I slowed the car. We were in front of a plain little house with a single cement step leading up to a gray door set in dirty stucco walls. The driveway had disintegrated to broken chunks of asphalt. "Here?" I looked around and didn't see anyone, but we were only a hundred yards from Lake Street.

"Yes. This is Mindy's house. She's got something I want to show you. Get out."

Okay. Now we were getting somewhere. Taking my keys out of the ignition, I got out of the car while situating the defense spray in my hand. As soon as I had the chance, I planned to zap Adam in the face, then run like hell for my car.

Would his glasses protect his eyes? Walking around the back of the car, I decided I'd angle up under his glasses. He met me at the trunk.

"Adam, where's the oven cleaner?" He didn't have it in his hand.

He stuck his hands in his pockets. The jingling started. "All I want you to do is see what I have to show you, and talk to you. I don't need the oven cleaner."

Guess I wasn't going to need my escape plan after all. I followed Adam up a strip of cracked sidewalk to the front door. A single pot with a cactus that had a purple bloom on it stood next to a push broom leaning up against the house.

Before we could knock, the door swung open and a small woman stood there. I immediately thought of a pixie. She had short black hair framing a pale face and electric-blue glasses that made her dark eyes pop out. Shorter than my five-foot-five, she had on her waitress uniform of denim shorts and burgundy T-shirt with BBQ SHACK stenciled across her thin chest. Her clunky boots made me think of Adam's Velcro tennis shoes.

"Adam, I'm glad you got here. Baby's agitated, and when Baby gets agitated so does Mom."

From the inside of the house, I heard the faint noise of a game show, mixed with intermittent yaps of a small dog.

"Told you on the phone I'd be here as soon as Samantha listened to reason."

I frowned at Adam. "When did you call her?"

He patted the lump in his plaid shirt pocket. "I used my cell phone while waiting for you in your car at the grocery store. Mindy didn't think the oven cleaner would work." Adam flashed his first small smile—it looked like the goofy grin of a golden retriever.

I couldn't see him as a murderer, but I was worried about him showing up where I happened to be in the grocery store. I wasn't a believer in coincidence. "How did you find me at the grocery store?"

The grin died. "I followed you. I knew the police would be around Heart Mates, so I waited until you got in your car and followed you. I had to talk to you." He turned from me. "Mindy, did you pick it up?"

She put her hands on her hips. "Not an *it*, a *she*, Adam. Did you tell her"—Mindy angled her head toward me—"about Faye deciding not to sign the divorce papers?"

Adam bounced on his Velcro shoes. "Told her the

police will think I did it. But you have the proof I didn't. Show her."

Mindy fixed her gaze on me. All eyes behind those large framed glasses, she said, "Adam didn't kill Faye. He loved Faye, loved her enough to give her the divorce she wanted if it made her happy. But Faye and Adam were spending time together, working on a website for her printing business, and when Adam took Faye the divorce papers last night, she didn't want to sign them. She wanted to stay as they were and keep working on herself and her life. Maybe get back with Adam, but first she had to work on herself."

I turned to look at Adam. He was still rocking on his feet, jangling his keys. "Why didn't you tell me that?" Why had he scared the hell out of me by just blurting out that he'd been at Faye's room last night and the police were after him?

"I thought I did. I said she didn't sign the divorce papers and that we were still married."

He was clueless. For all I knew, that had meant he killed Faye before she signed the papers. Mindy's version gave me a better picture of Faye and Adam rebuilding a broken relationship. Faye herself had told me that Adam was helping her with her website and some computer software. Giving up on Adam, I looked at Mindy.

"I'm still not sure what you want from me."

"Someone else killed Faye, and we have to make the police find out who it was." Mindy snapped her mouth together, her bottom lip quivered. The trembling spread to make her small chin wrinkle. Tears welled in her eyes and spilled down her face. "Faye's my best friend. We worked together at the BBQ Shack for almost six years before she quit. I can't believe she's dead."

Mindy didn't wail or whine. Her voice was soft and

feathery. Broken with grief. My own eyes burned. "I'm sorry, Mindy. I knew Faye too. It's all so awful."

Wiping her tears away, she nodded her head. "Adam said you found her this morning."

"Yes." I didn't want to think about it. I just wanted to go home, change clothes and . . . what? Forget that a friend of mine had been murdered?

Mindy turned her slight body and bent over, picking something up. When she stood, she was holding a small animal carrier-type cage. "Here she is, Adam. I picked her up this morning before . . . Oh, God, I don't know if I can go to work. Maybe Hal should just close the BBQ Shack today."

Adam took the carrier. "Thanks, Mindy. I—" His words broke off in a violent sneeze.

Mindy took the cage from him and held it out to me. "Here, you hold her. Adam's allergic. Besides, this is what he wanted to show you. This was his gift to Faye."

"Allergic to what?" Could this day get any stranger? I lifted the carrier and looked through the wire mesh. A tiny gray fur ball with slate-blue eyes stared back. "A kitten? How does a kitten prove you didn't kill Faye?"

Adam started to open his mouth to answer, then scrunched up his eyes behind his glasses and let out a string of sneezes.

Mindy answered, "He bought the kitten for Faye. She always wanted a cat, but Adam was too allergic to have one. He wouldn't go out and buy her a kitten, then kill her." She made the statement as if it explained everything.

Looking back at the carrier, I spotted the eyehook latch. Unlatching it, I reached inside just as the noise of the TV and yapping dog got louder.

"Oh, no!" Mindy tried swinging the door shut, but a small black poodle darted out, yapping and snarling.

"Ouch!" I yanked my hand out of the carrier, and the kitten came out too. Her sharp little claws attached her to my hand.

A new voice howled, "Baby! Baby! Baby!"

I dropped the carrier. "Ouch, get it off me!" I tried to grab the kitten, but the dog was hopping up and down at my legs like some kind of manic jack-in-the-box. Terrified, the kitten climbed up my arm and wrapped herself around my neck. It felt like a thousand needles were piercing my skin. Desperate, I danced around in circles, trying to get hold of the cat, while the damned dog jumped up and down and barked. Someone kept crying, "Baby! Baby! Baby!"

Adam's violent sneezing added to the racket.

"Mom! Get back in the house!" Mindy screamed.

"She's stealing my Baby! She's a Baby-stealer! I'll stop her!"

The cat arched up and hissed into my hair just as I came out of a desperate turn of trying to grab the animal off my neck.

That's when I saw a gray-haired old woman grab the push broom, swing it high over her head and advance on me.

"Mom, no!" Mindy bellowed.

I jumped back. Too late I remembered that I had been on a cement step. I flailed my arms desperately, catching a glimpse of three shocked faces staring at me before I landed flat on my back in the dirt.

Somehow, the kitten had managed to get off my neck and cling to the neckline of my shirt. It stood up on its spindly little legs, blue eyes staring at me.

Then it peed.

3

Finally home, I grabbed my purse and glared at the little gray kitten curled up in a ball on a bath towel. I'd broken the carrier cage when the kitten buried her claws in my hand and I flung the carrier onto the cement. The kitten had stayed attached to my hand. I wondered if I had a sign on my back that said "Sucker." Scooping up the towel and kitten, I didn't exactly remember agreeing to take the kitten. Somehow it had been decided for me since Adam was allergic and Baby—I shuddered remembering that poodle—hated kittens. No one said a word about Mindy's mother—and the fact that she was clearly deranged.

I do, however, remember agreeing to help Adam. The police and the whole town were likely going to leap to the conclusion that Adam Miller had killed his wife.

Once the town had leaped to conclusions about me. First they'd pegged me as the stay-at-home mom who didn't care that her husband was out doing anything with panties. Then, after Trent's death and I'd had my boobs done, shed a few pounds, along with yards of material on my skirts, the town tried again to peg me. Except that I was a work in progress and refused to be pegged. Now Adam was going to face that same small-town scrutiny with Faye's murder. I felt a kinship with him.

And having spent some time with Adam, it didn't take me long to understand Adam's problem—he was one of those computer geeks who had trouble communicating with people.

I went into the house. Actually, it was Grandpa's house. He'd built it thirty-some years ago on a plot of land in the middle of nowhere. Now, on this side of Grand Avenue there were custom homes, while the other side had tract homes and an elementary school. Closing the door behind me, I looked around.

Not exactly what one usually thinks of as a custom home. It was strictly one step up from the trailer that my mother grew up in on this very plot of land, although she tried to deny her poor beginning. My boys and I loved living in the small three-bedroom house with Grandpa. A sharp bark brought me out of my thoughts.

I slipped off my shoes and walked barefoot across the decades-old brown shag carpet to the dining room that was set in the corner of an inverted *L*. The carpet gave way to yellowed linoleum. Straight ahead, eighty pounds of highly agitated German shepherd stared at me from the other side of the sliding glass door.

The kitten started hissing and stretched her front claws over the edge of the towel to dig into my forearm. Grabbing her around the middle, I pulled her safely back onto the towel and looked at my dog on the other side of the slider. "Hold on, Ali."

Turning right, I walked through the kitchen and passed the refrigerator, where a quick right then left took me into the hallway. The boys' bedroom was on the right. I turned left into the bathroom the boys shared with

Grandpa. Pulling back the shower curtain, I set towel and kitten in the tub and shut the bathroom door.

Heading back to the kitchen, I tried to sort out what I needed to do. Swallow some Tylenol, take a bath, call Angel, and don't forget about the dog food in the trunk. . . .

I slammed into a wall of flesh. Hard male flesh.

"Babe."

His chest was covered in a white tank top stretched tight enough to reveal hard muscles. Swallowing, I looked up into a set of dark Italian eyes. "Gabe!" I paused to force air back into my panicky lungs. "You scared the daylights out of me! What are you doing here?" I reached out to grab hold of the counter to steady myself. Damn, wouldn't you know he'd show up when I looked like hell and smelled worse?

He ran his gaze over me. Then turned and went to the back door to let Ali in. She tore through the kitchen, skidded a left around the corner and went right for the bathroom where the cat was. I could hear her sniffing and whining at the closed door.

Gabe shut the back door, turned and gave me a look. I'd never seen him use that look on anyone else. He raised one winged brow higher than the other and his dark eyes narrowed, while his mouth thinned into a crooked line. That look pretty much said, *What the hell kind of trouble have you stumbled into this time?*

"I suppose you heard about Faye's murder." I went to the cupboard and pulled down a bottle of Tylenol.

"I heard. Word is that you found her."

I nodded and passed by him to get to the sink. He smelled shower fresh. Probably hadn't had a cat pee on him all day. God, could this day get any worse?

"Rough. But there's more. Want to tell me?"

I swallowed the Tylenol and faced him. Gabe was uncanny. I'd never met anyone like him. He had lived danger, knew it and understood it. He had been a cop in Los Angeles until a bullet to his knee forced him to take an early retirement. He'd moved out to Lake Elsinore and opened Pulizzi Security and Private Investigative Services. He knew things I could never hope to understand. We had a relationship that scared me to death. Gabe was a few years younger than I was, and I knew that one day he'd want to marry and have children.

I'd already been there, done that. Not even for hot, sexy Gabe would go I down that road again.

Avoiding his question just a little, I asked, "What makes you think that?"

His bad-boy grin rolled over his face, while his gaze slow-traveled over my coffee- and cat-pee-stained chest. "Any time you start ruining clothes and getting twigs in your hair"—he reached behind me and pulled out a toothpick-sized weed—"I know you're in trouble."

He had a point. I did have a bit of a pattern with that. He was close. Too close. "Uh, you might want to back up. I had a run-in with a kitten today. The kitten won."

He looked down at me with his intense dark-brown, almost black, eyes. At roughly six feet of two hundred rock-solid pounds, he towered over my five-foot-five in heels. "That explains the smell. Why were you wrestling kittens?"

Heat crawled up my face. "It's a long story and—"

He tossed the twig he had pulled from my hair into the sink and put both his hands on my shoulders. "This isn't going to be a normal story that an average woman would tell, is it? Like maybe you rescued a terrified kitten from a dog and the shaken kitten peed on you."

I shook my head, feeling my mouth twitch into a smile. "Normal stuff doesn't happen to me."

"Honey, stuff doesn't just happen to you. You have a gift for tripping over trouble."

Lifting my chin, I glared at him. "Yeah, well, I saved

your butt when you decided to play hero and ended up chained to a gas pipe in Detective Rossi's garage." Actually, Ali and I both saved Gabe, but I didn't want to dilute my point with facts.

He grinned. "A normal woman would have left and called the police."

"What's the matter, Gabe, wishing for a normal woman in your life?" Nothing like a bad day to yank my insecurity out.

"Nope. I don't wish for things, Sam. I make them happen."

The sudden shift in him robbed me of any cute comebacks. With anyone else, I might think that was a boast.

Not with Gabe. There were many things I did not know about him or his work. I could ask, but I didn't. I tried to keep the personal and professional separate, but Gabe zigzagged across those lines and kept me confused. He was teaching me how to be street smart and take care of myself. And I knew that I kept him amused. But beyond that, what was in it for him? Besides the occasional hot sex?

The truth was that I was scared to scratch the surface of our relationship. My dismal history with men included my bio-dad leaving long before I was born. I had grown up with a string of my mom's men parading temporarily through my life. I had vowed not to be like my mom and to do better. I'd gone to Heart Mates to find a good, solid man and ended up with panty-boy Trent. For thirteen years, I had bought his line about how he, as a condom salesman, was doing a public service. He did not judge, but provided protection for those who might have a lapse in judgment. What he'd really been doing was running drugs sealed up in those condoms.

Needless to say, I no longer trusted my judgment about men when it came to me. Stepping back so that Gabe's hands dropped from my shoulders, I said, "Tell you what, I'm going to go take a quick shower, then I'll explain everything, okay?"

Heat leaped into his eyes. "Want me to wash your back?"

Yes! Wait, no! Cripes, I wanted him to wash my back and keep going, but I also wanted to think. Gabe in my shower was not going to produce any rational thinking. With a quick glance at my watch, I gave him my pat excuse. "The boys will be home soon. You stay out here and keep Ali from eating the kitten I stashed in the boys' bathroom. Oh, and would you bring Ali's dog food in for me?"

He watched me with those silent dark eyes. "I could make you feel better, Babe."

Damn it, he could. And not just physically. I turned and made my way down the hall before I gave in to the temptation of Gabe.

When I came back out, Grandpa was home with the boys. They were laughing and talking. I heard Ali barking and a kitten's annoyed meows. Jeez, what were they doing? Running a hand over my still-wet hair, I padded down the hallway. I had pulled on a pair of jeans and a T-shirt.

Everyone was huddled on the living room floor between the TV and coffee table. "What's going on?"

Joel looked up. "Hey, Mom! Gabe said we should let Ali get to know the kitten."

I had an instant image of Ali's powerful jaws clamped tight with a gray tail sticking out. Rushing forward, I pushed aside Joel and TJ.

I was just in time to see Ali nudge the kitten with her wet black nose.

The kitten swiped at the dog's nose with her tiny paw.

Ali jumped back, sneezed and sat down, looking confused.

Sighing, I glanced over at Gabe. "How do you know Ali won't, you know, eat her?"

"She won't."

I gave up. Gabe was the one who found Ali for us. I later discovered that Ali had been tossed out of the police dog academy for stealing beer. She's a lovable lush, but also a highly trained police dog. Ali once saved my life by taking a bullet meant for me. I will buy her beer for the rest of her life.

All that didn't mean I totally trusted Ali not to eat the kitten.

Joel said, "Mom, she's cool. What should we name her?" At twelve, Joel was swiftly leaving boyhood behind. But every now and again, I still saw glimpses of the little boy in him. "Sorry, honey, we can't keep the kitten. We have to find a home for her."

"Told you!" TJ reached across me and shoved at Joel's shoulder.

"Enough," I told them. TJ had just turned fourteen. Full of teenage hormones, he also had a too-serious side that I wished I could soften. He was named Trent Junior for the father who let him down. He had his father's slender build and sandy hair, but not the total irresponsibility. When I looked at my two sons, I remembered my vow—face things head-on, deal with them and protect the two sons I loved more than my own life.

"Mom?" TJ tucked his arm back to his side. "You okay? I heard about Faye and that you found her and all."

I put my hand on my sensitive son's shoulder. "I'm okay, TJ."

Grandpa poked his head out of the kitchen. "All right, snacks are almost ready!"

Getting up from the floor, I went into the kitchen to

help. Grandpa was taking a cookie sheet full of s'mores out of the oven. My mouth watered at the rich toasted-marshmallow-and-melted-chocolate aroma, but the sight of Grandpa suddenly made my eyes sting. I knew I should scold him for the junk food he was feeding the boys, but I couldn't. We all adored him. In his seventies now, he was retired from his career as a magician. Aside from the occasional charity magic show, he spent his time now either gossiping with the vast senior citizen network in Lake Elsinore, surfing the Internet or whatever it was he did online, and helping me raise the boys.

"Hey, Sam. You feel better? Gabe said you looked pretty haggard."

Getting a plate out of the cupboard, I went to Grandpa and kissed his weathered cheek. He wore a mustard-colored shirt and green pants that slid down his bony hips. His almost nonexistent hair was combed to the side. But his milky blue eyes told the story. A sharp and crafty man resided in that aging body—only a fool would underestimate him. Helping him transfer the s'mores to the plate, I said, "Yeah, I'm better. I am just so sick over Faye."

He put a hand on my arm. "I know."

Once the boys put the kitten back in the bathroom, we all gathered around the table. Gabe put a cup of coffee in front of me, then took the closest seat. I stared at the file I had brought home from work. The one about Faye.

Joel asked, "Mom, where'd you get the kitten?"

I might as well tell them. With a deep breath, I launched into the whole story, starting with meeting Adam at the grocery store and ending with the fall off Mindy's cement step.

No one made a sound.

Gabe cleared his throat. "Let me see if I get this— you were kidnapped by a geek wearing Velcro shoes and brandishing oven cleaner, then attacked by a kitten, a poodle and a crazy lady with a push broom, who not only pushed you off a porch step, but also talked you into taking a kitten you don't want? That about right?"

Before I could think of a reply, Grandpa spoke up. Pushing his plate back, he fixed a serious expression on his craggy face. "That's totally R-O-T-F-L-M-B-O."

Everyone else at the table burst out laughing. Tears rolled down their faces. Joel wheezed with laughter, and Gabe doubled over in his chair. Ali got up from her place by the sliding door and ran around the table barking.

"What? I don't get it?" I looked around. Grandpa had just said a bunch of letters. "What did that mean?" I yelled that last part.

Everyone stopped laughing. Finally, Gabe managed to say, "R-O-T-F-L-M-B-O is e-mail shorthand for 'rolling on the floor laughing my butt off.' "

"At me?" I asked for clarification. And stared at Gabe.

"Uh-oh," Joel said, giggling, "you're in trouble now, Gabe."

He grinned at Joel. "Yeah? If your mom tries any sudden moves, I'll go get the kitten out of the bathroom."

Ali barked and ran back to the bathroom, apparently thinking that was a splendid idea.

I had to laugh. The very idea of street-tough Gabe using a kitten in self-defense crossed the line of absurd. Seeing smirks all around the table, I decided to ignore them and called to the dog, "Ali, get out here and leave that kitten alone."

She walked back into the dining room with her head hanging down and her ears laid back. Then she went to the refrigerator, stuck her nose into the seam and barked once.

"Not now, Ali. Later tonight you can have a beer," I told her.

"Mom?"

I looked back at Joel. "What?"

"Don't we, like, have to get the kitten some food or something?"

I hadn't thought of that. "I guess. Do we have some tuna?" What do cats like?

Grandpa stood up. "I'll take the boys to the pet store and we'll get a few things." Seeing my face, he held up a blue-veined hand. "Just to keep the kitten alive until we find a home for her. Hey! Maybe I can train her for a magic trick." His milky blue eyes narrowed.

"Grandpa, we are not keeping the kitten!"

"No? Oh, well, then, we'll just get a few cans of food. Come on, boys."

They stood up and TJ looked at me. "Mom, are you taking on this case and investigating Faye's murder? Do you think it could get dangerous?"

I looked my son in his worried blue eyes. "I told Adam that I'd help him. I doubt it'll be dangerous, and you know I'm not a private investigator."

Gabe snorted.

Joel jumped in. "But you sometimes work for Gabe so that makes you a sort of a PI, right, Gabe?"

Trying not to smirk, I turned to look at Gabe. Somehow, without any effort on my part, my two sons were building a bond with him. There was probably a little hero worship involved given that Gabe was—well, Gabe. Ex-cop, private investigator and very cool in a boy's eyes.

Now everyone, including Grandpa, looked at Gabe.

Without a pause, he directed his dark gaze around the table, then fixed on Joel. "Actually your mom is more of what we call a *surveillance agent* that I contract part-time to assist me."

Joel smiled. "Cool, surveillance agent!"

TJ's serious face softened with a boyish grin. "Yeah, much better than dating expert. Or romance broker."

* * *

The boys and Grandpa left. Alone with Gabe, I toyed with the file on Faye, feeling the intensity of his gaze. He sat next to me at the kitchen table.

"Surveillance agent?" I cringed at the thought of Joel and TJ chattering away to Eddie at Eddie's Critters pet shop, telling him that I was a surveillance agent on a case. "Eddie's married to Jan and she works at the library—the whole town is going to think I'm investigating Faye's murder!"

"Relax, Babe. Your grandfather is distracting TJ and Joel from the news of Faye's murder by buying the kitten a food dish and litter box. They'll forget all about the surveillance agent stuff when they get there."

I looked up at him in surprise. "Do you really believe that?" TJ and Joel had spread it around town that I was doing private investigating when I was attacked by a thug looking for drug money Trent had stolen. Gabe had done some work for me by doing a background check on my clients and I asked him for help. The boys managed to twist that into a whole new career for me.

The bad-boy grin slid over his mouth. "Nope, but I thought you wanted me to lie."

I traced my finger around the paper clip holding together the pages of Faye's file. I couldn't avoid the subject any longer. "I agreed to help Adam. To kind of look into this for him. The whole town's going to turn against him and think he did it." I knew this town well. I focused on feeling the thin, circular metal of the paper clip beneath my finger. "I suppose I could get into trouble taking money for investigating when I'm only a—surveillance agent."

"Uh-huh. Tell me exactly what happened when you found her."

I did, while going over and over the paper clip with

the pad of my finger. I ended with, "She was holding my brochure when I found her. The brochure she designed for Heart Mates. *Get Hot With Heart Mates*—that was the slogan. Faye had loved it and planned to design the brochure around that. God, poor Faye."

"Sam."

I looked up at Gabe. "Detective Vance warned me to stay out of it. How can I do that, Gabe? She was my friend. She died holding the brochure to my business. I was supposed to be helping her—what if I got her killed instead?"

"Stop it."

Startled, I blinked. His face had a set of dangerous features: black eyes, mouth that was just on the lean side, hard cheeks, a nose that might have been broken and all arranged in fashion that compelled females to spend a lifetime trying to tame him. It was sexy as hell, but right now his face was blank. A chill skittered along my bare arms. "What?"

"The brochure. It was in Faye's hand? Think hard, Babe."

I didn't have to. "Yes. I saw it and thought she had just fallen asleep on the table holding the brochure."

Gabe didn't move. "And you are sure the detective told you he thought she'd been strangled?"

My hand went to my throat. "Yes."

He shook his head. "Doesn't add up. This isn't just about you looking into this for Adam. I think you are in trouble here, Sam."

No. Panic set in. I'd had some trouble. Thanks to my panty-stealing dead husband, I'd had a whole lot of trouble. I didn't want any more trouble. Gabe's fingers slipped around the wrist of my hand holding my throat. When he tugged my hand away, I realized I'd been squeezing my own throat. Time to get a grip. Taking a deep breath, I forced myself to concentrate. "Trouble how?"

He kept a hold of my hand. "The brochure. Think, Sam. If someone tried to strangle you while you were holding a paper of some kind, what would you do?"

As soon as he put it that way, I knew the answer. For a second, the small sunny dining room spun around me. "Drop it and fight back. Oh, God, you think the killer put that brochure in her hand *after she was dead*?" I shuddered. Detective Vance's questions about Faye's connections to Heart Mates, how well I knew her, and wanting Heart Mates files all came tumbling back in a confusing rush. "You're saying that Vance thinks Heart Mates is involved? Or me? Because of that brochure?" The warmth of his hand contrasted with the chill of fear.

"I think we'd better find out what the connection of that brochure is to the killer."

"But the police . . ." I trailed off, remembering the last time I had been involved with the police. Pulling out my determination, I stiffened my spine. "The police have their own agenda. They only tell me what they want me to know." And the biggest lesson I had learned. "I have to look out for my sons, myself and Heart Mates."

"Right."

I was on a roll. I would find out exactly . . . "Uh, Gabe, what exactly am I supposed to do? I mean I'm not the police, I can't just, you know, get fingerprints and stuff."

One side of his mouth tilted up. "First, you're back to working for me. Our client, for the record, is Adam Miller, who has hired us to investigate his wife's last days. Then you just do what you're good at, Babe—nose around. Start there." He glanced over at Faye's file. "Find a reason to chat with the men she dated. Look for what's out of place, who seemed angry with Faye, Heart Mates, or both. But be careful."

That was insulting. "I'm always careful." Sort of.

He arched a brow, his mouth edging into a grin. "You got into a car with a man who might have killed his wife."

I knew that was going to come back to bite me in the butt. I waved a hand, dismissing his concern. "Adam didn't kill Faye. Besides, you said we're working for Adam."

"Prison's full of convicted felons claiming to be innocent. When I was a cop, every citizen I arrested claimed to be innocent. I'm more concerned about finding out the connection between that Heart Mates brochure and Faye's killer than getting paid by Adam. But working for Adam gives us a legitimate reason to investigate."

"Okay, okay, I get your point," I only half conceded. "But I don't think Adam did it." I hadn't realized how strongly I'd come to believe that. Lifting my chin, I stared at Gabe. "You should have seen him, Gabe. He bought Faye a kitten that turned him into a dripping, sneezing, mucus-spewing mess, just because she loved animals and couldn't have one while they lived together." I added the clincher. "He wears Velcro shoes!" I dared him to try and picture a murderer wearing Velcro shoes.

"Shoe prints. Could be he wears cool shoes to commit murder, then geek shoes to throw everyone off the trail. Sort of like Superman and Clark Kent."

Sighing, I said, "Trust me, Gabe, Adam was born to wear Velcro shoes. The Superman cape is more your size." Damn, I hadn't meant to say that.

He leaned forward. Close enough to smell the scent of his Irish Spring soap. Close enough to make my stomach flutter. "I'm Superman? Does that make you Lois Lane? Stacked and fearless?" He lowered his gaze to my breasts.

I'd been naked beneath his cape with him. It was a hot and mind-blowing place. My problems began when I got out from under the cape and started writing romance novels about us in my head. Superman and Lois Lane. Right. This Lois Lane fully intended to get the strong and determined heroine thing right, but screw the happily ever after. It didn't happen. "Back off, Superstud, my kids and Grandpa will be home soon."

He put a hand on my jean-clad thigh and leaned closer until his mouth was an inch from mine. "So?"

Damn. "So? I'm a mom, not a . . . a . . . what exactly is Lois Lane? A reporter, but like, didn't she have a cool moniker?" Nerves had me babbling. "I don't need Superman to save me—I want my own moniker."

His grin slow-crawled over his face. "Gee, Babe, it sort of takes all the fun out of it for me if I can't save your sweet ass once in a while. You know, just to keep in practice." His hand edged up my thigh.

My concentration was slipping into a hot pool of lust. It wasn't just the physical thing, it was the mind thing. From the time I met Gabe, he believed in me. Simple as that. I might screw it up once, but by God, I'd go back there and get it right the second time. Or maybe the third. Point is, Gabe didn't fly in with his cape on to save me.

He was teaching me how to save myself.

How can a woman resist that? I leaned in to kiss him when the door flew open. "Mom! We're home!"

I looked into Gabe's black eyes. "They're back."

"Guess that means you won't be coming to my bat cave with me?"

"That's Batman, not Superman."

"My phone booth then? Where the hell does Superman live?"

His voice was clipped with the hard edge of frustration. This was a part of our problem. I wouldn't leave my kids to go sleep with a man. Not even a Superstud like Gabe. They'd already lost their dad, and I'd grown up with a mom whose main goal in life was to catch a man. I didn't want my boys growing up that way. "Sorry, hero-boy."

4

ROMANCE BROKER BROKERING DEATH?
I stared through tired, bleary eyes at the morning newspaper headline. I hadn't even had my coffee yet. "Oh, no."

Grandpa spun around in his computer chair, looking fresh and chipper. "Clever wording, huh?"

He wore a white shirt with dozens of multicolored Zorro Z's stamped all over it. It hurt my eyes almost as much as the early-morning sun streaming in the sliding glass door. "This is going to be bad for business, Grandpa. No one's going to come to a dating service where the women are murdered. How'd the press get this, anyway? Faye only dated two men through us." I hadn't slept well thanks to a mewling kitten stashed in my bathroom, dreams of murder, and thoughts of Gabe. My head throbbed, and I was stiff from yesterday's fall off the cement step at Mindy's house. I washed down two extra-strength Tylenol capsules with my coffee.

Shrugging, Grandpa turned back to tap away at his computer. "They claim a 'source close to Faye' told them."

I tried to think who would do that. Adam? But why would he do that if he wanted me to help him? Detective Vance? Again, why?

Because he doesn't like me. Why didn't he like me? It was a little insulting, to say nothing of ego deflating.

Sipping my coffee, I scanned the article. Mostly speculation and a mention of my, and Heart Mate's, *past troubles.*

"What are you going to do, Sam?"

Setting my coffee down, I studied my grandfather. He had stepped in when my bio-dad made tracks before I was born. I loved him dearly. When Trent died and I discovered that we were broke, Grandpa opened his house to us. He'd been a better dad to my sons than their own father had been. And I knew that right now, whatever decision I made, Grandpa would support and help me.

Who needed a real dad?

"Gabe and I talked about that last night. He's concerned that the brochure in Faye's hand connects her murder to Heart Mates. He's agreed to let me help Adam by snooping around under his license, provided I focus on what the connection between the brochure and Heart Mates might be."

Grandpa pointed at the newspaper. "If someone's out to get Heart Mates, do you think they could be behind that article?"

"I hadn't thought of it like that. Maybe." Picking up the paper, I searched for the byline. The author was one of the staff writers who covered the Lake Elsinore area. I doubt the reporter had anything to do with it, but could someone be feeding the reporter information?

"What about Adam Miller?" Grandpa asked. "Do you think he might have done it?"

Pushing my hair back off my face, I said, "All night, I

tried to think of something, anything, Faye ever said that indicated Adam had the ability to murder her. You know, when the files at work were changed, Faye was completely exasperated, but not scared. Not threatened." Shaking my head, I tried to get the feelings I had into words. "She talked about him as being absorbed in the computer game he was creating and forgetting about her. Absorbed in his dreams, forgetting that she might have a dream. Faye characterized his flaws as being too focused, unable to communicate with people like he communicated with his computers. He didn't try to control Faye's movements or friends, nothing like that."

"He doesn't sound like a murderer. But that doesn't mean he's not. Sam, you have to be careful."

"I think Gabe will be doing some checking on Adam, Grandpa. He'll see if he has any priors, any kind of history of violence or mental instability." I sipped more coffee. The kids would be up soon, and my morning would turn into a whirlwind of lost shoes, missing homework, packing lunches, getting breakfast and general craziness. I loved these few minutes before it all started.

Then the boys would pile in the Jeep with Grandpa for a ride to school. Ali and I would both stand at the front door missing them already.

Grandpa swung back around and started tapping on his computer. "Want me to look around and see what I can find on Adam?"

I had to smile. "Sure—as long as you stay out of the police files and other illegal sites." Grandpa had some far-reaching connections through his Multinational Magic Makers magic community, the "Triple M" for short. Even Gabe was impressed with the stuff Grandpa could find. But, as stealthy and sneaky as Grandpa was in these endeavors, I knew that it was possible one day he was going to get caught. Not from my own experience, since I am having a good day when I can turn my computer on at work. But I'd read accounts of the Secret Service storming schools for stuff kids did on the Internet. I didn't want them bursting into our house to haul Grandpa away.

Although it would be fun to watch them try to cuff him. Grandpa is a pretty good escape artist, but somehow I doubt the police would be as entertained by his skills as his audiences have been.

"Excellent. I'll get right on it after my coffee meeting this morning."

I rolled my eyes at his back. The *coffee meeting* was a regular morning ritual of a bunch of retired gray-hairs getting together at Jack-in-the-Box to gossip. Grandpa went faithfully every day after he dropped the boys at school. A couple of months ago the big topic was if Rosy Malone was really going into the hospital for gallbladder surgery. Grandpa cracked the mystery by breaking into her medical records via the Internet to determine that Rosy was having some cosmetic work done.

"Okay, you snoop around on Adam and I'm going to talk to the two clients who dated Faye. Gabe ran the standard background check on them that we do on all our clients. No problems turned up. But it's a place to start. God, it would be awful if it turned out a Heart Mates' client killed Faye." It was awful enough for her to have been murdered, but if I was in any way responsible . . .

"Uhhh, I looked over that file you brought home on Faye this morning too." Turning from his computer, Grandpa went on, "Sam, about that brochure that Gabe thinks might connect the murder to Heart Mates . . ."

He had my full attention now. "Yes?"

Using one finger, he tapped the file on the table. "Jim Ponn, one of the two men Faye dated, owns Ponn's Printing."

That had been in my files, but I hadn't put it together. That made Jim and Faye competitors. In a small town there wasn't a lot of room for competitors.

Lake Elsinore's city council fed Main Street oodles of money in the hopes of revitalizing business. Matched awnings hung over doorways, trees decorated with clear lights lined the street and freshly painted park benches were strategically placed. But Main Street remained the same, antiquated and no match for the bright, shiny superstores.

Driving down Main Street, I passed what had become something of a landmark, Guadalajara's Mexican Restaurant, and spotted clusters of day workers hovering in an empty field up the street. Laborers waiting for someone to come by and pick them up for any kind of temporary work. Any job to pay for food. I lived in fear of joining them if I didn't get my dating service solidly into the black and growing.

According to town legend, the evening brought out a few ladies of the night, but the town leaders regularly swore they had rid the town of those particular working girls.

Ponn's Printing sat between an antique store and a bakery. The big glass window had the curving letters of the business name stenciled on it. Finding a coveted parking space in front, I sat for a minute and reviewed my plan.

The kitten meowed. She was my plan. I picked up the box I had found for her since the carrier broke when I flung it down on Mindy's front porch. I planned to casually ask Jim Ponn if he wanted the kitten.

And then what—casually ask him if he happened to murder Faye?

While getting out of the T-bird, I decided I'd have to work on that last part. A few folks made their way down the sidewalk holding cups of coffee and pastries wafting a warm cinnamon-sugar aroma.

Inside the shop, the air had a thicker, musty scent sharpened by whiffs of ink. I set the kitten box on the long counter in front that kept the customers from wandering into the back. Behind the counter, music thumped from a boom box set on a stool. Arranged precisely in the tight space, several big copier machines hummed and spewed documents. Scattered computer monitors blinked against the fluorescent glare of the overhead lights. The tanned linoleum floor was snaked with cables controlled by liberal amounts of silver duct tape.

Jim Ponn turned from the computer monitor he was studying. His big shoulders sagged slightly at the sight of me. He used an ink stained hand to smooth down his blond mustache before he punched a last key on the keyboard and came over to the counter.

"Sam, what can I do for you?"

I had met Jim for the first time when I did the interview to sign him up with Heart Mates. He had bought out this print shop after years in construction, changing the name and expanding the services to include some designing. A decade of swinging a hammer showed in his thick shoulders and arms. The slight paunch of his gut and red complexion made me think of too much beer and high blood pressure. I remembered Jim as being a kind of quiet but a nice guy. Maybe a little embarrassed to use a dating service. Hardworking came to mind.

"Hi, Jim. I just came by to—well, a couple of things really." Nerves had me babbling. "You know about Faye, right?" I watched for his reaction.

His thick upper body deflated a bit. "Yes, the police were here yesterday."

"Oh, well, yeah, about that." I shifted the kitten box around on the counter, thinking. It would be a bad start for Jim to think that I suggested the police interview him. "Uh, I found Faye in her motel room, and the detective on the case asked for all the files on her. I had to give them the information about who Faye dated through Heart Mates." Pausing for a breath, I debated the best way to draw Jim into a discussion about what he told the police. Then I blurted out, "What did you tell them?" I tried not to wince at my less-than-polished questioning technique. This always looked easier on TV.

His face tightened. "Look, I'm busy here. Is there something you need?"

This was not going well. I reached into the box and pulled out the kitten. She mewled and splayed out her stick legs like a cartoon. I couldn't even get a kitten to cooperate today. "I sort of ended up with this kitten that was supposed to go to Faye. You know anyone who wants it?"

Jim stared at the kitten while brushing his mustache with his hand. "She loved animals. Talked about how she couldn't have one while she was married." Lifting his gaze to mine, he went on. "I only dated her twice. She was sweet, but needy, you know?"

Surprised that he started talking, I didn't want to interrupt the flow. I pulled the kitten to my chest to comfort her. I prodded with, "Needy?"

"Yeah, like always wanting approval. She was just a kid, really."

"Twenty-six," I told him.

He ran his hand over his whole face. "Sad. Guess maybe her ex-husband wasn't such a pansy after all." He dropped his hand to the counter. "Not that I think it's right what he did, killing Faye. I only meant that, you know, a man who lets his wife earn the money while he plays with computer games? Not a man in my book. That's why she left him."

My mouth snapped open to defend Adam and say that I was investigating Faye's last days at his request. But I thought better of it, calming myself by stroking the soft baby fur on the kitten. She had burrowed into my peach sweater, making a tiny little motor noise in her throat. Jim obviously jumped to the same conclusion that everyone else would—that Faye's husband had killed her. He'd probably told the police his belief too. But rather than challenge that, I thought of the brochure connection and changed the subject to see what he'd say. "Faye was starting her own business."

His face closed. "Don't know anyone who wants a cat. Gotta get back to work."

I stalled and pushed the point. "I just sort of wondered if you helped Faye. Maybe gave her a few pointers since she was starting a printing business too?"

"I didn't even know she was planning that. She asked me all those questions, used me . . ." He broke off, his face turning a steaming red. "I have to get back to work. Come again if you need any kind of print advertising, business cards, that sort of thing." He turned his back on me and returned to his computer.

Guess he didn't want the cat—or competition. He clearly wasn't going to answer any of my questions, like when was the last time he saw Faye, or where he happened to be Monday night when Faye was murdered.

Still I had one more question. "Jim, before I leave"— or he threw me out—"I just have one more question."

Intent on the computer screen, he didn't look at me. "If I answer, will you leave?"

Nothing like outstaying a welcome. "Yes, but this is

important. Do you know who Faye's first client was? You know, the first brochure she designed?"

"No, but if it were me, the first one I would design would be my own."

"Oh." Setting the kitten back in the towel-lined box, I walked out. Well, yeah, that did make sense, didn't it? Had Faye made some brochures to advertise her own business? And was Jim lying or did he really not know? He would have known if he killed her, since Faye was holding the brochure. And I assumed it was the brochure for Heart Mates. I realized for the first time that I wasn't one hundred percent sure that's what it was. But it had looked like it was. Faye and I had decided on blue and poppy for the colors. For some reason, I distinctly remember the colors of the brochure in her hand, like my horrified mind had taken a snapshot.

I was pretty sure it was the Heart Mates brochure. I'd have to find out for sure, I suppose, by asking Detective Vance.

Going back to my car, I settled the kitten box on the passenger seat. Maybe I should give her a temporary name. Without warning, Ali's face popped into my head. She had stood at the front window and watched me getting into the car with the kitten. Ali's liquid brown eyes had been huge and sad, her perky pointed ears drooping against her skull. In Ali's dog world, I had betrayed her by taking the kitten with me and leaving her home. How could I make her understand that I was looking for a home for the kitten, while Ali had a home with us? I'd never give that dog up and neither would the boys or Grandpa. I was going to have to make it up to her.

But right now, I needed to figure out who murdered Faye, and how it might be connected to Heart Mates. Until I learned otherwise, I was going to assume that the brochure in Faye's hand was for Heart Mates. Vance had asked me about it, which now struck me as odd. He would have looked at it and known it was for Heart Mates if that were the case. So why had he asked me? Gabe was right, there was something odd about the brochure, making it my best clue. Getting my legal pad out, I made quick notes of the conversation with Jim while it was still fresh in my mind.

Dated Faye twice. Didn't say where they went. Seemed disturbed by her death, but disturbed how? Implied she asked him lots of questions about the printing business, but he didn't realize she was going to start her own company. Angry? Motive for murder? Considered Adam a pansy and a murderer. Claims he didn't know what brochure Faye designed first and assumed it would be an advertising brochure for her new business. Note: Had Faye designed one for her new printing business?

I reread the notes. Had I missed anything? Starting the car, I backed out of the parking space and headed for the freeway. My plan was to jump on the I-15 South, get off at Railroad Canyon and head up to the Wal-Mart shopping center on Grape Street where Dominic Danger's coffee place was. *Smash Coffee.* Interesting name. Dominic had dated Faye once. Would he turn out to be as interesting as the name for his coffeehouse?

Names. While merging into the freeway traffic, I thought about names for the kitten. A temporary name. Just until I got rid of her. Glancing at the critter curled up in the box, I decided it had to be a name to fit a little gray dwarf with slate-blue eyes.

Sneezy?

Nah, too stupid.

Smelly? PeeWee?

The ringing phone saved me from the dwarf names rattling around in my head to keep me from thinking about murder. With an eye on traffic, I reached to the floor and yanked the ringing phone from my purse. "Hello?"

"Sam! I hear you're on a case!"

"Angel, where've you been? How'd you hear that? I've got so much to tell you!" I had tried several times last night to reach Angel.

"Busy. I have a new career. Well, more like an investment. And, you know, I hear things."

Angel had a new career every week. Her hobby of stalking her ex-husband tended to get in the way of a solid career. The high-tech equipment she used to stalk her ex made sure she did indeed *hear things*. Since Angel had come out of the marriage with a good sum of money and had the wisdom to invest it well, she didn't need a job to pay the bills. This new career had to be interesting. "Tell!"

"Nope, not yet. I'm working on it. I want to know all about this murder case you're on."

"Obviously you heard about Faye. There's so much I have to tell you. Do you know there's a new detective in town? Logan Vance is his name and he hates me. Isn't that strange? Says he read all about me in the newspaper."

"Maybe he's gay."

I laughed and had to hit the brakes when a car in front of me slowed down. "Anyway, he doesn't want me to nose around, but Adam Miller, Faye's husband, asked me to."

"What does the Italian hunk say about this? Did you talk to Gabe about it?"

"I'm on his payroll."

"Cool, maybe he'll sexually harrass you."

"God, Angel, you never change!" Keeping an eye on the traffic, I added, "Gabe's not as convinced as I am that Adam didn't kill Faye. He's more concerned that Faye had a Heart Mates brochure in her hand when I found her. He thinks that might connect her murder to Heart Mates."

Angel was silent for a minute. "But you believe Adam, Sam?"

"Yeah, I do." I almost shot past my exit. With a quick jerk of the steering wheel, I cut off a man in a high-riding SUV. He laid on his horn behind me. I ignored it, figuring he was one of those Type-A personalities, and steered off the freeway. "More now that I talked to—" That horn wouldn't quit. I glanced up in my rearview mirror. "Oh, shit!"

The big SUV that I cut off to get to the off ramp loomed up in my rearview mirror and kept coming with its loud horn blaring.

It was going to run me over. Like a monster truck over a trash can.

I dropped the phone and grabbed the steering wheel with both hands. Straight ahead at the bottom of the off ramp was a red light with busy cross traffic. On my right, a shallow ravine waited and beyond that, the motel that Faye had been murdered in.

What if the murderer was behind me? Every instinct screamed not to let him trap me. I had to get away.

Fighting to control my panic, I swiftly reviewed my options. The SUV barreled closer, looking like a car-eating monster in the mirror. Though the driver's seat was much higher than my T-bird, I made out a man wearing a dark hat and sunglasses hunched forward over the wheel.

He had enough speed to squash my car like a bug. I didn't want to be squashed. As hard as I tried to think of options, all that came to mind was racing down the off ramp and praying I could turn right into the thick cross-traffic zooming along Railroad Canyon Road.

It might be suicide.

Or it might save my life.

I was three fourths of the way down the off ramp. The red traffic light was only yards ahead. Trent had al-

ways bragged about the power this bird had, and Blaine
rattled off V's and 8's trying to explain to me.

Oh, God! The SUV's front grill filled up my rearview
mirror.

I was out of time, and out of ramp to stop the car. I
glanced at the speedometer; the needle danced around
forty-five miles an hour. Then I looked up into the mirror.

The SUV bore down to an inch from my taillights.

I punched the accelerator, rocketing the car forward.
Committed now, I prayed and held on with both hands.
No need to honk my horn since the SUV behind me
still blared its horn.

A postage stamp–sized opening appeared in the sea
of cars zooming by. My field of vision narrowed. Hitting
the corner, I stomped on the brakes, strained every muscle in my arms turning the steering wheel right.

Squealing, the car slid around the corner, caught hold
of the pavement and straightened out into the flow of
traffic.

I made it!

My ears pounded with adrenaline, and it felt like my
heart might leap right out of my chest. Keeping one eye
on traffic, I searched my rearview mirror.

The SUV sat on the off ramp, its nose part way into
traffic. He couldn't squeeze into the opening that my
little T-bird could.

God, I loved this car!

But what had that been about? My hands started to
shake, and my cell phone rang. Looking around, I saw
that the box had slid off the passenger seat onto the floor.
Inside, the kitten lay curled up next to my cell phone, fast
asleep.

Letting the phone ring, I paid attention to my driving,

deeply scared now. Had someone just tried to kill me? Why?

Because I had cut them off while on the cell phone? The state of California was considering legislation to ban cell phone calls while driving. A lot of people got angry at careless cell-phone-chatting drivers. But would they go so far as to try and run them over?

Or had this been something else altogether? Jim Ponn had seemed pretty angry about Faye using him to learn about the printing business. Could he have gone to talk to Faye and lost his temper and killed her? Since I left Jim this morning, had there been enough time for him to jump in his car and chase me? Why? To scare me off? Kill me? What kind of car did Jim drive? Had the driver looked like Jim? I couldn't be sure—same bulk maybe.

How did I get myself into these things? I was headed the wrong way to go to Smash Coffee. Pretty shaken up, I decided instead to go to the office first and calm down.

Maybe even find Detective Vance and see what he knew. Like me or not, he was going to start spilling information.

5

I felt a little safer once I got to work. Letting the door close behind me, I set the kitten box on one of the folding metal chairs in the waiting area of Heart Mates. Then I went back to the door and looked out at the parking lot to see if a white SUV had followed me.

"Expecting someone?"

Caught in my paranoia, I squared my shoulders, brushed down my long peach sweater over my brown suede skirt and faced my assistant. "I ran into a bit of trouble this morning, so I'm being a little cautious."

Blaine moved aside his half-eaten croissant sandwich oozing bacon and cheese to stand up. Arching his neck, he looked out the window at my car in the parking lot. "You get in an accident or something? The T-bird okay?"

Blaine's real love always came through. I crossed my arms over my chest. "If you cut yourself, do you bleed motor oil?"

"So the car's okay?" He glanced over at me.

Sighing, I gave up. "Some idiot in a huge SUV tried to run me over. The bird's fine."

Sinking back into his chair, he picked up his sandwich. "Did you outrun him? That T's got a 'D' 312 V-8 engine under the hood. You should be able to outrun most of the gutless cars being churned out today."

I held up my hand, trying to ward off a serious lecture on the innards of my car. "I just floored it off the freeway ramp and made a right turn into cross traffic with my eyes closed. It worked. The SUV chasing me got stuck waiting for the light."

A look of intense pain crossed his face. Shaking his head in disgust, Blaine set his breakfast sandwich down and picked up a stack of small, square papers. "Every time you find a body, we get busy. Then the article in the newspaper this morning . . ." He trailed off and shrugged, holding out the messages to me.

Taking them, I browsed through ten messages. Four were from my mother.

I threw those in the trash can by the coffee set up on the TV tray at the end of Blaine's desk.

Two were from reporters. I looked up at Blaine. "What did the reporters want?"

"To know how it felt to discover the dead body of a client. And any comments on the allegation that Heart Mates might have a killer on its client list."

My adrenaline rush of fear thickened into anger. "Ghouls." I started to toss those in the trash too, when I thought better of it. Checking the names of the reporters, I kept the one who wrote the newspaper article this morning. I could call him back and ask who the "source close to Faye" was. He probably wouldn't tell me, but it was worth a try. I threw the other one away.

The last four were appointments this afternoon for new clients. Four! Maybe I wasn't going to have to join the day laborers on Lake Street. I really didn't look my best at dawn anyway.

"Sam, why is that box meowing and ringing at the same time?"

That's the thing about Blaine. Not much ruffled him. Hiring him away from the garage where he had worked on and restored our classic cars when my panty-stealing husband was alive had been one of my better business decisions. At the time, Blaine was the only one I could think of who had the right qualifications. He could operate all the video equipment—still camera, computer, printers, scanners—and he was big enough to deter the occasional client who had the wrong impression of a dating service.

Turning to the box, I said, "Let me take this call and then I'll tell you." The kitten appeared seriously put out by the ringing phone judging by the way she kept hitting it with her tiny gray paw. I picked up the phone. "Hello."

"What happened?" Angel's voice was breathless with worry.

"I don't exactly know. I sort of cut it close to this guy behind me when I was changing lanes to get off the freeway and the next thing I know—he's chasing me." Walking back to the door, I glanced out to the parking lot, which really was more of a parking strip. No big white SUV. "I lost him so I'm fine now. I'm at work."

"God, Sam, you scared me! I thought you'd been in an accident."

It was getting harder to hear Angel over the mewling kitten. I had an idea and went over to the box to scoop up the bundle of fur. "Sorry about that, Angel. I have another problem, though. I've got this little gray kitten—think you'd want it?"

"Can't. Hey, Sam, I have to run. Just wanted to make sure you are all right. Let's get together soon and talk about your case. Bye."

The phone disconnected. Taking it away from my ear, I stared at it. That was very weird. Angel always wanted all the details now. Right now. Hmmm. Hugging the kitten to my chest, I tucked the phone back into my purse hanging on my shoulder.

Could my best friend be avoiding me?

"You left out the part about cutting off the guy while talking on the cell phone." Blaine's voice carried male disapproval.

"I had to change lanes!" Never mind the fact that if I'd been paying more attention to the road instead of Angel on my cell phone, I might have been able to change lanes a little sooner. That would have prevented the mad dash across the right lane to make the exit. Glancing down to see the kitten studiously kneading my sweater with her tiny little claws, I thought about the re-action of the guy in the SUV. Returning my attention to Blaine, I decided to get his point of view. "Uh, you're a man."

"Last time I checked."

I rolled my eyes, but continued, "Do you think a quick lane change that might have cut this guy off would really cause him to chase me down? It felt like he was going to run me over."

Picking up his cup of coffee, Blaine shrugged. "Road rage happens. Cutting guys off while yakking on a cell phone might do it. Or maybe he just wanted a better look at the T-bird."

"Just the same, I think I'll call Vance."

Blaine gulped some coffee. "The detective? He had some questions yesterday when he picked up the papers. I answered them."

"What questions?"

"General stuff about Faye and her dates through us. What we did about the profile of Faye that was tampered with. Our security measures. I went over the usual stuff, like we never give out addresses and every match is done with both clients' permission. That kind of thing."

"Okay, sounds like you handled . . ." I stopped talking when the door opened and I turned to see Mindy walk in.

She stopped just inside the doorway, her dark eyes framed in blue glasses looking around. "So this is Heart Mates."

Her brown eyes were dimmer today—from disappointment in the atmosphere of my dating service, or grief? Dark circles under her eyes suggested grief. With her chin-length hair bunched up into an oil gusher on top of her head, a long Harry Potter T-shirt over a denim skirt that ended an inch above the tan ankle socks and clunky boots, it looked like Mindy had dressed in the dark.

"Mindy." I tried to guess why she was here. "What happened? Have the police found Adam? Has he been arrested?"

She turned her gaze on me, then looked at the kitten I held. "Sam, hello. Uh, no, Adam's okay. I came to talk to you about Faye's funeral service."

"Oh." I took in a painful breath and tried to get my thoughts organized. The kitten was now kneading and chewing on a section of my sweater directly over my right breast and next to the strap of my purse. I pulled her off and walked over to set her in the box. "Okay, uh"—I looked up at my assistant—"we'll be in my office."

Blaine said, "Want me to bring you and Mindy some coffee?"

I glanced at the nearly full pot of coffee at the end of Blaine's desk. That gave me something to do. "Thanks,

Blaine, but I'll get it." Going to the TV tray, I said, "Mindy, would you like some coffee?"

"Please. With sugar."

"Okay, go on in my office, it's right through there." I pointed to the cubicle door. "Make yourself comfortable."

Taking a minute, I filled two cups with coffee. Mindy got one of our Styrofoam specials, while I took my customary heart-stamped mug. I had buried my grandma, then my husband in short succession. Now I had to bury a friend. But it was going to be worse for Adam and Mindy. And what about Faye's family?

"You okay, Boss?"

Blaine's brown eyes studied me much like they might a sick car. Forcing a smile, I said, "Yes. Yes, I am. It's tough, but then, so is life." I walked to my office meaning what I said. I would face life and deal with it. Once I had hidden behind my role as a wife and mother, playing it safe in baggy dresses and immersed in volunteer work. All worthy and admirable things to do—unless one is using them to anesthetize oneself and pretend life really is a romance novel come true.

I handed Mindy her sugared coffee and took mine with me around the desk. Sitting in my chair, I set my coffee down, took my yellow pad out of my purse and dropped the purse into the bottom drawer of my desk. It felt good to get that off my shoulder. I flipped over the page with notes from my chat with Jim Ponn to a clean sheet and looked up at Mindy. "Okay." I took a sip of my coffee. "What can I help you with?"

She was twisting her cup of coffee in her small hands. "Adam wants to have the service on Saturday. It'll be a memorial service. I'm working on the details." Holding her cup, she leaned forward in her chair. "Here's the thing, Sam. Adam needs to be able to go to his wife's service. You have to find out who really killed Faye by then."

"By Saturday? Mindy, today is Wednesday. That's only three days!" Maybe this was why real private investigators needed a license that would imply some sort of training. Three days to find a killer? Jeeze.

"Cops always say the trail goes cold after twenty-four hours."

She was serious. "Mindy, that's on TV. In real life—" I stopped talking. What did I know about finding murderers in real life? Except for my husband's killer, and it took me a year to discover the mistress who poisoned him with his own peanut allergy. Three days!

"Sam, please." Mindy's small, perfect chin tightened and she sat back in her chair. "Adam will pay you. We both want to know who killed Faye. And why. Why would someone do that? There's no one else who's going to care and fight for Faye. The police, if they can't pin this on Adam, they'll just stop looking. But if you push and snoop to keep this case alive, and find the murderer, then the police will have to arrest him."

"Mindy, you're giving me way too much credit. Besides, what about Faye's family? Surely they'll pressure the police. I know Adam really can't right now since he's afraid they won't listen to him, but what about her parents and siblings?"

She blinked behind her glasses and gulped some coffee. Every breath appeared painful for her. "There's only Faye's mom, and she's not coming. Not even for the service."

I knew my face betrayed my outrage. God, I couldn't imagine that. My mother drove me crazy, constantly tried to change my life, drag me into real estate and has never actually told me the truth about who my bio-dad is. Or rather, she's told so many stories that I don't know which one might be the truth. In fact, my mom regularly tried to change reality to make it what she wanted it to be. But she loved me.

And she loved my children. I made a mental note to call my mom back today.

"Don't you see, Sam? Someone has to help Faye. I mean I know she's dead . . ." She stopped talking, looking down at the cooling coffee in the Styrofoam cup.

I stayed quiet, letting her have a few moments to fight down the grief. Talking to her in the relative calm of my office, I noticed that Mindy had a really cool voice. Smooth and seductive, an interesting contrast to her pixie size and haphazard manner of dressing.

Finally, I said, "I can try, Mindy. But you and Adam have to help me. I knew Faye first as a client, then we were becoming friends, but our connection was about business. She was trying to become independent and learn to trust her own decisions. I need to know more about what brought her to that point." I'd only found Faye yesterday morning. It was still hard to believe a vibrant, bubbly woman was dead. "Faye talked about her marriage and her need to build her own life. But she never talked about her mother."

"Faye was an only child. Her dad abandoned them when Faye was in middle school, and her mom always kind of blamed Faye. Her mom moved up to Northern California with some guy Faye's last year of high school. Faye was not invited to move with them." Mindy was more in control of herself, but her voice tightened with anger.

Picking up a pen, I wrote *Faye* on top of the yellow sheet and started taking notes. "I'm sorry, Mindy. I don't know what to say. Obviously you've known Faye a long time."

"We met in high school. Faye and I had something in common, I guess. Neither of us fit in, and both of us had difficult mothers at home."

Right. The mom with the poodle who thought I was a baby stealer. "That's rough. Is your mother feeling better today?"

She held the cup in both hands, drinking some of her coffee before answering. "Mom has good and bad days. She was diagnosed with Alzheimer's about two years ago. I quit college and came home to take care of her. Before that, my mother was always a little unbalanced. The doctors don't think that's connected to the Alzheimer's."

And I thought I had problems. I was beginning to really admire Mindy. She could use a little fashion advice, though.

"So you and Faye had loneliness in common?"

"That and a need for attention. We both decided to take drama. Drama kids in high school—they're part of the freaks-and-geeks crowd. Faye was so much better than I was. She just shined. She learned to really come out of her shell. I fell back on getting good grades, but the two of us, we became best friends."

Freaks and geeks? Mindy was the geek and Faye was the freak? High school was a cruel place. "Was Faye popular with the guys?"

Mindy shook her head. "No, not in high school. Faye always thought she was too heavy. And her mom made it hard for her. Then when her mom left her last year in high school, Faye worked and rented a room. She didn't have time. When she did date, she was . . . you have to understand that Faye was needy. She desperately wanted to be loved."

It was a strange thing to be seeing a whole new picture of Faye. But it made her desire to become self-sufficient more understandable. And more tragic. Here was a woman who was getting it together and now she was dead. "How'd she meet Adam?"

"I introduced them. I was going to college at Riverside Community College. Adam did some tutoring there with Computer Science stuff." Mindy took a breath to continue, then just stopped.

"Mindy? Where did you introduce them? How old were you and Faye?"

"Around twenty. It was at the BBQ Shack. I invited Adam to come see me there when I got off work. I figured we'd hang around for dinner, then maybe go out to a movie or something."

"Oh." I got the picture. Mindy had intended the dinner as a date and Adam had thought it was friends. With Adam, I could see that. He wasn't particularly observant, but what about Faye? Had she realized? "Did Faye know you liked Adam?"

"Adam and I were just friends."

Friends? I didn't think so, but I left it for now. "How did Faye and Adam get along?"

"Great. Faye was interested in Adam's work. She didn't know a whole lot about computers, but she liked listening to him explain things. And she felt that he needed her. Faye could put into words what Adam was trying to say. She believed in his dream. For the first time in her life, someone needed her. Faye loved that."

"Did she love Adam?" I wondered what Mindy's feeling were on that. She didn't seem upset, but then that would have been, what, six years ago? Faye was twenty-six now, so yeah, six years ago.

Mindy gazed off into the past, the coffee in her hands forgotten. "I think Faye wasn't sure. I mean she thought she loved him in the beginning, but after four years of marriage, after struggling with working at the BBQ Shack and then doing all she could to help Adam get the financial backing to sell his computer game, I think she didn't know. She hadn't dated much. And once Faye found a good source of funding, Adam didn't need her anymore. The investor took over contacting companies, writing proposals, and generally making Adam marketable. Faye was a little lost."

I understood that. I had lived my life through others and ended up lost too. That was the thing I had connected with in Faye. "How did Adam take it when Faye left him?"

Her gaze snapped back to me. "He was devastated! He never saw it coming. I did. Faye did. Everyone but Adam. God, he's clueless sometimes!"

Uh-oh. Now I was seeing some real and deep emotion in her. But I wasn't sure if it was a frustrated friend who watched the marriage of two people she cared about fall apart, or something else. "Did Adam love her, Mindy? Do you know?"

She sighed. "Yes. He did. No doubt. The trouble was that Faye changed and Adam didn't pay attention. Once he lost her, he paid attention. And lately, Adam took an interest in Faye's dreams. They were discovering each other. . . ." She shrugged, then looked at the watch strapped to her wrist with a thick brown band. "I have to go, Sam. Someone's staying with Mom and I need to get back." She set the coffee down and stood up. "The service will be Saturday at noon. Please, try to find Faye's killer by then. Adam has to be able to go."

I looked up at her, trying to think rapidly. "Wait, Mindy, I need to know a couple more things." I wasn't sure what upset her, so I headed in another direction. "What about the two men she dated through Heart Mates? Uh . . ." I glanced at my notes. "Jim Ponn and Dominic Danger. Did she ever talk about them?"

"Some." She smoothed her Harry Potter T-shirt. "She was looking for men who had something in common— you know, starting a business kind of thing. She was going in another direction from Adam. Maybe thinking they could help her, I don't know."

"Help her?" I remembered what Jim had said about Faye using him. "You mean she picked the men solely on the condition that they had their own business?" I had not seen this in Faye. Ambition, yes, but using people? That would mean she was using my dating service too. Had Jim Ponn figured that out? Sort of poetic justice that he'd kill her and leave my brochure in her hand? Could that have been some kind of message to me? Or to the world in general?

"Maybe. She never said that exactly. She dated that Jim guy twice. Now Dom, she liked him, but only dated him once, then saw him as a friend. They sort of became buddies. He and Faye talked about doing some kind of community theater play. I can't think why he'd kill her."

"Did you meet either of them?"

"No." Mindy glanced down at her watch. "And I really have to go now. I have someone staying with Mom."

I stood too. "Mindy, how do I get hold of Adam?"

"He's got my cell phone. I can give you the number, but you can call me too. He's laying low and supposed to be working on finishing the demo of his game for a presentation meeting next month." She leaned over and wrote down the number across the top of the legal pad I was using for notes.

"Thanks." I went around the desk to walk her out. As I watched her leave, I wondered—did Mindy love Adam?

"Boss, we have the clients coming in a few minutes."

Turning from the door, I sighed. "Yeah."

Blaine opened his bottom drawer and pulled out

some clipboards with the information sheets and the permission for a security check that Gabe conducted. "Getting tired of the dating game, Boss? Should I starting putting out resumes?"

That was the problem with a cubicle for an office— no privacy. The kitten started complaining. Going to the box resting on the folding chair, I said, "You know better than that, Blaine. I love this place." Lifting the kitten, I glanced around Heart Mates. Okay, so the threadbare steel-gray carpet, dingy walls and water-stained ceiling were a little tacky. A nice couch and a quaint antique table covered in the latest issues of happy couple–type magazines would be an improvement. Right now I had folding chairs and TV trays littered with fifty-cent copies of used *National Geographics* left over from Joel's last science project. I did have a *Bride's Magazine* in there somewhere that was at least the current year.

Maybe I didn't have a lot of clients yet, and maybe I was a wee bit behind on the lease for the computer equipment—but I was going to make it. Certainly the payment from Adam and Mindy would help me get caught up on the bills.

Blaine's thick, blunt fingers lined up four clipboards, one on top of the other, each succeeding one laid right below the shiny silver clip. "Oh, good. Now I can run out and buy that new car."

I don't think I'd ever authorized the purchase of those clipboards. I wondered where Blaine got them, but figured asking might be a case of finding out more than I wanted to know. "Ha-ha." I headed toward my office with the kitten in tow. I'd stuck some of those little cans of cat food with the pop-top in my purse. "I'm just trying to make some extra money to pay your salary," I yelled over the wall while digging through my purse. Ah-ha. Pulling out the can, I read the label to see the dead fish flavor. Sounded yummy. Wrinkling my nose, I headed back out to the reception area.

"Right." Blaine looked up at me with a silly grin. "And impressing your PI boyfriend has nothing to do with it. Or showing the town that you're not just a dumb housewife."

Shrugging, I set the kitten in the box, popped the top of the food and set it in the box for her. Woohoo, now we had a new aroma to add to the general ambiance of the office. Picking up the box, I took the kitten and smell into my office. We'd use the interview room for the clients.

I heard the front door open and Blaine greeting the new clients. I headed out to the reception area to get to work.

Leslie Lee was the last of the four new clients and perky as hell. The interview room was two or three times the size of my cubicle office. The oak dining table from my married days sat on one end, while the other was set up for taking pictures and videos; it had a TV and VCR mounted on the wall in the corner. Romantic travel posters covered the walls.

Ms. Lee had been browsing through the still-shot albums and screening videos for over an hour.

Faint from hunger for lunch, I had a hard time remembering that I needed clients. The first three clients had been happy with the interview and my solemn promise that my assistant and I would get right to work looking for several matches.

Not Leslie Lee. She wanted to look through the pictures and videos herself. And ask a million questions. Grudgingly, I had to admit that she showed intelligence in asking about security. She even took notes about our policy of contacting each client with a potential match, and only releasing phone numbers at their approval. We never gave out addresses and we handed out a little safety sheet to each client. That was Gabe's suggestion. It detailed safe ways to conduct the first meeting, such as setting up a double date with friends in a public place. Mostly common-sense stuff.

But now Ms. Lee's thoroughness had surpassed impressive into annoying. I needed chocolate and caffeine. Right away.

"So, if I pick a guy, but he's not interested in me, then you will not give me his phone number or any contact info?"

I sighed. "No. We have strict policies to protect all our clients' privacy, Ms. Lee."

"Call me Leslie!"

"Right." I had to end this. "Uh, Leslie, why don't you go home and think on this today and sleep on it tonight. You can come back and browse through the albums and videos again, but in the meantime, Blaine and I can run our state-of-the-art matching program for you. That will narrow your search to those who have the same interests as you. Right now, though"—I looked down at my watch for impact—"I'm afraid I have to run out for a business meeting." With a Big Mac, fries and Diet Coke. Supersized.

She looked up from her notes. "Oh! Of course! I'm just so excited now that I decided to be brave enough to do this."

"Sure, understandable. And I promise we'll get back to you with matches no later than the end of the week." I stood up and walked Leslie Lee out of the interview room, past Blaine working at his computer and out of the office. I closed the door behind her.

The clicking of Blaine's two-finger wizardry on the computer stopped. Turning to him, I said, "I'll be in my office. Everything okay with the files?"

"Sure. I'm going to lunch anyway. I'll finish entering the new client information into the company files this afternoon. The computer will have matches before I go home today."

"Fine. How about we work on those in the morning then?"

Turning off his computer, he stood up. "You're the boss. I'll be back after lunch." He went around his desk and left.

I locked the door behind Blaine and headed to my office to make some phone calls. I needed to talk to the reporter who wrote the article in this morning's newspaper, check in with Gabe and mention the car chase this morning and have a little chat with Detective Vance. Lunch would have to wait.

Grabbing the phone messages, I dialed the newspaper reporter's phone number. Mac Finch answered his own phone. "Uh, hello, this is Samantha Shaw of Heart Mates dating service," I went into my professional-woman mode.

"Ah, yes, Ms. Shaw. Thanks for returning my call. Do you have any comment on the death of Faye Miller? Or the fact that the police are investigating her ex-husband? Word from my sources is that Adam Miller was livid about Faye dating through your agency and may have killed her for it."

My face and chest puffed up with outrage. Somewhere in the heat blowing crosswise in my mind, it occurred to me that these outrageous allegations were being made in a voice that was so ordinary and bland that, for a second I thought I was sleeping through my high school biology class again.

But I was awake now. Forcing myself to breathe, I focused. All I wanted to know was where he was getting his information. "I have no comment on that, but I have a question for you, Mr. Finch." In my mind, this guy was bald, bland and wore bifocals. "I need to know who your sources are. It's clear that someone is feeding you information, much of it inflamed or false."

"I'm afraid I can't tell you. I never reveal my sources, but I do fact-check to the best of my ability, Ms. Shaw. If you feel something is in error, I will do my best to correct it."

Uh-huh. I'm sure he was a nice guy just trying to pay his nice mortgage, but I still didn't trust him. "Thanks anyway," I said and hung up.

Maybe Vance could tell me. Pulling out my purse, I dug through my wallet and found Vance's card. I dialed and got voice mail. Naturally. "Detective Vance, this is Sam Shaw. I had some things to discuss with you about . . ." I froze.

A rattling noise came from the reception area. Was it the door? Someone trying to get in? Blaine? No, he had a key. I forgot the phone clutched in my left hand.

I strained and heard nothing. Ready to chalk the noise up to my imagination, I jumped at a tapping, like a key against the window.

Probably it was nothing. Some kids, or a potential client. Quietly, I set the phone back down in the cradle and reached into my bottom drawer. I dug in my purse for my keys, where I kept a small canister of defense spray.

The front door rattled violently. Jerking my hand out with the keys, I sat frozen.

Should I call 911? But I'd just called them yesterday for Faye. Was there a limit? Cripes, that was stupid. I picked up the phone.

Then I set it down. I'd call, the cops would come and it would be nothing. Or maybe my mother. I still hadn't called her back. Possibly even the mailman. That car chase this morning had spooked me.

Sucking up some fake courage, I stood and stiffened my spine to my full five-foot-five in heels. Grasping the little can of defense spray next to the gold bear with the imitation diamond in its belly, I walked softly out to the reception area.

The kitten was batting the can of cat food around her box. I looked at the front door. It was an older door, with a window set in the top half. Walking to the big window by Blaine's desk, I leaned over the stacked trays filled with bills and files to peer outside.

I jumped back and screamed. A huge white SUV roared by the window, damn near scaring the body fluids right out of me. The truck squealed out of the parking lot onto Mission Trail Drive. My heart did a bone-bruising jig around my chest. Dizzy with fear, I crossed my legs to keep from peeing myself the way the kitten had.

The white SUV or truck had looked like the same one that chased me off the freeway this morning.

6

After the SUV was gone, it took me about four seconds to decide what to do—I snatched up the kitten and got the hell out of Heart Mates. As a card-carrying member of the Chicken-Shit Club, I didn't want to be forced into a pointless act of bravery if my SUV stalker came back. Once I was in my car, I wasn't sure what to do next. But I did want to get out of there, so I started the car and backed out of my parking space.

Calling Detective Vance wouldn't do any good since he was out of his office.

Making a left turn onto Mission Trail Drive, I thought about Gabe. Maybe I should call him. Reaching for my cell phone, I had second thoughts. My cell phone chitchat while driving appeared to be what sparked this whole chase/stalking thing.

I checked my rearview mirror and nearly chicken-clucked when I spotted two white vehicles in the sea of cars behind me. But one was a Ford Escort, and the other one some kind of beat-up sedan. No big white SUV.

Was I overreacting? Maybe all this was a coincidence,

or whoever was in the SUV wanted something innocent from me. Who did that driver look like? I had an impression of a thick neck and shoulders like Jim Ponn's, but the hat and sunglasses mixed with my fear made it hard to see any identifying features. Jim had a red-blond mustache. Had that man in the SUV had a mustache?

When I came to the red light at the intersection, I made a decision. Turning right, I headed up Railroad Canyon Road to the Wal-Mart shopping center. I'd go to Smash Coffee and talk to Dominic Danger. According to the file on Dominic, he owned the Smash Coffee Shop— which filled Faye's requirements of business owners for dates through Heart Mates, at least according to Mindy.

Once I got there and safely parked my car, then I would call Gabe from the parking lot.

Staying alert for white SUVs, I swung a right on Grape Street, then hooked a left-hand turn into the Wal-Mart shopping center. To the right of the huge Wal-Mart, a strip of smaller stores lined up on the edge of the parking lot. This shopping complex was the pride of Lake Elsinore. We once had a Kmart and a movie theater that had been the city's Camelot. They both stood empty and abandoned.

Parking in front of Smash Coffee, I sat for a long minute and lusted over the new, clean suites. The front window had a motif of a spiky-haired stick man juggling what looked like a large fancy paper coffee cup with wisps of steam, a bean grinder spilling out some beans and a bottle of flavoring that had a pour spout used on liquor bottles in bars. SMASH COFFEE was splashed across the bottom of the window in bold black letters. Beneath that read, *Take the Smashing Challenge* in colorful letters tilting back and forth like a preschooler's wobbly writing.

What was the smashing challenge? Being money challenged, and a reverse snob, I bought my to-go coffee at McDonald's. I couldn't see paying three dollars when I could get change back for one dollar at the McDonald's drive-through.

For a place like this to stay in business in blue-collar Lake Elsinore, it had to have a hook. Not an I'm-rich-enough-to-pay-for-this hook. That was Temecula, our upscale wine country that had its own mall cousin-town a few miles south on the Fifteen Freeway. Temecula had a mall. Elsinore had used appliance and auto-parts stores. We did have a cool Outlet Center, but I'm pretty sure that didn't count. Outlet Centers are about getting a good deal on designer goods, and everyone knew you had to leave upscale towns to do that.

The kitten woke up and sneezed. Looking over at the little gray ball of fur, I hoped Dominic Danger would take her. She opened her slate-blue eyes wide and fixed an imperial stare at me.

Damn, that pint-sized feline packed some heavy attitude. Bored with me, she turned to stretch her little body out and paw at some threads on the towel.

I reached past the kitten on my red vinyl passenger seat and grabbed my purse off the floor. Getting out my cell phone, I punched up Gabe's number and pressed SEND.

While it rang, I looked around for any large, white SUVs. There had to be at least a dozen large white vehicles in the huge parking lot. With Wal-Mart on the other side, a Vons grocery store on this side, this was a Soccer Mom Mecca.

Gabe's answering machine message sounded in my ear. I thought fast. No doubt he was working on some case. Somewhere. Hopefully, just not in some beautiful blonde, or sultry brunette's bed. Annoyed at the turn of my thoughts, I said, "Gabe, it's me. Talked to Mindy this morning. I have three days to find Faye's killer before the funeral. Adam has to be able to go to his wife's funeral. Also, some nut is stalking me. Call me later."

I disconnected and got out of the car, scooping up the kitten box and heading purposefully into Smash Coffee. The rich scent of fresh-ground coffee beans hit me full force. I looked around. The right side of the shop had a long counter built over a dozen or more clear glass containers of coffee beans. Behind the counter lined up rows of sparkling machines, presumably for grinding and making coffee. On the end of the counter stood a nose-high glass bakery case filled with breads and pastries.

Hunger pains viciously attacked my stomach. I forced my eyes away from those. My thighs thanked me.

The walls were painted a light pecan color and trimmed with glossy white molding. Leafy green plants trailed along the ceiling and the tops of the walls to create a sort of jungle effect. The floors had a rough-finish tile that matched the pecan walls. Glass-topped wrought-iron tables and cushioned chairs were scattered on the left side of the shop.

It felt like an outdoor patio, cozy and warm.

And silent. Done cataloging the shop, my gaze slid to the cluster of women covering two tables. Very silent women, all staring at me.

My instant hot flash, clammy hands, racing heart, dry mouth and sudden fear of the telephone told me I'd stumbled onto a PTA meeting. What if they asked me to head up a committee? Maybe bake twenty-five dozen perfectly decorated cupcakes in fifty-nine minutes? Or—I tried not to faint—help with a fund-raiser? I froze in place.

"May I help you?"

Pulling myself together, I remembered that I was now a different person. I'm no longer the soccer mom, PTA mom and all around dump-it-on-the-stay-at-home-mom anymore. I'm a businesswoman. I had a purpose. Fixing my biggest smile on my face, I turned to the man behind the counter. He didn't look like the picture in Dominc's file. "I'm looking for Dominic Danger."

"And who are you?" The man's serious dark eyes bore into me. His hair was cut mercilessly short. From his near six-foot height, he could almost be a model for one of those expressionless mannequins. On his lean frame, he wore navy blue slacks and a sport coat over a cream-colored mock turtleneck. It looked like he did algebra equations for fun. Balancing the kitten box on my hip, I held out my right hand. "I'm Samantha Shaw. I own the—"

"Samantha Shaw. Yes, I know who you are now."

Dropping my ignored hand, I blinked. His voice did not thunder or rant, but it contained a refined sneer. Like what he was really saying was, *I know who you are now, the town slut.* "I see. Well, is Dominic in? Or do you know where I can reach him?"

"Haven't you done enough, Ms. Shaw? You leave Dom alone. He's just wrecked over this murder, and then the unfortunate matter of the police questioning him. We know who sicced the police on him, now don't we, Ms. Shaw."

The hostility spewed from him along with the accusing words. Interestingly, his tight-skinned face did not really change expression. Made me want to look for a hand stuck up his butt and controlling him like a ventriloquist's dummy. The daggers of heat piercing my back reminded me of the PTA women behind me. Lifting my chin, I kept my voice smooth. "Who are you? Do you work for Dominic? I doubt he'd be pleased to hear of your attitude."

He stared down his skinny Michael Jackson nose. "I'm Tristan Rogers, co-owner of Smash Coffee. And Dom needs me to protect him from the likes of you. He's too emotional. I warned him not to go to your sleazy dating service."

Gurgling and hissing from the coffeemakers competed with the howl of fury echoing in my head. All coffee slurping from the PTA women behind me ceased. Looking into Mr. Moron Mannequin's dull, dark eyes, I considered the pepper spray on my key chain. All that waxy skin would contort, then melt off into a pool of remorseful asshole.

Okay, I was pissed off.

"Listen here, Rogers. I've had a bad day. In fact, I'm having a bad week. A dead woman fell on me yesterday, and believe me, buddy, getting trapped under a dead body makes it personal. I want to know just who the hell killed her. You got a problem with that"—I held up my free hand in case he was stupid enough to think he was allowed to talk—"I don't care. You want to stop me from talking to Dominic, then you'd best close up shop and buy a gun, because I'm not about to be stopped by a pretentious coffee boy!" I whirled around with the kitten box in my arms and slammed out of the door.

Breathing hard, I stood in the bright sunlight. The day was cool, but my temper was still red hot. How dare he call my dating service sleazy? I worked damn hard to make it respectable.

"Sam?"

I jumped and looked down at the kitten in the box. Feeling stupid, I realized that the voice had not come from the box but from behind me. Turning, I saw Linda Simpkins, the PTA president, and several other ladies watching me. They had followed me out of Smash Coffee.

Perfect. I'd made a fool of myself in front of the PTA that predicted my downfall once I'd left their ranks. Pasting a smile on my face, I said, "Hello, Linda, ladies."

"Sam, we all heard about Faye. It's just dreadful. Uh, what you said in there about finding Faye's killer—are you investigating?"

How to answer? These women were part of an extensive phone tree that I had left over from my volunteer days. I'd been ruthless about side-stepping excuses, and I always had a backup plan. If I couldn't talk the mother into, say, working the cotton candy machine for several hours, a chore sure to cripple your back, then I'd have a second option related to that particular mother's skills, like maybe donating flowers or painting a backdrop for a play. I had a Rolodex full of names, numbers and skills. I'd used that phone tree when I'd done some investigating in the past. I decided to be frank. "Yes, I am. Faye was one of my clients at Heart Mates. Client safety is paramount to me."

Linda stuck her hands in the deep pockets of the jean dress she wore over a long-sleeved shirt. "You don't think her husband did it? I heard he did. It's all over town that he killed her for going to Heart Mates."

A million things whipped through my head. "No, I don't think he did it." It took a lot of control to keep civil.

Eyeing me, she sighed. "Things aren't always as they seem, are they? Is there anything we can do to help?"

I realized she was talking about the time that I helped her out. Linda had discovered some very private videotapes missing of her and her husband. She had come to me for help. Working with Gabe, I'd found those tapes. If videotapes of Linda and her husband doing the wild thing had surfaced—it would have ruined Linda. Not many communities want their PTA presidents and soccer moms to star in sex videos.

"I am interested in what you might know about Faye. Had you met her?"

"She called me and offered to send me some information on her new printing business—you know, for PTA or soccer stuff. We use Ponn's Printing. I thought it kind of odd, since she didn't have kids, that she thought to call me. When I asked her how she came across my name and number, she just said that she'd read about some stuff the PTA had done in the town newspaper. And my number is listed in the phone book."

"Sounds reasonable." But I was thinking. Had Faye done more than pump Jim Ponn for information? Had she been stealing his clients? It left a bad taste in my mouth. That wasn't really the Faye I thought I knew. "Linda, what did you tell Faye when she called you? Did you meet with her or anything?"

The web of fine lines around her wide brown eyes deepened. "That's the funny thing. I did agree to meet with her and hear her pitch, but she called me Sunday night and cancelled."

"Did she say why?"

"No, well, not really. She just said that, while she'd be glad to take on any business I could bring her if I was ever dissatisfied with my current printer, she didn't want to steal clients." Linda looked troubled. "I hadn't met Faye in person. I have seen a picture of her now, in the newspaper, but she sounded almost tearful, as though she was desperately trying to be professional."

I tried to see it. Faye in her motel room, on the phone with Linda, trying to—what? Right a wrong she had done? Or had she been afraid? Maybe someone had threatened her? God, she had only been twenty-six years old—had she gotten herself into trouble of some kind? I didn't know. Linda's face mirrored my anxiety. "Anything else?"

"Not that I can think of. Do you think she got in over her head, Sam?" Linda was a mother and disturbed by the thought of a young woman getting into trouble.

"I don't know. But thank you for telling me this. Uh, maybe you could ask around and find out if anyone knew Faye? Any information might be helpful."

"Yeah." Linda nodded, her brown eyes troubled. "I'll put the word out."

Small towns. I'd have more gossip on poor Faye than the tabloids did on celebrity divorces. Sadness had me look away toward the front window of Smash Coffee. "I appreciate you leaving your coffee to come out and talk to me."

I saw her reflection in the window shrug. "We only come over here to see Dom anyway. Since he's not here today, it's not as much fun."

"You know Dominic?" I turned back to Linda and shifted the box. Boy, I was tired of lugging this kitten around.

"Oh, yes! He's divine."

I blinked. I had never heard Linda talk like that. Divine? "How?"

A new twinkle in her eyes softened the crow's feet. "He's just fabulous! People come from all around to watch his little shows when he makes coffee! He's famous for it. Did you ever see that Tom Cruise movie about the bartender? He's like that—making a whole show out of filling your order. And then there's his Smashing Challenge."

I'd seen Dom's photo in his file. I tried to picture him juggling coffee the way Tom Cruise had juggled liquor bottles in the movie. Seemed kind of dangerous. "What's the Smashing Challenge?"

"A customer can come in and sort of make up a coffee—like say . . ." Pulling her hands out of her pocket, she waved them in excitement. "Pumpkin Ice Frappe. If Dom has the ingredients, he mixes up the concoction. The customer only pays for the drink if they like it. It draws tons of people on the weekends. I can't believe you haven't heard about it, Sam."

Actually, I had. It just hadn't clicked into place. Mainly because my mother had gushed on and on about it. Apparently the real estate community also adored Dominic and Smash Coffee. My mind spun with thoughts. The kitten started mewing complaints.

"Oh." Linda leaned in to look into the box. "What an adorable kitten. Did you get it from Eddie's Critters? Eddie has a nice pet shop," Linda commented. "He just loves animals. He's brought several animals to our schools to teach the kids about caring for them. He and Jan just do so much for the community."

"Uh, this was Faye's kitten." Looking at all the women standing close enough behind Linda to catch every word, I said, "Anyone want a kitten? She needs a good home."

They were all gone before I finished the last sentence.

I stared down at the little kitten. She looked like a piece of burned coal cooled to a fuzzy gray. Maybe I'd start calling her Coal. But that was a boy's name.

Setting the box in the car, I fired up the bird and thought about my options. Clearly, I was stuck with the kitten for a while longer. Hunger contracted my stomach. Sliding the car into reverse, I backed up and spotted the Crazy Chicken place at the edge of the parking lot. They had a drive-through. Perfect.

While ordering the high-fat, high-calorie, high-death-rate broiled chicken with lots of corn tortillas and salsa, I thought about the case. Jim Ponn looked good considering the brochure in Faye's hand. Jim had the print shop, appeared angry, and Linda had said Faye mentioned she didn't want to steal clients. If Faye had somehow gotten hold of his client list, or he'd told Faye who some of his clients were, then that gave him reason to be angry. Jim was big enough to surprise-strangle a woman Faye's size.

Edging the car forward in the post-lunch line, I thought about Dominic Danger. What would be his reason to kill Faye? I had no idea. Mindy said they had become friends, rather than a love interest. Tristan "the Mannequin" Rogers sure was protective of Dominic. Why? He'd called Dominic *too emotional*. What did that mean? Had Dominic gotten *emotional* and murdered Faye? Why would Tristan protect Dominic? The obvious answer would be the business they both owned.

At the pickup window, a boy half my age caught sight of my car. His mouth hung open, revealing braces with black and red colors. I had the hard top on today, with the portholes. "Sweet."

"Thanks, how much for the food?"

"Huh?" My bag of food hung in his big hand as he scanned the car with his eyes.

"My food?"

"Oh!" He looked surprised to see the steaming bag in his hand. Finally he told me the amount. I paid him and left, heading back to the office. All the way there I watched for large white SUV types. The kitten's meowing distracted me. The bag of food sat next to her in the car, and she appeared to be trying to get to it. Reaching in the bag, I broke off a tiny chunk of chicken, burning my fingers in the process, and stuck it in the box.

That shut the kitten up. Now if only I could solve my other problems as easily. If Dominic was not at work, he was likely at home. I'd look over the file when I got back to work and get his home address.

Right after I checked to make sure Blaine was in the office and no white SUV stalkers were hanging around.

Blaine and I spent the afternoon working together to input all the information about the new clients into the computers. Then we ran the cross matches and left the rest for tomorrow. Tired, I trudged into my office and got my purse out of my desk. I shoved aside cat food and diet bars to find the file on Faye that Blaine had given me. Shuffling through it, I found the interview sheet on Dominic Danger.

There was his home address.

That meant I didn't have to beg and wheedle Blaine into searching it out for me. For once something went right. Returning the papers to my purse, I turned around.

Blaine stood in the doorway. "Off to your job moonlighting as a PI?"

Busted using the copies he had made for me, and only one day after I'd told him I wouldn't need them. Slinging my purse over my shoulder, I brushed past him. "You can stay here and gloat. I'm going home."

His laughter followed me out.

Driving home, I realized that I hadn't heard from Gabe or Vance. Or my best friend Angel.

I was starting to get a complex.

Turning right onto the hard-packed dirt road that led to the house, I parked by Grandpa's Jeep and sighed in relief. I'd made it home without a single car chase.

Lugging the kitten into the house with me, I called out, "I'm home."

Ali darted between my legs, barking madly, and dancing up on her hind legs to see the kitten. Or eat the kitten. It was hard to know which. Bent over the controls of a Nintendo game, the boys nodded in acknowledgment. Grandpa looked over from where he was parked in front of the computer. "Hey, Sam. Haven't started dinner yet. Got some real interesting stuff to tell you."

Ali tried a new tactic of nose-butting the kitten box. "Ali, no," I scolded. She slunk off to her blanket by the sliding door.

Dropping the kitten box by the boys, I said, "You two take care of her." Walking by Grandpa at the computer, I kissed his shiny head with the scraps of gray hair. "Let me change and you can tell me while I start dinner."

"Okay."

I came out of my bedroom dressed in a pair of faded jeans and a short purple T-shirt that left about two inches of belly showing. Barefoot, I went into the kitchen and opened the freezer. Pot pies?

"What's for dinner?" TJ yelled.

"I don't want stupid Marie Callender pot pies again!" Joel added.

I shut the freezer and tried the refrigerator. Didn't need a psychic to know a trip to the grocery store was in my future. Wonder if I could afford pizza? Too bad it was Wednesday. Tuesday was taco night at Del Taco.

"So what'd you find out today, Sam?" Grandpa pushed a button to set the printer to chugging and spewing documents. He came in and leaned against the sink.

Four eggs, less than half a gallon of milk, a package of tortillas, bologna and cheese in the meat drawer, a bag of salad, half an onion and a whole bell pepper, five beers, assorted sodas, half pitcher of Kool-Aid. From that, I had to make dinner. Taking out two beers, I closed the fridge and decided I'd let my subconscious mind work on dinner. Maybe Grandpa had a magic solution.

"Mom? Do you know what's for dinner yet?" TJ asked again.

"It's a surprise."

Twin groans floated in above the take-over-the–world Nintendo sounds. "Have you two done your homework?"

"Ah, Mom."

Opening the beers, I handed one to Grandpa while aiming my serious mom voice to the living room. "Homework now."

Ali stood up and barked. Going to her dish, I dumped half my beer in there. "That's all for now, Ali. I think you need to be on guard tonight."

"Trouble?" Grandpa asked, then drank a sip of his beer.

I gave him a rundown of my chat with Jim, being chased, talking to Mindy and having three days to find Faye's murderer, and my meeting with Tristan. "I brought home Dominic's address. Tonight, I'm going to go by there. What did you find on Adam?"

His beer forgotten on the counter, Grandpa hitched his pants up his skinny hips and went back to his computer. "Nothing real good on him. Got his car registered with DMV—it's a tan Toyota Corolla. I have the license plate number." He took the papers out of the printer and held them up.

Stopping at the table, just a few feet away from the printer, I groaned. "Grandpa, you broke into the DMV files?"

"I had access."

"I'll bet." Access didn't mean *legal* access. Distinctions like that didn't always bother Grandpa and his far-reaching Triple-M magic buddies. "Did you find anything else? Has he been in any kind of trouble?"

He glanced at the papers in his hand. "Lots of parking tickets. Some he pays on time, some he don't."

"DMV records?" Gabe asked as he walked into the dining room area bearing two large boxes of pizza. TJ and Joel were right behind him. I hadn't heard a knock or the doorbell ring. I suspected that TJ and Joel either heard Gabe's truck pull up or smelled the pizza. They probably dashed outside to greet him and avoid homework. My crack guard dog barely lifted her nose from slurping her beer. Ali treated Gabe like one of the family.

"Not me," Grandpa lied to Gabe. He handed me the papers from his printer and went into the kitchen to rummage for paper plates.

Gabe set the boxes on the table, got out a slice of plain cheese pizza and plopped it down in Ali's food dish, next to her licked-dry beer dish.

She barked once and set to work on the pizza.

Going to the fridge, I pulled out two sodas for the boys and a beer for Gabe. Shutting the door, I turned.

Gabe stood there. "Hi, Babe."

He looked good. Little more spiffy than usual in a white button-down shirt tucked into black jeans. His belt emphasized his lean waist and hips. Black hair combed back to reveal black winged brows over his dark eyes.

Olive skin covered his Italian bone structure. Overall, he gave the appearance of slightly civilized danger. I held out a beer. "Hi."

Ignoring the beer, he put his hand behind my head and kissed me.

Full hands made resistance hard. His mouth on mine made resistance damn near impossible. God, he tasted good. Strong and male. But my kids . . .

He pulled back and took the beer. "Hungry?"

Yes. Damn it. Glancing over at my kids, I saw they were busy staking out their pizza. Grandpa looked up and winked. "Not really," I went for the safe answer. "Had a big lunch while Blaine and I worked this afternoon."

"Got your message. You have three days to find a murderer and someone is stalking you. Slow day?"

I couldn't help but laugh. "Didn't ruin any clothes. Of course, there's still tonight."

He dropped his gaze down my purple short T-shirt and tight pants. Heat flared his eyes to a dark and wicked hue. "I might be talked into damaging your clothes. For the right reason." He lifted a single questioning brow.

What we had here was one hot and horny Italian. What we also had was one loving-it, generic white-bread, old-enough-to-know-better woman playing with the hot and horny Italian. Not for a single minute did I delude myself into thinking that fact escaped Gabe. Did he like the chase? What would happen if I stopped running and he could have me whenever he felt like it?

Probably the same thing that happened with my husband. I'd bore him into stealing other women's panties. That absurd thought made me smile. No way could I picture Gabe talking some dumb bimbo into sex, then stealing her panties. The smile faltered. I could picture the sex part, and God knows Gabe wouldn't have to try hard for that. He just wasn't the panty-stealing type.

I took the kids their sodas and sat down before I gave myself whiplash with my thoughts.

Grandpa scooted his computer chair over and snagged himself a loaded piece of pizza. Gabe had brought one plain cheese, mostly for TJ and Ali, then one with everything but anchovies for him, Grandpa and Joel.

How hard had it been to button these jeans? No-pizza hard? One-slice-of-cheese-pizza hard? Or go-for-it easy? I gave up the math and took a slice spilling over with olives, mushrooms, pepperoni and other artery-clogging ingredients. Before digging in, I asked Gabe, "Did you come up with anything on Adam?"

Setting his beer bottle down, he smiled. "Figured I'd look?"

Pride made me cocky. "Figured you'd look there and try talking to your contacts to get any info on Faye's murder."

He nodded once, his idea of a compliment. "With Adam I came across the same as Barney. Didn't get much with Faye either. I'm waiting for more info on that. Autopsy is today, so maybe I'll get something tomorrow."

The pizza stuck in my throat. Washing it down with the last of my beer, I forced myself to get past Faye being cut up to determine how she was murdered. "I'm going to try to catch Dominic Danger at home. His business partner, Tristan Rogers, was hostile to me so I think I'll stick to Dominic's home to talk to him."

Grandpa said, "That might be a problem, if you're trying to avoid Tristan Rogers."

We all looked at Grandpa. "Why's that?" I asked.

"Tristan lives with Dominic. At least he has the same address as Dominic."

"I only learned about Tristan and Dominic being business partners today. How did you get so much information?"

Grandpa set his slice of pizza down. "Well, remember we were talking about the connection of the brochure and Jim Ponn? I got to wondering what the connection might be with Dominic. You know, like maybe Faye was designing a brochure or some other advertising for them. Unsure how to find that out, I decided to research Dominic's business, Smash Coffee. They have insurance, and the insurance files list Dominic and Tristan as partners in the business. It also lists their home address. It's the same for both."

"Hey, Grandpa, that's cool!" Joel dumped the crust he was holding and got a fourth slice of loaded pizza. "Can you teach me to do that? Like could I find out where my teachers live?"

"No!" I had visions of stink bombs thrown at the teachers' houses. Or some other magic concoction that Joel picked up from Grandpa.

"That's what you get when you ask Gramps in front of Mom," TJ solemnly informed Joel.

I narrowed my eyes on my oldest son. Hmm, that bit of info was going straight into the *Things To Watch For* file.

TJ stood up with his plate and soda can. "I'm going to go do my homework." He dumped his stuff in the trash and went down the hallway.

Joel stared after his brother as if he were a traitor.

"You too," I said.

He got up and left.

I turned back. Damn, Tristan and Dominic lived together. Now what? "I think I'll drive by, maybe see if I can spot something, or figure out if Tristan is gone." Looking to Grandpa, I said, "Do you know what kind of car Tristan drives?"

"Black Accura. Dominic drives a yellow Mustang."

I turned to Gabe. "How about we go take a look?"

"I got work tonight, Sam. I can cancel if you are spooked. Tell me about this stalker of yours."

I ran down the chase and someone at the locked door of Heart Mates, then tearing out of the lot in a white SUV.

Gabe turned to Grandpa. "What kind of car does Jim Ponn drive?"

"White Ford truck."

"Not exactly a Suburban but could be mistaken for one in a time of stress." Gabe had his gaze fixed on me. "Think you want me to come with you? Since you're only going to Dominic's, and you'll take your pepper spray and stun gun, you should be okay."

"I—"

Gabe pulled out his cell phone and cut me off. "I'll cancel."

"Like hell." The words spilled out, surprising me. I did want him with me on this one for some reason, probably because I had no idea what I was doing. But I didn't want to need him for something like this.

Gabe stared at me.

I stuck my chin up. "You go to work. I'll be fine."

"I'll go with her, Gabe. Don't you worry, I'm carrying. I'll protect Sam."

Both Gabe and I whipped our heads around to look at Grandpa. "Carrying *what?*"

His blue eyes twinkled. I never saw Grandpa's hand move, but I heard the click. I remembered that click. A six-pack of tattooed thugs had once pulled one of those on me to try and steal my car. The overhead light bounced off the silver blade. "Ohmigod, Grandpa, that's a switchblade!"

Pride softened the wrinkles on his face as he tilted the knife back and forth in the light. "Ain't she a beauty?"

7

Grandpa was still grousing about Gabe taking away his switchblade when I went back to change my clothes. My short purple T-shirt would make people remember me when Grandpa and I snooped around in Dominic Danger's apartment complex. We were going to take his black Jeep to look less conspicuous. So unless I wanted to go undercover as a hooker, the T-shirt had to go.

Hearing a commotion in the living room, I assumed my mother had arrived. I didn't like leaving the boys alone at night, especially when a woman had just been murdered yesterday and I didn't know who was following me around in a white SUV, or why.

Anyone stupid enough to try something with my mother on duty was likely going to end up owning a fixer-up house and no memory of buying it. Mom was smooth in her chosen profession.

Wish I could be that good in mine. But I will be. One day I'll have the most talked-about dating service in Southern California. Maybe I'll even franchise.

And still do a little PI work on the side?

I yanked off the purple shirt and pulled a long-sleeved black shirt out of my drawer. Holding it up, I saw the huge white lettering that read *Romance Readers Rock*. It looked like a neon sign, but it was the only long-sleeved black shirt I had besides a turtleneck. I didn't want to wear a turtleneck.

Part of being a good private investigator was to be flexible. I turned the shirt inside out and pulled it on. It was dark, who was going to see?

Well, Dominic Danger for one, if I found him home alone. If Tristan Rogers was there, I had two choices. Leave and wait until I could talk to Dominic alone, or use my stun gun on Tristan and talk to Dominic. I liked the second option, but since Tristan had specifically said Dominic was emotional, I guessed I'd have to go with the first plan.

Too bad. I really didn't like Tristan. He'd called Heart Mates sleazy.

After tucking my hair under a black baseball cap, I gathered up my black fleece vest with the zippered pockets from my soccer-mom days that I had stored my stun gun and pepper spray in. I went out to the living room.

The boys were settled at the table with glasses of milk and a big tin of cookies. My mom got a lot of free baked goods in her job and oftentimes brought it to TJ and Joel. I ignored Joel slipping Ali a cookie and turned to find my mom and Grandpa on the brown checked couch.

"Samantha." Mom stood up. She wore casual clothes of straight-legged cream-colored pants and a mint-green knit top. Her blond wedge cut was perfectly smoothed.

Mine was tucked up under a baseball cap. "Hi, Mom. Gramps and I won't be long—"

"Samantha, I brought you a cassette tape to listen to. *Get Rich With Real Estate*. Side one is *Residential Properties* and side two is *Commercial Properties*. Listen to this tonight while you and Grandpa are looking at the senior citizen complexes. I gave the pamphlets and maps to get to the better senior facilities to Dad."

My right eye started to quiver as soon as Mom said *real estate*. But I was lost on the pamphlets and old-folks-home comment. "Senior citizen complexes?"

Grandpa got up off the couch behind Mom holding a stack of glossy papers and maps. "When I called Kathryn to ask her to watch the boys, I mentioned that you and I were going to take a gander at a few of them senior places. I told her that I wasn't ready to move or anything, but I wanted to look."

Ah, a covert operation. My eye calmed down. Mom had plans for both Grandpa and me. Grandpa should sell this house and move into a senior citizen complex to spend the rest of his days playing bingo. I should go into real estate and snag a man. Ugh.

Mom thought TJ and Joel were perfect already. That was something all of us agreed on.

Still holding out the cassette tape, Mom narrowed her eyes. "Why is your shirt on inside out, Samantha?" Her gaze rolled down me. "Shouldn't you wear something more, uh, grown-up? Those jeans are tight."

My right eye quivered again. The left one twitched. I felt like I was trapped in *I Dream of Jeannie*.

Thrusting the tape into my arms, Mom rushed to her purse on the couch. It was a cream and mint-green bag. How did my Mom manage to have everything so perfectly accessorized? Coming back, she held out a piece of paper. "This is the Paleolithic Diet, from the Stone Age. You don't eat anything that you can't catch or find growing. No grains and no milk."

Holding on to the dreaded real estate tape, I stared at the papers. Did I look like a dinosaur to my mother?

"Thanks, Mom, but I'll stick to my diet bars." I had those starvation bars stuffed in my desk at work for emergencies. I liked the chocolate, fudge and café latte flavors. I didn't suppose the crazy chicken lunch and pizza dinner was going to help my thighs much.

"Try it, Samantha. Once you get your thighs slimmed down, dump that dating service and get your real estate license—"

"Mom!"

Both my kids stopped sneaking cookies to Ali and stared at me.

Taking a breath, I calmed down. TJ and Joel lost interest and went back to eating.

Looking at my mom, I suddenly thought of Faye. Her mom wouldn't be coming to her funeral. My mother changed facts to suit her view of the world, was desperate for me to grow up, get a real career, a man, and was in general an annoying pain in the tushy, but she loved me. I loved her.

Of course, that didn't mean I was going to let her turn me into a real estate agent. "Mom." Bringing my voice down several octaves, I picked up my black, fully stocked vest and slipped it on. "Heart Mates is my career. I don't have time to read your diet. We need to go find Dominic Danger." I was halfway to the front door when I realized what I'd said. *Slap me stupid!* My plan was to keep on going and pretend I hadn't slipped.

"Dominic Danger from Smash Coffee? What are you seeing him for? How would he know of a good senior complex? Gay men are good at decorating, but what do they know about senior housing?"

I froze with my hand on the front door. *Gay men?* Turning around, I glanced at Grandpa.

Balancing the colorful pamphlets Mom had given him, he shrugged.

My mom's ivory skin had a dull flush. *Uh-oh*. Being the Real Estate Queen of Lake Elsinore and surrounding areas, my slip about Dominic had led her to believe we had sought real estate advice elsewhere.

Like I'd willingly talk real estate to anyone!

But gay? Leaving the door open, I walked a couple of steps back into the living room. "Mom, what do you know about Dominic Danger?"

She lifted her chin. "I know he's not a real estate agent."

Right. "Uh, Mom, I was going to talk to Dominic about Faye Miller. Actually, we were going to stop by on the way to check out senior housing and ask Dominic if he might like Faye's kitten." Probably it would be best if I acted like we were actually taking the kitten with us. Glancing at Grandpa, I said, "You put the kitten in the Jeep, right?"

"I plumb forgot."

I narrowed my eyes at him, trying to warn him not to play dottering old man in front of Mom. His daughter was not likely to be fooled.

Grandpa winked behind Mom's back. "I'll go get the little critter and we'll be ready to go." He dumped the pamphlets on me and headed for the bathroom where the kitten was stashed.

"Mom, how do you know that Dominic is gay?" Gay! Why would a gay man go to Heart Mates? Hmm, maybe I should consider branching out? Nah, what did I know about providing mates for gay people? Hell, probably as much as I knew about straight people, but I was wandering off the subject of Dominic.

"Haven't you ever seen Dominic do his Smashing Challenge? He's gay." My mom picked up the *TV Guide*. "Is *Diagnosis Murder* on tonight?"

Joel groaned at the table.

"Mom, do you have any other reason to believe Dominic's gay?"

Flipping the pages of the *TV Guide* with her tastefully polished nails, she glanced up at me. "Everyone knows he's gay. It's not like he talks about it. He just lets people think what they want."

If Dominic was gay, that might explain why Tristan was so protective of Dominic and hostile toward me. If he cared about Dominic in a personal way, he wouldn't want the police questioning him, I supposed. And he surely wouldn't want him going to a dating service. But why would Dominic come to Heart Mates if he was gay and in a relationship?

A furrow appeared between Mom's taupe-lined eyes. "You're not getting involved in Faye Miller's murder, are you, Samantha? Everyone knows that Faye's husband killed her for going to Heart Mates. It's all over town. That dating service is nothing but trouble. What you need to do is distance yourself from that whole mess. You listen to that tape in the car. Once we get you into real estate, we'll work on getting you a decent husband." Her face cleared and she tossed the *TV Guide* onto the coffee table. Going to the kitchen table, she pulled out a chair and delicately rubbed her hands together. Fixing her gaze on the boys, she asked, "Where's the cards?"

Grandpa appeared, carrying the kitten with his shuffling gait. I glanced back at my mom, watching her fingers fly as she dealt out a hand of poker.

She might have cleaned up to a sophisticated real estate broker, but my mom was still a magician's daughter. She was dealing from the bottom of the deck. Smiling, I followed Grandpa out to the Jeep.

* * *

Dominic and Tristan lived in an apartment building a mile or two from the house. Grandpa drove his aging black Jeep from the newly paved Grand Street with a spiffy double yellow line to the old two-laned, roughly paved deal with no street lights or sidewalks. It wound around some older homes into a densely shrubbed area on the right that hid a few homes and some kind of Arabian horse ranch. We passed some streets and empty land, until we came upon two sets of apartments on the left. These structures faced the Ortega Mountains, which loomed over Lake Elsinore Valley and helped hold the smog down over us like a smothering blanket in the hot summer afternoons. The view from Lookout Point up on the Ortegas was breathtaking.

But down here in the valley, with darkness surrounding us, the apartments looked isolated and eerie. Not run-down or full of graffiti or anything that I could really see. Just a feeling, as if the dark mountains had eyes. And we were being watched.

Or maybe I was losing my mind.

Fortunately, the apartments we were looking for did not have a security gate. We drove into the complex and began searching for the street. There were four main buildings spread out on a maze of streets and carports. "Any idea which apartment is Dominic's? Or where he and Tristan park?" How was I going to know if Tristan was home or not if I didn't know where he parked?

Grandpa drove the outside street that made a square around the entire complex. "I have the address, but we'll have to get familiar with the layout to find it."

"Looks to me like it's a big square divided into fours, with a big complex plopped down in the center of each smaller square. Streets run in and out of that, with carports on both the inside streets and the outside square. This is impossible to figure out."

It was about eight o'clock. We passed a couple of men working on a two-toned, black and primer paint truck. They glanced up as we passed but didn't seem too interested in us.

Still, I was beginning to wish we'd brought Ali. My stun gun and pepper spray didn't make me feel as safe as my dog. The kitten in the box on the floor at my feet wasn't a confidence booster. "Wait. Grandpa, back up to those men."

He slammed on the brakes, threw the Jeep in reverse and backed up. "Why? What are you going to do?"

"Ask for directions."

The two men looked up again as we slid to a stop at the back of the truck they were working on. They were on the passenger side of the Jeep. One wore a light wind-breaker bearing the name of the town's minor league baseball team, The Storm. It was unzipped to show a hairy chest and a slight paunch. He was bald and in his fifties. The second man was younger, wore jeans and a greasy shirt that made me think he was the owner of the sick truck. Probably the older man was helping the younger man out. Probably he'd help me too.

Neither looked too dangerous. I jumped out of the Jeep, snatched up the kitten box and walked over. They had hung lights from the carport. Two long orange outdoor extension cords ran to the apartments. They watched me approach silently. "Excuse me, but I was wondering—" My mouth went dry and the scent of dirty grease climbed up my nose. Up close, they looked tired and suspicious. Not so helpful. "Um, if you could tell me where Dominic Danger lives? I have this kitten for him."

Both men glanced into the Jeep and back to me. The younger man carried a wrench, and they both walked to the back of the truck. The older man said, "Look, Raoul, she's got a pussy and wants to give it away."

Uh-oh. Reacting with female instinct to the crude word, I started backing up toward the Jeep. With the box in both hands, I couldn't get to my pepper spray. I shifted the box, while backing up, to get one hand free. Then I worked the zipper open on the left side of my vest pocket that held the pepper spray. "Dominic is expecting this *kitten.*" I tried for the firm self-confidence I used on my kids, but my voice quivered. Fear released the floodgates, giving me an adrenaline rush. It sounded like the roar of the ocean washing over my brain. The kitten stood up and looked at me curiously.

"For free?" The grease-stained younger one was about four steps away and holding the wrench. His dark eyes bled insolence as he raked his gaze over me. "I can always use free . . ."

I didn't wait to hear what he said. Praying I had left the door to the Jeep open, I whirled around and rushed to the opened door, dropped the kitten box on the floor and leaped in after her. My heart banged up my throat. Sweat-popping terror drenched my body. My vision narrowed. Grandpa sat white-knuckled in the driver's seat, and my thoughts narrowed too. I had to protect Grandpa, myself and the kitten. In that order.

With my butt on the seat, I shoved my left hand in the unzipped pocket and latched on to the pepper spray. With my right hand, I reached out to pull the door closed. "Drive!"

The passenger door didn't budge. I looked up.

Grease Boy stood there with his wrench, holding on to the door. "That your pimp, pussy girl?"

I heard Grandpa's roar of anger and the sharp, unmistakable click. My own fury rode up and exploded. Seeing the older man coming up behind Grease Boy with what looked like a hammer, I yanked out the pepper spray, shoved it in the direction of their faces and depressed the tip.

"Shit—" The cussing exploded and quickly deteriorated to moaning.

I grabbed the door and pulled it closed. "Get us out of here, Grandpa!" The words were barely out of my mouth before the Jeep leaped ahead and picked up speed. I looked into the side mirror and saw both men on their knees clawing at their eyes.

Relief poured over me. I was just about to ask Grandpa about that click I'd heard, when I glanced ahead of us and screamed, "Grandpa!" We both spotted the dark green car sliding backward out of a parking space. Right in front of us.

Grandpa slammed on the brakes. Everything went into slow motion. The Jeep jerked, slowed, and slid right into the left rear brake light and fender of the green car. Metal crunched, and the red plastic shell around the brake light shattered.

In only seconds, we came to a tangled stop. Stunned, all I heard was the idling of two car motors and our breathing.

The owner of the Taurus got out of the car. A tall, well-shaped silhouette in the amber lights of the carports. Buttoning his suit jacket, he approached the driver's-side window.

For the second time tonight, my heart went into overdrive. Detective Logan Vance. We'd just hit the car of Detective Vance. He leaned down and peered into the Jeep. His square jaw did a tighten-and-scissor motion before he sucked in a breath and said, "Samantha Shaw. Why am I not surprised to find out it's you riding up my ass?"

I blinked and shoved the pepper spray in my hand down into the map pocket on the door. Could this night get any worse? What if Vance found out I'd sprayed the two yahoos about six car spaces back? Had he heard their swearing?

And what about Grandpa? That click I'd heard—I didn't even want to think about that. No better time than the present for Gramps to use his faster-than-the-eye-can-see skills to hide the switchblade he must have pickpocketed back from Gabe.

Would Vance arrest Grandpa for hitting his car? Fighting for composure, I said the first thing I thought of. "Detective Vance. What are you doing here? Do you live in these apartments?" Glancing at the covered carports, I noticed that he was parked on the end, closest to the cross street, and that the space he was in was not covered like the others. That usually indicated guest parking.

Vance didn't live here, then. He was a guest. Or on official business.

Looking at the antennas poking out of the dark green Ford Taurus Vance had been driving, my head spun. Ohmigod! We had just hit an unmarked police car.

"Step out of the car, please."

We both complied, with Grandpa breaking out his license and proof of insurance, all the while calmly talking as if he'd just met up with an old friend. Not slammed into the car of a Lake Elsinore police detective. While the two of them exchanged information by the driver's-side window, I casually looked back to where I'd doused the two potty-mouth thugs with pepper spray. They had disappeared. I guessed they must have gone into the apartment to get the pepper spray out of their eyes.

Returning to Grandpa and Vance inspecting the damage to the cars, I had a look for myself. The Jeep had a broken headlight. The Taurus had a shattered brake light, and the bumper was pushed up into the trunk on the left side. Damn. Vance had to be pissed.

Grandpa shuffled back to the Jeep to copy down Vance's information. I sucked up some courage and wished I were home watching reruns of *Diagnosis Murder* with my mother.

"Uh, are you going to get in trouble for this?" I tilted my head toward the damaged car.

His nostrils flared. "Why are you here, Shaw?"

His brown eyes looked tired. Had he been working nonstop since Faye's murder? Lake Elsinore had its share of crime, but murders were not a daily occurrence. And most of the murders tended to be disputes that escalated into murder. Faye Miller did not fit the type. Vance had really stepped into it for his first murder in the town. But to answer his question, I thought maybe I'd skirt around the truth. No use burdening him more, given his dire warnings for me to stay out of Faye's murder. "I have a kitten in the car. I was looking for Dominic's apartment to see if maybe he wanted the kitty. Then we, uh, Grandpa and I, that is, were going to look at some senior citizen complexes." Mom had bought our cover story, why not Vance? I thought I saw his right temple throb, but I couldn't be sure in the dim lighting.

"I don't believe you. I think you are investigating without a license and hindering a police investigation. Those alone are arrestable offenses. On top of that"— he glanced at the Taurus—"you and your grandfather assaulted a police officer."

"You can't believe that!" I was getting a full-body workout from the constant adrenaline rushes. "We just didn't see you backing out! It was just an accident. And I'm not investigating!" Not exactly. More like asking questions. Under Gabe's license, but I was afraid to point that out since he might pull Gabe in for some infraction or other. The truth was, I wasn't exactly up to speed on the legalities of private investigating. To prove my cover story, I ran around the Jeep and dumped all the pamphlets and maps from the backseat into the kitten box. The kitten jumped and began hissing at the papers intruding in her space.

I hauled the box back around the Jeep and set it on the hood. "See!"

Vance glanced inside, not at all impressed. "Another thing, Sam. I've had a complaint about you. Actually, Tristan Rogers filed a complaint at the police station today. He said you were harassing him and bringing animals into his place of business. That's a violation of the health codes, unless"—his light brown eyes sank to the kitten in the box, then slid back to my face—"you're claiming that's a working cat. Maybe a Seeing Eye Kitten."

Tristan Rogers. That weasel. "I merely stopped by to talk to Dominic to see if he wanted the kitten. Dominic wasn't there, and Tristan was rude. Why would a petty harassment complaint warrant a detective's attention anyway?"

Vance smiled. A full-blown sun-god smile complete with dimples. "I'm investigating you, Ms. Shaw. It's part of my job. Finding you here where you don't belong makes me want to take a closer look." He ran his gaze over me. "Nice outfit. Guess wearing your T-shirt inside out is the trend. I wonder what I'd find"—he hooked a single finger on the edge of my vest and tugged—"in all those zippered pockets?"

Seductive. Smooth. He moved like he was slicing through warm water, sleek and powerful. His finger never touched my body. Yet my nerve endings jumped to life. I knew Vance hated me. Which meant he was playing with me. Thirteen years of marriage to a player sharpened my instincts. No way was I gonna let some cop on a mission play me. Bringing my arm up quickly, I used a move Gabe had taught me to smack his hand away. I said nothing.

Dropping his hand to his side, he went on, "You don't have a permit to carry a gun. Maybe I should search you to make sure you're not carrying."

Damn, he had been investigating me. I clenched my teeth so hard my ears popped. *Focus!* I had to think. Protecting my family was the most important thing. I did not want to piss off Vance enough to make him arrest Grandpa or me. But I also had a job to do. Three days to find Faye's killer so Adam could go to her funeral. I was here to see Dominic, and I needed to know if Tristan the Weasel Mannequin was hanging around. "What did Tristan say?"

The smile dimmed. "Nothing. He's not here. I was on my way to your house next."

I had to get control of this situation. Two could play the charm game. "Look, Vance, somehow you and I got off on the wrong foot. How about we just start over? Why were you coming out to my house?" My head throbbed with the effort to stay calm. "Since we've had this little run-in, maybe I can save you the trip."

Vance shifted on his feet and studied me. What was he thinking? My nerve endings were sending out mixed signals and giving me a headache. It was almost like Vance and I had a connection that I didn't know about, but he did. I hated being out of the loop.

Finally, he said, "You left a message on my voice mail, remember? An incomplete message. You might try finishing your sentences before hanging up."

"Huh? Oh, yeah! The stalker." God, I had to keep my thoughts straight.

His whole body went rigid. Rolling up on the balls of his feet, he leaned forward. "Faye Miller had a stalker? I didn't find a police report on a stalker." Reaching into the inside pocket of his jacket, he pulled out his notebook. "Tell me what you know."

I swallowed and knew I was going to burst his first-real-lead-of-the-case bubble. "Not Faye, me. Some lunatic in a white SUV chased me off the Fifteen Freeway, then tried to break in to Heart Mates at lunch."

Disappointment sagged his broad shoulders. "Oh. You have the stalker." He sighed. "Go into the station tomorrow and file a report."

He didn't care. Damn it, why had I thought he would? Tristan filed a report claiming I'm harassing him, and Detective Vance is policeman on the spot, following up on the report. Me? He probably hoped the stalker would kidnap me and spirit me off to Mexico.

"Sam, everything all right?" Grandpa came up and handed Vance some papers.

"Fine, Grandpa." I glared at Vance.

He did a small smile that barely touched his dimples. That smile made me want to smack him. It screamed "hysterical female" at me. "Someone will contact you tomorrow regarding this accident." Turning to me, Vance hardened his face. "You stay out of my way, and out of my case."

Slamming down my hands on my hips, I said, "Did it ever occur to you, Vance, that I might be able to help you? That two of us working together might solve this case?"

He snorted. "You? A date finder for losers? Go back to getting your excitement from your little romance books, Ms. Shaw. Slice and dice the writers in your critiques if it makes you feel more powerful. But leave real life to the professionals."

"Now you've gone and done it," Grandpa hooted like a sick owl as he headed back to the Jeep and climbed in. "Oh, yeah, you fixed yourself good for sure." He slammed the door and started the Jeep.

Grabbing the kitten box off the hood, I meant to walk

away. Vance grabbed my arm. "I swear if I see, hear or even smell you near this case, I'll arrest you."

I looked up into his eyes. The weird amber lights from the carport dotted the brown with specks of yellow. I was tired of being pushed around. "What's the matter, Detective, do you need handcuffs to get a date?" I yanked my arm out and strode toward the Jeep.

"I know about your PI boyfriend, Sam. Investigating without a license is a crime, and Gabe Pulizzi could be in trouble for letting you run around under his license."

I stopped so fast, the poor little kitten yowled as she slid across the box. Anger shoved out any thread of judgment I had left. Spinning on the toe of my athletic shoe, I got up in his face. "Gabe Pulizzi can take care of himself. Don't make the mistake of tangling with him, Detective, or you'll be looking for a job as a bag boy in the grocery store." Raw fury pumped my blood. "And if Gabe didn't destroy you for messing with him, I will."

Vance's forehead wrinkled in confusion. "That's pretty strong loyalty to your boyfriend, considering he's working late tonight doing some *private consulting* with . . . well it's none of my business. You know what they say"—his face cleared to hard cop—"once a schmuck always a schmuck." He got in the Taurus, slammed the door and started the car.

The urge to strike back welled up in the back of my throat like vomit. Vance had stabbed deep into my weakest spot with unerring accuracy. I shoved it away. Hard. Avoiding what I didn't want to know was a skill I'd become exceedingly proficient at in my thirteen-year marriage.

Revenge was a skill I was honing now. I walked around the Jeep and climbed in next to Grandpa. The Jeep moved while my thoughts swirled in red haze of pain.

Detective Vance would pay for that.

And Gabe? Just what the hell was Gabe doing tonight? He'd said he had work, but he hadn't said anything about private consulting.

"Sam?"

My chest hurt when I tried to suck up some air. "Hm?"

"Misdirection. It's the oldest trick in the magician's handbook. If Vance distracts you from what you set out to do tonight, he wins."

I turned to look at Grandpa. He knew me so well. He understood my anger at myself for allowing my husband to make a fool of me in this town for years. He understood even my quietest anguish of my bio-dad wanting nothing to do with me. He was my rock. I reached deep for an ounce of courage. "No way in hell is he going to win, Grandpa. Let's go find Dominic Danger."

8

We went around to the back of the apartment complex and parked. I forced my mind onto the task at hand. "Vance had to have been parked close to Dominic's apartment. I guess we'll have to get out and walk around to find it." And hope we don't run into the truck-fixing thugs I'd zapped with the pepper spray.

"His apartment's right there." Grandpa pointed over the steering wheel to the building in front of us. Near as I could tell in the amber lighting, the two-story complex was painted an orange/pink color with white trim. White cement steps with wrought-iron railings led upstairs to the second-story unit. Grandpa seemed to be pointing to the ground-floor unit directly in front of us. "How do you know that?"

"This." He held up a business card.

I took the card. On the front was Detective Vance's name with assorted professional details. I turned the card over and my shell-shocked gears ground into action. There was a hand-drawn map on the back. Oh, boy.

"Grandpa! How'd you get this from Vance?" I knew, of course. Jail was a sure thing.

Grandpa shrugged. "He must have picked it up when he got his insurance proof out of his car. When he handed me the papers, I palmed the card. He'll think he dropped it."

I laughed and leaned over, kissing Grandpa's weathered cheek. "You're amazing, Grandpa, you know that?"

"Gotta keep my skills up, Sam. That's all." He brushed it off.

"Which reminds me." I'd forgotten about that click I'd heard. "You swiped that switchblade back from Gabe, didn't you?"

"Now, Sam—"

I put my hand up. "Get rid of it, Grandpa. Between you and the boys, a weapon like that is bound to be trouble. Gabe"—I winced slightly and refused to think about the things Vance had said about what Gabe was doing tonight—"told you that a switchblade bigger than four inches is illegal in California. If Vance had found that on you, he would have arrested you for sure."

Gramps' blue eyes narrowed. "I'm not so certain."

He had my attention. "What do you mean?" Grandpa was a good judge of people.

"Well, I can't put my finger on it. He wants you out of his case, no doubt about that. But he sure knows a lot about you for having only known you a couple days. Think I'm going to have to take a gander into Detective Vance's life."

Future visits with Grandpa behind the bars of a federal penitentiary did not appeal to me. "No! He's a cop, Grandpa. It's hard to get information on a cop without breaking into places you shouldn't be."

Gramps smiled. "We'd better talk to Dominic before Tristan gets home." He got out of the car.

Misdirection. No one was better at it than Grandpa. Scooping up the kitten box, I followed him up to the door of Dominic's apartment. Maybe our luck would hold and the two tool-wielding thugs wouldn't see us. I knocked on the door.

The door swung open. "What now?"

I stared. The man standing there wore only a pair of blinding orange sweatpants rolled low on his lean hips. Nothing else. He looked like his picture—rumpled blond locks, narrow face with decent bones and green eyes— eyes that were bloodshot and swollen.

Grandpa broke the ice. "We're looking for Dominic Danger. My granddaughter and me are on assignment with the Pulizzi Agency."

Gabe was going to be thrilled to find out Grandpa was working for him too. "Uh, I'm Sam Shaw from Heart Mates. I'd like to talk to you about Faye Miller, and this little guy here." I looked down into the box to see that the kitten had burrowed into the papers I had tossed in there. "She's Faye's kitten. She needs a home." I talked fast, expecting Dominic to react like Tristan.

He opened the door wide. "Oh, sorry, I thought you were that detective. Call me Dom. Come on in."

We walked in. While Grandpa introduced himself, I looked around. Kitchen on the left, living room on the right. Straight ahead looked like two bedrooms separated by a bathroom.

The place was a mess. I blinked in surprise, given Tristan's uptight appearance from this morning. On the kitchen counter was a blender half full of some greenish substance. Cucumber slices decorated the white counter top. The living room had bookcases along the wall by the front door and a couple of green recliners facing them. Typewritten papers were tossed everywhere, some face down, some face up as if they been thrown in the air. On one of the chairs, a slice of cucumber sat on both arms.

Dominic had been giving himself an eye treatment in the midst of the chaos. I didn't know what to make of that.

"Please, sit down." Dom used a lanky stride to walk over and scoop up his cucumbers, then swept the pages off the second recliner. He dumped the cucumbers on the kitchen counter, grabbed a folding wood chair from the small dining table between the kitchen and living room, turned and straddled the chair. "I'm trying to get Tristan to drop the harassment charges, Sam. I told the detective that Tris has been under a lot of strain lately."

Strain? From my short meeting with Tristan, I'd have thought he was the type to give other people strain, not suffer from it himself. Setting the kitten on the floor, I took the chair closest to Dom. From my vantage point, I could see the bookcase was stuffed with books. A little thirteen-inch TV was crammed in the center.

I began, "About Faye—" To my surprise, huge tears welled up in Dom's eyes.

"She talked about you a lot. She wanted to be like you." Dom sniffed and reached for a glass on the table. It had that green stuff from the blender it in. "Oh, sorry, would you like some? It's a health drink to rid the body of toxins."

Ugh. Think I'll keep my toxins. "No, thanks." I took a moment while Dom drained the thick liquid in his glass to sort out my thoughts. Hearing that Faye talked about me and wanted to be like me was hard. But I needed to focus on her life and what I didn't know about her to find who killed her.

Could Dom be her killer? Could his grief really be remorse? He had a slender build but not weak. Wiry muscles moved nicely under his smooth skin. "I understand that you only dated Faye once through Heart Mates."

Dom put the glass down. "The dating thing didn't work out, but we became friends. We had common interests. Spent a lot of nights watching movies from my video collection. I'm really going to miss her."

His voice trailed off and his gaze blankly wandered to the bookcase. I didn't think he was studying books, but looking inside to some memory. If he was acting, he was very good. "Uh, Dom, I'm wondering why you picked Faye. You know, to date." I was also wondering if Dom was gay and why the hell a gay man would come to Heart Mates. Couldn't quite figure out how to frame that question.

His vivid green gaze slid back over to me. "She had awesome hair. I have great hair." He gave his head a practiced shake. His blond highlights danced. "It looks better when I haven't spent two days drinking gin-and-tonics. A day of this stuff"—he picked up his glass—"and exercise will have me back in shape. But Faye, she had awesome hair."

"Uh . . ." That was a little peculiar. "So you, what, saw Faye's still-shot picture and decided you wanted to date her?"

"Yep. Like I said, awesome hair."

Uh-huh. "But it didn't work out for you two?"

He crossed his arms over his chest and stretched out his long, orange sweatpant-clad legs in front of him. "I think we both needed a friend more than a date. Faye was trying to get her business off the ground, and I had experience with that."

That fit what Mindy had said about Faye picking men who had their own businesses. "That didn't bother you?"

Surprise flittered across his face. "No. Faye was smart. She needed to learn how to run a business and I knew how. Well, Tris does more of the boring stuff, but I"— he unfolded his arms and thumped his chest—"have the flair."

I glanced over at Grandpa. He was reading a type-written page he must have picked up off the floor. Going back to Dom, I tried to think how to ask the next question. "Okay, I see what Faye got out of being friends with you. But why did you come to Heart Mates? What were you looking for?"

He glanced at Grandpa reading the page. "A leading lady."

Well, I'd never heard it put quite that way before. Very dramatic. "A leading lady like a wife?"

"Sam, I think Dom means for a play."

I turned to look at Grandpa. "A play wife?" Dom didn't want a real wife? What did that mean?

He held up the papers he was reading and waved them at Dom. "Did you write this play?"

"Tristan did. But he was against me going to Heart Mates to find our leading lady. I, of course, am the male lead."

Oh, *a play*. Now I got it. "What's the play about?"

His eyes glittered. "It's brilliant! It's a romantic comedy caper about a man being chased by two women because he's won the lottery, but one of the women turns out to be a man. Of course, it's just community theater."

He was using my dating service to find talent for his play. Faye had been using us to find know-how and maybe even clients for her printing business. Didn't anyone want to find love? "So did Faye agree to be in your play?" I remembered Mindy said that Faye had been in drama during high school. And that she'd been very good at it.

"Yes, but she wanted to lose some weight. I told her

to try jump rope. You know, she lived in that motel and there wasn't a lot of room for exercise. Jump rope is great exercise." A small, sad smile lingered on his face. "She didn't want to meet Tristan until she got thinner. But in the last week, she'd been getting a stronger sense of herself. Said Tristan could take her the way she is or find another leading lady."

That was the Faye I knew. Apparently that was the Faye that Faye wanted to be. To others it might sound contradictory, but I understood the desire to be strong. What I didn't understand was who killed Faye and why. I couldn't see any reason Dom would kill Faye. "Was Faye afraid of anyone that you knew of?"

Dom's smile died. "No. And she wasn't afraid of her husband either. She had real conflicting feelings about him. Said that when she left him, he had been more interested in his game than her. But lately, she said her feelings were changing. She told me that Adam was seeing her differently now. As a woman with her own hopes and dreams, not just an extension of his dreams. I don't believe the rumors that he killed her."

Me either. I was kind of at a loss. Faye and Dom seemed to have a legitimate reason for having found each other as friends. I still didn't know if Dom was gay, but what difference could that make to finding Faye's killer? "Can you think of anything else?"

He closed his eyes, leaning his head back. "Faye had a secret. Something that really tormented her. She never told me what it was, and I didn't press." Opening his eyes, he looked at both Grandpa and me and said quietly, "We all have secrets. I just tried to be her friend."

I believed him. "Dom, can I use your bathroom? Maybe you could take a look at Faye's kitten and see if you want her. That is, if you're allowed to have cats in these apartments." I stood.

Dom got up. "Bathroom's right there." He pointed to a door between two other doors. Then he went to the box and picked up the kitten, talking softly to her.

With him distracted, I glanced into the first bedroom. A large TV sat on a dresser facing the bed covered in a brightly colored bird-of-paradise tropical quilt. Rows of VCR tapes were stacked on the floor along the wall by the bathroom. On the other side of the double bed was a rack with free weights and two jump ropes. The sight of those jump ropes clogged up my throat. I pictured Faye diligently jumping rope, trying to get into good enough shape to be Dom's leading lady. Swallowing, I decided this was Dom's room.

Ducking out, I looked back and saw that Grandpa had engaged Dom in conversation. Grandpa glanced at me and barely nodded.

Emboldened, I passed the bathroom to look into the second bedroom. Another double bed, this time pushed up against a wall and covered in a bland blue spread. The focal point of this room was one of those compact but highly organized computer desks that had a place for the monitor, printer, and machine drive thing. A neat row of books marched across the back of the workspace on the desk. It was dark in the room, except for the moving light of the screen saver on the computer. I recognized a few of the books by sight from years of critiquing romances—the magazine I did the critiques for often sold these books so I was quite familiar with them. Several were from a very popular *Writer's Digest* series and there was the thick *Literary Marketplace* tome. A writer's books. I certainly didn't see any romance novels. This had to be Tristan's room.

Grandpa coughed and I whirled around and hurried into the bathroom. Quickly ridding myself of the beer from the pizza dinner, I washed my hands and walked back out. "So, Dom, do you want the kitten?"

"Can't. Tris doesn't really care for animals."

No shit. He didn't exactly seem like the caretaking type. "Uh, where is he, anyway?" I glanced around at the mess. The pages from Tristan's play had obviously been thrown in a fit of anger.

Dom sighed. "We had an argument about the play. I told him I didn't see how we'd find anyone as perfect as Faye. Between the police questioning me and other pressure, Tris got upset. He never really wanted to meet Faye and let her audition for the part. Anyway, he . . ." Dom's green gaze rolled over the scattered pages of the play. "He got his Alpha Smart and stormed out to go work on his latest project."

These guys, Tristan and Dom, were opposites. Like Al Gore rooming with Kato Kaelin. "How'd you and Tristan meet?"

"A screenwriting seminar a few years ago. As an actor, I like to see how the writers work since I am the one who interprets their pieces. Tristan spotted my talent right away. Then I ran into some trouble, and Tristan helped me out."

I think Dom and I knew two different Tristans. "So Tristan's friendly?"

"He's . . . selective. He grew up with his mom and grandma. His childhood was a real downer." Dom thumped his naked chest. "I, on the other hand, grew up in a big family. Five kids. I'm the youngest and they all love me." He grinned.

Seeing that smile, I could picture his family sheltering and taking care of the youngest boy. That gave me a better impression of Tristan and Dom. I had no idea if they were a gay couple, but I began to see maybe how they complemented each other. Tristan took care of the daily details that would escape spoiled family-baby Dom, while Dom brought life to Tristan's boring mannequin life. That explained why Tristan was so protective of Dom when I was in Smash Coffee this morning. I still didn't like him, though. Looking around the paper-strewn living room, I put my hand on Dom's arm. He had nice solid biceps. "Do you want me to help you clean this up?"

He shook his head. "Nah. Tris is temperamental. You know how writers are. He probably went over to a writer friend of his in these apartments. They'll have cognac and a bitch session, then write for a while and he'll come back a rational man again."

"If you say so," was the nicest thing I could think of to say. Rational man and Tristan Rogers just didn't fit in the same sentence to me. More like a tightrope waiting to snap would be my description. "By the way, what's an Alpha Smart?"

Dom shrugged. "Some kind of portable little word processor do-dad Tris can use to work on his book anywhere, then hook it up to his computer and dump the work in there. He raves about it all the time. Kind of boring."

Grandpa jumped in. "They're real nifty little machines. They run for hours and hours on just two double batteries. But you can't hook up to the Internet with them."

For an addicted Internet snoop like Grandpa, that's a real drawback. Smiling at Dom, I took my hand off his arm and got a business card out of my wallet. After handing it to him, I picked up the kitten box. "Call me if you think of anything else about Faye, okay?" I turned to the door, then looked back. "What's Tristan writing now? Another play?"

"He's working on a novel that's a suspense thriller. That's his big dream. Mine is acting. Tris wants to be a serious novelist."

"And Smash Coffee?"

Dom smiled. "Smash Coffee will one day finance our dreams. It's going to be a huge chain, bigger than Starbucks!"

I liked his style. In fact, I liked Dom.

I didn't sleep well. Tossing and turning my back into one huge cramp, I dragged myself out of bed even before Grandpa was up. Stumbling into the bathroom, I tried to clear my brain of Detective Vance, SUV stalkers, Dominic, Faye and Gabe.

I trusted Gabe. I did.

I snapped on the bathroom light. The kitten yowled, her tiny gray body stretching as she blinked in the bright glare. Then she looked at me and yowled again.

Sighing, I turned to the mirror and damn near yowled just like the kitten. My hair stuck out in frizzy curls. Bags bigger than my luggage were puffed up under my eyes, and I had deep lines across one side of my face where I'd spent my single hour of slumber with my cheek pressed into the pillow.

I needed coffee. And sleep. And Gabe to not be out doing other women. Staring at my sallow complexion, I said, "What are you going to do about this?"

Turning on the faucet, I splashed my face with cold water. Drying it, I peeled off the T-shirt I'd slept in and left the bathroom. From my dresser, I pulled out a pair of black bike shorts and a sports bra top. Winning the fight to stretch the spandex over my body, I pulled on a big white tank top. Then I stuffed my feet into socks and shoes. Running shoes.

Going back into the bathroom, I grabbed the baseball hat I had tossed on the floor last night. The kitten stared at me, her slate-blue eyes huge in her itty-bitty face.

"I'm going for a run." Yeah, like I ran. I did take Tae Kwon Do lessons. Sometimes. About once a month.

And if my run happened to take me by Gabe's house? Maybe I'd notice if he came home last night? A coincidence.

The kitten hissed and batted at a dust mite.

Grabbing up my hair, I put the hat on and tugged the end of my hair through the back. Quickly, I brushed my teeth. Ignoring the kitten, I left the bathroom and trudged down the hallway.

Ali padded out of the boys' room and cocked her head at me. Grandpa was almost always the first one up. Ali figured it must be an emergency.

"I'm going for a run."

She stared at me, then sneezed and headed for the front door. Shrugging, I opened the front door and went outside with my dog. Dang, it was cold!

Ali sat down and watched me. I bent over at the waist and touched my toes. So far, so good. I added a little bounce. Standing up, I thought that felt pretty good. "Okay, we'll start with a little walk to warm up." I took off down the steps and walked through the dirt toward Grand Street, turning left.

Ali paced me.

The air was crisp, not quite cold enough to see my breath. The Ortega Mountains surrounded me from behind, full of pinkish colors with the rising sun. Down below on my right, I caught a glimpse of the still lake over the tops of the houses. Ali and I walked quickly, breathing in the cool air and the quiet morning. Cars passed with commuters getting ready to hit the freeway and sit in the daily gridlock that plagues Southern California. My neck and back were already loosening up.

We came to the park that adjoined the middle school.

The well-kept field between the playground and the school was packed on weekends with soccer. Now it was empty. Ali and I crossed the street to the park; then she took off running, stretching her legs on the dew-touched grass. I plodded along the sidewalk that stretched along the edge of the park. Ali raced all the way up to the playground equipment at the top of the hill, then cut in and out of the swings and slides, sniffing around and kicking up clouds in the sand.

Smiling as I watched her, I picked up my pace and actually considered jogging. Hearing a car turn up the street, I checked for Ali, but she was fully engrossed in playground smells. Pumping my arms, I set off into a slow jog up the rest of the hill. My first goal was to get to the corner, where I could turn into the housing tract and I'd be on a downhill slope. I was only yards from the corner now and dead even with the playground on my right. There was a steep, grassy slope that went down to the playground. Many evenings I drove by here and saw kids riding pieces of cardboard down the slope.

I kept jogging, determined to make it to the corner. My lungs burned in protest of willful exercise. Damn, I was way out of shape, while Ali raced around the playground like a puppy.

Hearing a squeal of tires from my left, I whipped my head around.

The white SUV! It turned onto the street and skidded toward me. I stopped, staring at the huge, white front grill—it got larger by the second. It was going to hit me! Turn me into road kill.

Fear kicked in, snapping me out of shock. I spun around and dove—right out into the air over the grassy slope. I slammed down on the hill and rolled to the bottom, right smack into a cement picnic table.

I heard the SUV skid and hit the curb. Praying that

nothing was broken, I held on to the cold cement bench and pulled myself to my feet. Ali came running to me, already growling low in her throat. The SUV sat with one wheel up on the sidewalk curb above us. The motor idled and the driver door opened.

Gasping, I felt the hair on Ali's back rise and stiffen beneath my hand. Ali and I had been in a chase before, and she'd ended up shot. That time she'd only been nicked, but I didn't want her shot again. "Stay with me, Ali!" I started edging around the table, trying to figure out our situation. There were houses across the street and on the street right around the corner. The backyards of those houses were facing the park.

Looking back at the SUV, I saw a big man stumble around the front of the truck. He was lurching and weaving as if drunk.

Ali gave a single growl, shot out from beneath my hand, raced up the hill, and launched her eighty pounds of furious German shepherd body fully onto the man's chest. He was knocked flat on his back.

Stunned, I sucked in a breath and ran up the hill. "Ali!" I got to the sidewalk. I could see Ali's back, her long tail stiff and quivering. She had both her front paws on the man's chest and growled every few seconds. The man lay perfectly still.

Cautiously, I went around Ali's body and looked.

"Oh, my God! Eddie!" It was Eddie Flynn. He owned Eddie's Critters Pet Shop and was married to Jan, the town librarian. "Ali, down."

The growling stopped, and Ali stepped off Eddie's chest. He looked terrible. His faded blue eyes were red-streaked and puffy. His normally reddish complexion paled sickly. Sweat glistened thickly on his high forehead and upper lip. His once thick dark-gold hair faded to wheat-colored strings that screamed for a shampoo and Rogaine. Eddie used to be a decent football player in high school, but these days he looked more the part of the faded ex-jock. Still, he didn't usually look this bad. Not even Ali could have scared him into looking that sick.

But what was Eddie doing here? What was going on? "Why the hell have you been chasing me, Eddie?"

He groaned. I reached down and grabbed his hand, helping him off his back. He grunted up to a sitting position, then stood up. Staring up at him, I thought he was going to fall down again. Reaching out, I put my hand on his arm to steady him. However weird this was, I was not afraid of Eddie. Exasperated, I said, "Eddie, what's wrong with you? Have you been drinking?"

He shook his head no, then swallowed loudly over the noise of his Suburban's idling engine. He took a shallow breath, opened his mouth to answer and threw up all over me.

The warm, foul-smelling splash hit me in the chest and ran down my shirt, legs and arms. "Jeeze!" In reflex, I jumped back, but it was too late. I was covered. Dancing around in disgust, I ripped off my over-sized tank top and tried wiping off the barf. My stomach heaved, but there was nothing in there except an ounce of toothpaste-tasting water from brushing my teeth.

Eddie fell to his knees and finished puking. The sound sent waves of nausea washing through my stomach as I swiped over and over at the warm, used liquid on me. Ugh!

Ali whined and went down the hill by the picnic table. From there she sat down and stared at us. Smart dog; she wasn't getting puked on.

"I'm sorry, Sam." Eddie was on all fours and looked worse than before. His voice was thready and tired. Slowly, he got to his feet and went to his truck.

I stared after him. Now what? Was he going to run me over?

He came back with a container of baby wipes. Eddie didn't have kids, but he uses his white Suburban for transporting animals that made messes. Taking the wipes, I tossed the tank top into a nearby trash can. I didn't want it. Yanking out handfuls of wipes, I tried to take a shower in them. Meanwhile, I glared up at Eddie. "Start talking. Right now, I'm ready to get in your car and run *you* over and leave you for the buzzards. Why have you been stalking me?"

He began breathing deeper. Taking a couple of wipes, he ran the wet cloth over his mouth, face and neck. "I haven't been stalking you, I've been trying to talk to you."

"Eddie, are you drunk?" It was the only explanation.

"No!" He looked up at me, his swollen eyes painful to look at. "I'm not drunk. I need your help. Look at me, Sam, I'm a sick man."

He did look sick. And beaten. His thick football shoulders were slumped. I noticed that he did bear a resemblance in build to Jim Ponn of Ponn's Printing. With a baseball cap on and my terror, I could see how I might have thought it was Jim chasing me. Sighing, I looked around. It had to be six-thirty now, and full daylight. The street was still quiet. "Eddie, turn off your truck and come sit down at the picnic table." I went down the slope, feeling a few stiffening aches from rolling down the hill and slamming into the cement table.

And I was cold.

Eddie sat down across from me with his hands wrapped around a big silver travel coffee mug that he'd filled from the water fountain. Ali went a few feet away to sniff around a tree. I looked at Eddie. "What's this about, Eddie? If you wanted to talk to me, why didn't you come by the house, the office or call?"

He stared at his thick-fingered hands holding the travel mug. "Jan can't know, Sam."

Uh-oh. Sounded like a marriage problem to me. I'd never pegged Eddie and Jan for that kind of thing, though. Eddie had never given Jan a second look during high school, and then he'd left for college on a minor football scholarship. He'd landed back in town less than a year later. An old story, the big star in the small-town high school didn't always translate to big star at a bigger college. He basically flunked out and didn't do so hot on the field. Back in Lake Elsinore, Eddie floated around to a few jobs, settled into a delivery service, then was in an accident. He got a settlement from the accident and went to the library to find out about small businesses.

He met Jan there when she helped him with his research. They got married and Eddie opened his pet store. They had done well in the community. Jan and Eddie did a lot of community work and seemed devoted to each other. Jan had the ex-football star who would never look at her in high school, and Eddie had grown up enough to appreciate a woman like Jan. Or so I thought.

I dug deep and tried to pull out a little tact. "Eddie, I don't know if I should be the one you talk to about this." Given that my husband screwed around on me, I wasn't real sympathetic.

His eyes slowly lifted to mine. "You're the only one I can talk to. No one else can know. I just . . . I need to know."

Maybe I had this wrong. But no, Jan wouldn't screw around on Eddie. Women who wore long flowered skirts, pink jackets, pearls and Jergens lotion did not screw around on their husbands. My curiosity was piqued almost enough to ignore the sick vomit smell. "Know what?"

He looked around and leaned forward. "If she's poisoning me."

"What?" My voice bounced off the hills and trees surrounding us. "You think Jan is poisoning you? You've
lost it, Eddie."

"Shhh! No one can know about this. I'll pay you
whatever you want. I just have to know if she's poisoning me. You see how sick I am."

He did look sick. Not just the one-day kind of sick,
but long-term. His hair was falling out, and his skin
sagged from his eyes to his jaw. He appeared thinner
than the customary ex-jock-plus-regular-beer thickness
he'd been carrying around for a few years. But Jan poisoning him? "You think Jan is trying to kill you?"

"No, not kill me." He stopped talking and dropped
his head to stare at his hands and the travel mug. His
high forehead gleamed sickly in the brightening sunlight. "I think she's just making me sick. She could kill
me, I suppose. . . ."

"If this is true, and frankly, I'm not sure you aren't a
little nuts, this is something you have to tell the police."
Why did everyone come to me?

He jerked his head up. "No! No cops! No one can
know about this. I just want you to find out if I'm being
poisoned. That's all. If the town discovered Jan was poisoning me, it might ruin her reputation."

"You're worried about her reputation? She could kill
you!"

He shook his head. "I don't think she means to kill
me. You saw, I just get sick, then feel crummy for a
while. Until the next time."

This is why I'm never going to get married again.
Married people are insane. But Eddie looked in bad
shape. What could it hurt for me to—what did one do
on a case like this? How would I find out if Jan were poisoning him? "Eddie, what is it you want me to do?"

"Can't you, like, keep an eye on Jan? Just let me

know what she's doing? Maybe look around the house and see what she might be poisoning me with."

"Haven't you looked?"

He sucked up a breath. "I like the enemies I can see, know what I mean? On the football field, I know who my enemy is and I go after him. But this kind of thing, I don't know how to find out what she's doing. Remember when I got in the accident and got the settlement money?"

I nodded, wondering where he was going with this.

"I didn't know anything about how to research starting your own business. I just knew I wanted to maybe have a pet store. Jan did all that research stuff. She found out about small business loans, how to set up a business, everything. I know how to take care of animals and sell them to folks looking for a pet." He stopped.

"What are you getting at, Eddie?"

"Well, you know Jan works in the library. She could read books on anything and learn how to do it."

The light went on. "You mean like poison you with a household product or something so you wouldn't know?"

Running his hand over his forehead and stringy hair, he answered softly, "Yeah."

I still couldn't picture it. "Eddie, why would Jan do that? I thought you two loved each other."

"We do." Looking up at me with his red-streaked blue eyes, he leaned across the table. "I do love her. Jan's smart and she's helped me make something of myself in this town after I lost the football scholarship."

"That doesn't explain why she would poison you, Eddie." I was learning. I did not intend to step in the middle of something that would end up with me dead.

"Jan's a little . . . high strung. She likes things perfect. If I screw up, she has a way of making me pay for that."

"By poisoning you? Eddie"—I decided to try one more time—"you should go to the police."

"No! I love her. I don't want her in trouble. Please, Sam, just do this for me? I'll pay you. Don't tell anyone else and report everything you find to me. Okay?"

I could use the money. And now I was deeply intrigued. Love was my passion. I'd critiqued romance novels for thirteen years, now I ran a dating service, and I still didn't understand what made people in love do such bizarre things. But I wanted to. "Okay, Eddie. I'll do it." Quickly, I outlined a fee schedule, and Eddie agreed.

Getting up, he said, "One more thing—that woman you discovered murdered? Have the police arrested her killer yet? Or are they close?"

I shook my head. "No, not that I know of, Eddie. Why? Did you know her?"

"Saw her around. She liked animals and came in the shop sometimes. Said she couldn't have one since her husband was allergic." Eddie shuffled off to his truck.

I watched him go until I heard Ali whine. Looking over at her, I saw she was staying upwind of me. Catching a whiff of myself, I sighed. Now what? Home was twice as far as Gabe's house. "All right, Ali, let's go to Gabe's."

The thing was, I doubted Gabe would be at all shocked to have me show up on his doorstep at seven in the morning covered in vomit.

9

I stood across the street from Gabe's one-story, four-bedroom house. Most of the houses were two-story plans, but Gabe had picked the one story. He lived there alone. The front bedroom that opened off the living room functioned as his office. He could be sitting in there right now watching me out the window just to the left of the front door. Ali sat a little way from me on the sidewalk, whining. She knew where we were, and she was determined to go visit her buddy, Gabe.

Dogs apparently aren't plagued with second thoughts like humans. Gabe's black truck was absent from the driveway, which meant that he'd either parked it in the garage or he was gone. But at least there was not a strange car in the driveway—one that might belong to another woman.

Ali whined again. Looking down at her, I had to agree. Grandpa and the boys would be up by now and wondering where I was. I had no choice. Sighing, I started across the street.

Ali shot past me, barking joyfully.

"Ali!" I wailed.

Gabe's front door opened before I got up the driveway. I heard Gabe's rich voice talking to Ali. My stomach twittered with nerves. I rounded the corner of the garage.

First I saw Ali on her hind legs, her front paws on Gabe's naked chest while he scratched her ears.

Walking slowly, I took in his dark, straight hair carelessly brushed back and a faint sheen of sweat on his forehead and bare chest. He had on blue shorts and athletic shoes. All of which added up to a workout. I knew, from very personal experience, that Gabe had one bedroom turned into a gym. He looked hot, sexy and slightly dangerous.

Ali jumped down and Gabe's eyes shifted to me. I stood about four feet from him.

He sniffed once and ran his gaze over me, lingering on the black sports bra top, then lowering his gaze down my belly, hips and legs. Finally he looked me in the eye and arched one eyebrow. "Dumpster diving?"

Embarrassed tears suddenly burned my eyes. Gabe had been exercising and looked like an Italian hottie. I tried exercising and looked, and smelled, like I'd been run over by a septic truck. Life was not fair. Irritated at myself, I blinked back the tears and got defensive. "I need to use your phone. I'll stay out here if you bring me the cordless."

His gaze softened. "Calling the police?"

I shook my head. "Kids."

He opened the door wide. "Babe, go take a shower. I'll call Barney and the boys to let them know where you are."

Damn, he was being nice. I couldn't deal with nice right now. "Uh, you might want to move back." No way was I walking by him and giving him the full barf-a-roma treatment.

Grinning, he said, "Shut the door behind you. I'll

tell Barney that you are fine and make sure he can get the boys to school." Turning, he disappeared behind the front door to where his office was nestled into the fourth bedroom. Ali followed him.

Lifting my chin, I shucked off my shoes to keep from tracking vomit on Gabe's beige Berber carpet. Going in, I shut the door behind me and walked by the office without looking in. The living room on my right had a warm brown couch that matched a big square chair and ottoman across the brass-with-glass-inlay coffee table. There were some Western prints on the walls, lots of open land with buffalo roaming type things. The formal dining room attached to the living room still remained empty. I turned left, passing the kitchen/family room to hook a second left into the bathroom.

Closing and locking the door, I leaned back against it. The mirror looked back at me.

Ugh. Taking off my hat, I got a good look at smashed frizzy hair. I stripped off the black bra top, bike shorts, socks and thong. Opening the cupboard under the sink, I pulled out a couple of towels and wrapped my clothes up in one. I'd wash the towel and return it to Gabe later.

Dropping the towel-wrapped clothes on the floor, I went to the shower and turned it on full blast. Thankfully there was shampoo and lots of soap. Getting into the steamy tub, I stood under the hot, pelting water and started with my hair. Working from the top to the bottom, I restored myself to clean and thought about Gabe.

He was alone in his house. I wasn't a schmuck. I wanted to rub Vance's face in that little discovery. Of course, the fact that I checked up on Gabe meant that Vance had gotten to me. That annoyed me. Next time, I'd tell Vance to suck eggs. Gabe was one of the good guys. I knew we didn't have a real future, but he didn't lie to me and sleep around with other women.

God, how stupid would I look if he had done that? Thirty-something widowed woman goes after hunk five years her junior and he makes a fool of her? I'd never live that down in town. Turning off the shower, I grabbed the towel and dried off. Full of relief, I stepped out of the tub and onto the floor rug. The mirror was fogged. Pulling off my towel, I wiped a circle in the mirror.

I looked wet and tired. But at least I was vomit-free and smelled like soap. I could live with that. Finger combing my hair, I glanced down at the bundle of dirty clothes. Damn, what was I going to put on?

My choices were severely limited to either a towel or a washcloth. Not an oversized bath towel, but the standard barely-cover-breast-to-top-of-thigh size. It wasn't like Gabe hadn't seen me naked. Besides, maybe now was a good time to play it sexy for him. Grandpa would get the kids off to school. Maybe Gabe and I could spend a few minutes doing a little naked tumbling before I rushed home, dressed and went to work. I had to admit it was incredibly seductive to see him in the doorway with only his shorts on. Plus, nothing I did ever ruffled Gabe. He made showing up at his door before seven in the morning and reeking seem normal.

He just accepted me the way I was. Pretty cool.

Glancing back in the mirror, I made a face. Vance's comment had threatened me deeply, and if I were honest with myself, I'd probably have to admit that I was sort of marking my territory with Gabe by deciding to seduce him.

That was my plan—sex, then talk to Gabe about Eddie and needing to find Faye's killer by Saturday, which gave me a whole two days, then home and off to work. A full morning. Flashing a grin at myself, I figured *what the hell* and wrapped the towel around me. That was the kind of woman I was—seduce my boyfriend before running out to solve a murder and a spousal poisoning, match up a few lonely hearts and be home in time to cook dinner for my kids. I could do it all. Pulling the door open, I smelled fresh-brewed coffee. The house was silent.

I stepped out of the steamy bathroom into the cool hallway. Gabe in his shorts and bare chest lingered on my mind.

Vance and his snide insinuations fueled my bravado, made me want to prove that I was desirable. No better way to do that then with the always sexy, sometimes dangerous, Gabe.

The kitchen and family room were empty. A full pot of coffee sat untouched on the white tiled counter. I guessed that he was in his office. Clutching the towel, I went to the back door—it was one of those wood-frame-with-glass-in-the-middle types—and looked out to see Ali contentedly chewing on some kind of meat bone.

Now all I had to do was find Gabe. He'd ducked into his office to call Grandpa and the boys when I came in, so I figured I'd find him there. Maybe he'd be looking over his work, his dark hair falling over his face, big shoulders glistening in the morning sun.

I hoped he hadn't put a shirt on.

Briefly, I wondered if I had turned into a slut. Smiling, I headed out of the kitchen to the living room. I could hear movement and low muttering in the office. Bingo—I'd found him. Probably on the phone. This was going to be fun.

Now to surprise him. Sucking in a breath, I didn't let myself think. For once, I was just going to do something for Gabe and not think of consequences. So far in our relationship, he'd done the chasing and seducing. Time for a little role-reversal. I dropped the towel and rounded the corner into the bedroom-turned-office.

"Surprise!" I threw up my right arm against the doorjamb and thrust out my left hip to give Gabe a full view of my curves. My heart hammered in my chest.

I waited a beat, then looked around to see Gabe's reaction.

Ohmigod! He wasn't alone. A stunningly gorgeous brunette leaned over Gabe's chair, her long, shimmering hair falling over his naked shoulders and the surface of his desk. She wore a lace top held together over her excellent implants with a single tie. Her piercing blue eyes stared at me. Her perfect mouth dropped open.

I was going to throw up. Or die. Could I hold my breath and die? This was my worse nightmare. Frozen to the ground, humiliation exploded from my center and heated every inch of my skin.

Move! Do something! The words bounced inside my head, but no one said anything. Silence hung thickly.

I backed away—nothing could make me turn around to show my generous backside. Once out of their sight, I whirled around to run. To escape.

My feet tangled in the bath towel I had dropped on the floor earlier. Already in motion, I flew forward and landed facedown and spread-eagled. Berber carpet tickled my skin while humiliation compelled me to get the hell out of there. I struggled to climb up and managed to get to my knees. The towel was tangled around my feet. I kicked at it while clawing at the carpet with my hands, just like the damned kitten. Desperation drove me to keep going.

Please, God, don't let them be behind me! The view would be . . . Oh, God I couldn't think about it!

Finally, I kicked the towel free and lunged to my feet. Without looking back, I fled around the hallway corner to the bathroom.

I slammed the door shut, turned the lock and leaned against it. What the hell did I do now? Looking into the mirror, the red face of a panicked woman stared back at me. My hair was half dried to a curly frizz. "Shit, shit, shit!" I squeezed my eyes shut and prayed I would wake up from this nightmare.

I heard movement in the house. A door closed. A car started. Yeah, my hearing kicked in now. Why hadn't I heard the boyfriend-stealing bimbo come into the house? Or in Gabe's office? I grit my teeth in disgust with myself—because I'd been horny and focused on my stud of a former boyfriend.

Who was that woman hanging on Gabe?

"Sam?"

I jumped, whirled around and glared at the door. Gabe was on the other side of that door.

I was never going to face him again. I would stay locked in the bathroom until he left. He had to leave the house eventually. Then I'd get my dog and go home.

Maybe we'd move out of Lake Elsinore. Or the state of California altogether.

"Come on, Babe, open the door."

Yeah, right. Anger washed over my humiliation. I had trusted him. I'd gone to him naked and . . . I couldn't even think about it. Why did she have to be beautiful? "Eat dirt and die!"

Silence. I was pretty sure he wasn't eating dirt and planning to die. Gabe never gave up. He also had a handy set of lock-picking tools and a wealth of know-how. I started looking around the bathroom for some kind of help. Liquid hand soap in a pump by the faucet, a few towels—

A quick, metallic scrape, then a click snapped my attention back to the door. "Stay out!"

The door opened.

I grabbed the shower curtain, yanking it over my body as I backed up into the corner between the tub and toilet.

Gabe's powerful bare shoulders filled the span of the doorway, then narrowed down to his flat waist where his smooth skin disappeared beneath his blue shorts. I caught a glimmer of silver from the slim tool clutched in his right hand. His face was blank, except for his nearly black eyes. They fastened on me.

My mind bubbled and bounced from thought to thought until I sucked in a breath and halted the chaos. I would not be a coward. Whatever this woman was to Gabe, I would make him think it didn't matter to me. Like I ran naked in front of supermodels seducing my boyfriend every day. Lifting my chin, I glared at him. "Bet you were surprised."

"No more surprised than you." He leaned against the doorframe, his gaze turning watchful.

Ball back in my court. God, why couldn't I disappear? "I need some clothes."

"Apparently." He didn't move.

Shit. I couldn't make myself pull on my vomit-soaked spandex shorts and bra top. "Maybe you could get me some?"

He pushed off the wall with his shoulder, set the tool on the bathroom counter and stepped closer to me. "I have the feeling that if I get you something to wear besides my shower curtain, you'll disappear on me."

That's the idea. "Look, Gabe, obviously you're *busy*. Just get me something to wear and I'm out of here."

"Believe me, Sam, you have my full attention. You had my attention from the second you yelled *surprise.*"

"God"—I couldn't help myself—"how do I do these things? I swear this stuff doesn't happen to other people!"

A slow grin crawled over Gabe's face. "I'd lay money on that bet. You are one of a kind."

I narrowed my eyes. "Who is she, Gabe? Vance told me last night you were doing *private consulting.*"

He arched an eyebrow. "Vance, huh?"

All right, I was done. Gabe could play his games with the private-consulting bitch. Oops, I meant *client*. Glaring at him standing a whole three feet from me, I said, "I have two days to find out who murdered Faye, and now Eddie Flynn wants me to find out if his wife is poisoning him. Eddie threw up all over me this morning while I was out running. Believe me when I say I'm having a bad day. So I suggest that unless you have something to tell me about Faye's murder, you get me some clothes and get out of my way." Breathing hard with my speech, I looked up at the clear plastic rings holding the plastic shower curtain to the rod. If all else failed, maybe I could tear the curtain down and wear it home.

Of course, I'd have to steal Gabe's truck since I wasn't going to walk home wearing a shower curtain.

Halfway into the bathroom, Gabe took another step that brought him nose to nose with me. "You trying to piss me off?"

I blinked. "Are you trying to make me kill you?" Sort of an idle threat given his two hundred pounds of pure muscle. And damn it, couldn't he at least smell rank from working out this morning? He smelled good. Faint tang of Irish Spring mixed with a rich male scent. In spite of myself, a thread of desire curled inside of me.

He lifted a hand, slipping it around the edge of the shower curtain next to my clutching hand. "You trusted me enough to come into my office naked." He ripped the shower curtain away. Several of the plastic things holding it to the rod snapped. The curtain hung drunkenly and out of my reach, leaving me naked again.

Uh-oh. Every once in a while I tended to forget that Gabe lived by his own rules. But I refused to be intimidated. Or at least to not show it. "You're pissed 'cause I got naked and walked into your office? Big deal." Not the best boost for my ego.

"Get real." He leaned over me, one hand on the mirror to the left side of my head, the other hand on the porcelain wall of the shower. "You can come to me naked anytime. It's the mistaking me for your dead husband that pisses me off. You can trust me, Sam."

I could feel the heat of his body. What was it about Gabe and me? We had this combustible relationship that got hotter by the day. I couldn't talk to him like this. I was naked, and he . . . I dropped my gaze to his hugely distorted shorts.

We were going to end up doing it on the bathroom floor if I didn't get us out of here and me into some clothes. I didn't know if that was all bad or just partly bad. "Where's she now?"

"Veronica? She went on ahead to the studio for a script meeting. I'll meet her and the writers there later."

"You're working on a script?"

His gaze lowered to my mouth. "Consulting. Just like Vance told you. I do that sometimes. Veronica asked for some extra coaching for her part in a pilot TV show about a small-town private investigator."

Conflicting feelings swirled inside of me. Hollywood was beckoning Gabe. He looked like Hollywood. Somehow I didn't think a widowed mother of two sons who ran a dating service could compete with that. "You never told me."

He was doing an eye-search thing, and right now he was studying my breasts. I had a pretty decent pair of size C implants. He raised his gaze back to me. "Habit, Babe. I don't talk about work. All you have to do is ask, and I'll tell you what I'm working on."

I remembered him pulling out his cell phone last night, ready to cancel to help me. "You were with her last night?" I snapped my mouth shut. I didn't want to do this—play the wounded woman. But damn, he had me surrounded, backed into the corner of his bathroom. If this were a romance novel, Gabe would declare his desire for only me and we'd do it on the floor.

"Yes. I took her on a fake stakeout to show her what it's like."

But this wasn't a romance novel. And I wasn't going to be a fool. "I have to get to work."

He slid his hands in, capturing my head. "You weren't thinking about work when you posed in the doorway of my office wearing only your sex appeal." Then before I could answer, he leaned down, his mouth hot on mine.

"Gabe? Sam? I brought the clothes!" Grandpa's voice was close.

Snapping my head back and banging my head on the mirror, I heard Grandpa's shuffling tread in the hallway outside the bathroom. Christ, what next, the pope? I couldn't face one more person naked, and especially not my grandpa!

Gabe wasn't in much better shape given his huge hard-on.

Panicked, I shoved at him, trying to get to the shower curtain.

"Relax, Babe." He sighed, turned away and scooped up my towel-wrapped dirty clothes from the floor. Carrying them in front of his hips, he went out of the bathroom, pulling the door closed behind him.

I heard their voices in the hallway. Grandpa said, "I brought Sam these clothes. And I think she'd better take a look at this."

I heard the sound of paper crackling. Given how my day was going, it had to be another catastrophe.

"Let me see." Gabe's voice was moving away.

Curiosity ate at me. Getting another towel out from beneath the sink, I wrapped it around me and sat down on the edge of the tub. Eyeing the little silver do-dad that Gabe had used to pick the bathroom lock with, I picked it up. Inspecting it closer, I almost laughed. The highly skilled PI had used a standard skeleton key that came with most new houses. Next time I wanted to lock myself in a bathroom, I needed to check the molding over the doorway for skeleton keys.

Twisting the key in my hand, I waited.

Finally the door opened. Gabe came in and set down a pair of jeans and a T-shirt on the counter. "Barney's gone. He brought you these clothes. He's already dropped the boys at school."

"You asked him to do that when you called?"

Gabe looked at me. "Yes."

I glanced at the pile of clothes, including shoes and white cotton underwear poking out between the discreetly folded jeans. At this point, Grandpa in my underwear drawer wasn't my biggest problem. "Thanks." I was as confused as ever about Gabe.

His gaze lingered on me wrapped in the towel, and then he sighed. "Get dressed, Babe. We got a situation." He closed the door quietly.

A situation? What now? Getting up, I pulled on my clothes and tried finger-combing my hair.

Hopeless.

I went into the kitchen to find Gabe had poured coffee. He had a white tiled bar that separated the kitchen from the family room. He was sitting at the bar, reading the newspaper and drinking coffee. A second steaming cup sat at the place next to him. I went around him and sat on the stool.

He closed the paper and turned it so that I could see the headlines:

HEART MATES DATING SERVICE:
Exposé on Dating Service with Lurid History

I looked up at Gabe over the paper. "My day just got worse."

He nodded. "You can read it for yourself later. Here's the short version. This writer claims they went under-cover at Heart Mates to investigate if dating services are really a safe way to meet romantic partners. The author is anonymous for his or her own protection. They claimed they picked Heart Mates because it was in the news last year with the dope-dealing scandal and the death of a police detective investigating it. The author states you were cleared of any wrongdoing. The article goes on to say that with the recent murder of Faye Miller and Faye's connection to Heart Mates, dating services could be dangerous places. So this is a first of two parts in investigating dating services."

Fury blurred my vision. Who had done that? Who had come to Heart Mates and pretended to be a client when they had really been a reporter? And Faye! To use her horrible murder that way. I shivered, picked up the cup of coffee and took a sip. "What else?"

"Discusses your security measures, walking the reader through the joining process. The writer's conclusions come out in tomorrow's paper."

I looked into Gabe's face. "Can they do this? Can they say and imply things about Heart Mates this way?"

"Legally they might be on shaky ground, but do you have the money and time to go after them? They are banking that you don't. This stuff sells papers."

Heart Mates was my baby. I had to force myself to think. But Gabe was not emotional that way. He was clearheaded and factual. This article told him something—what? "When you said *we have a situation*, what did you mean?"

He turned his head, looking at me. "What do you make of this article, Babe?"

I ignored the endearment and focused. "Someone is trying to smear Heart Mates, me or both."

"Maybe," he agreed. He went to the coffeepot by the sparkling white refrigerator and refilled our cups. "Or someone is trying to divert attention from themselves."

I thought about that. "Like how?"

"Look at what you have so far. You find Faye with the brochure of Heart Mates in her hand. I got some information about Faye's autopsy, but we'll get to that in a minute. There's something about the brochure the police are holding back. Then these articles about Heart Mates start turning up. If the killer is not Faye's husband, Adam, or another client from Heart Mates, then it's convenient for the killer to get the police to look there."

"Misdirection." Like Grandpa's magic. I had to admit that made sense. "But how could the killer get the newspaper to write these kinds of articles?"

"Good question. You're thinking now. So it could be the killer's trying to misdirect the police, as you said. Or it could be the killer is specifically out to get you."

I stared back into his dark eyes. "Me? Personally? Why?"

"Don't know, but let's just say you do have a certain knack for stumbling into trouble."

"Thanks." I dropped my eyes to my half-filled cup of coffee. Embarrassment over my naked surprise tickled the back of my throat and made my eyes water. I shoved it aside. Faye was dead. Adam Miller wanted to go to her funeral in two days' time. I had to find out who murdered her.

"Babe."

Swallowing my own humiliation, I looked up at Gabe.

"You did surprise me. We're not done with that."

I centered myself. I had a job to do. "Yes, we are. Let's get back to Faye."

He touched my jean-clad leg. "No, we're not. That's a promise. But right now, I'm seriously worried about your safety. How about coming to my meeting with me this morning? Call Blaine and let him handle Heart Mates today."

Go with him? Facing Veronica wasn't high on my list of things to do, but somehow that Gabe would want me there, and worried about me, eased my mortification. "I can't, Gabe. I owe Faye this. Dominic told me that Faye was trying to be more like me. And if her murder is connected to me or Heart Mates . . ."

His mouth curved slightly, and he squeezed my leg. "I know, Sam."

He did know. Gabe still struggled with his own demons. Including the murder of his wife and their unborn son. His wife had called him, pleading with him to save her when gang members had been breaking into their apartment. Gabe had been on duty and unable to get there fast enough. Nor had he been able to get another patrol car or cop there fast enough. But the worst thing, the thing that still ate at him, was that his young, pregnant wife wouldn't help herself. She wouldn't get Gabe's gun down from the closet and protect herself and their unborn child.

There were many layers to Gabe's guilt, in his mind. That he hadn't got there fast enough, that the gang members were retaliating against him by killing his wife and baby and that Gabe had fostered his wife's dependence on him—the dependence that had rendered her incapable of defending herself.

I touched his hand on my leg. While I didn't fully understand the powerful and explosive passion between us, I was firmly caught in its hold. "I'll be all right. You go to your meeting. First, tell me what you got from Faye's autopsy report." I winced on that last sentence. Faye had been so alive and bubbly just days ago. Now she was dead and cut up.

His face settled back into a mask. "The police have determined that she was strangled by some kind of rope object that had white and blue nylon threads. There was no rape or sexual activity in the hours prior to her death."

"Strangled. Then the brochure was put in her hand. God." Thinking about it, I said, "In your experience, when an angry husband does that, does he rape his wife first?"

"Depends. Maybe if he went there to punish her, or establish his control over his wife, yes. But if things just got out of hand and he killed her, maybe not. Keep in mind, Sam, there was no forced entry. Faye let her killer into the motel room, or he followed her in when she came in. But she appeared to be dressed for bed and working. So I favor that she let her killer in."

From what I knew of Adam, and talking to Mindy, I didn't believe Adam did it.

The memory of Faye slumped over that table, then falling on me, cramped my gut. But I tried to hold on to the image and think. "So it's likely she knew who murdered her. And trusted him?"

"Didn't feel threatened by him is a better way to phrase it. Assuming it was a he. A woman could have strangled her, but I'd lean toward it being a man just on the strength it takes to strangle someone. Faye wasn't a small, frail woman."

I realized I had my hand at my throat. It was just so horrible. The thought of someone getting behind Faye, throwing some kind of rope around her neck and tightening it . . . "Did someone just walk into Faye's room with a rope? It doesn't add up. Adam says he went to have her sign the divorce papers and she refused. She said she wanted to think about it. Then Adam left and went to a friend's house. If he did it, would he walk in there with a rope? Wouldn't Faye be suspicious?" I couldn't see it.

"Strangling is often impulsive. It's a personal way to kill, and usually done in some kind of strong emotion like anger or fear. The murderer and Faye may have argued or disagreed and the murderer grabbed something in the room to strangle her. Maybe like the belt to her robe, but that wouldn't have nylon threads in it."

Nylon threads? "Ohmigod." My breath locked in my chest and the kitchen spun drunkenly.

Gabe took his hand off of my thigh and grabbed my arms to steady me. "Sam, what is it?"

His touch calmed me. Gabe would know what to do. "The nylon threads, a rope—Faye's jump rope. It always hung off her mirror, and it wasn't there when I went into her room the day I found her. It was white with blue threads and it was nylon."

His face tightened. "A nylon jump rope? That would fit."

I took a slow breath. "There's more." My mind tumbled backward to last night.

Gabe's fingers firmed on my arm. "What?"

"I saw two jump ropes in Dominic Danger's bedroom last night."

10

Ali sat between Gabe and me in his truck parked in front of my house. He was dropping me off on his way to Los Angeles, or more specifically, Hollywood. On the drive over, I caught him up on my interview with Dominic Danger.

"I can't think why Dom would kill Faye. He flat-out told me that he encouraged her to jump rope for exercise if she wanted to lose weight. That seems stupid to make any connection between himself and the murder weapon if he killed her. The jump ropes I saw in his room were bright orange, not white with blue threads like Faye's." I chewed my lower lip while picking dog hair off my shirt. Tired of waiting to see what Gabe and I were going to do, Ali plopped her head in Gabe's lap.

Gabe petted the dog. "So your suspects are Jim Ponn, Dominic Danger and Adam."

I glanced over. "I'm working for Adam. I'm trying to find Faye's killer so Adam can go to his wife's funeral without worrying about being arrested. He loved her."

"Don't rule Adam out. His car was at the motel the night of the murder."

I stopped fiddling with the dog hair on my clothes. "Adam told me he was there, Gabe. That's my point. Adam loved Faye enough to let her go by agreeing to the divorce. Faye's the one who decided not to sign the papers. How'd you find out his car was at the motel?"

"A source. The night clerk's office is across the parking lot from Faye's room. He saw three cars. A tan Toyota Camry that belongs to Adam. It was there often. Then a white truck with a shell or an SUV, he couldn't tell for sure. And a dark sedan, either a Honda Accord or an Accura."

"Jim Ponn has a white Ford truck. That's what Grandpa said last night. But Dominic drives a yellow Mustang, so his car wasn't there."

"Could have taken Tristan's car. Barney said it was a black Accura."

"Hm, that brings us back to Dom. I can't find a motive. He freely admits to being friends with Faye. What do I do?"

"Ask around about Faye. Talk to Adam again, preferably in person. Find out what he's not telling you. Clients usually only tell you what they think you need to know. Look at it this way—Faye let someone in to kill her. Learn enough about her life, and you'll know who she would let in."

That made sense. "Sort of get to understand the victim so I can think like her?" It made me sad. I'd been enjoying getting to know Faye while she was alive. And I'd been honored that she wanted my help in learning to run her own business and be a new woman.

"Right, but when you talk to Adam, take Ali with you as a precaution." He glanced down at the dog he was petting. When he returned his attention to me, his dark eyes were thoughtful. "Do you know where Adam is, Sam?"

"Mindy wouldn't tell me, but I have an idea." My best friend, Angel Crimson, had been avoiding me and she claimed to have a new investment. Adam Miller's computer game had an investor. Coincidence?

"Okay, stay vague on that so that you are not lying to the cops."

I met his dark eyes. "CYA?" Gabe had a thing about *covering your ass*. He often mentioned that when I was claiming to be working under his license. I think he had the idea that I might get him into some trouble. He didn't seem particularly worried about that, more like amused resignation.

A wicked grin curved his mouth. "Always, and especially with *your* mouth-watering ass."

The cab of the truck shrank. And heated. I tried not to think of posing naked in front of Gabe and his beautiful actress-client. I tried even harder not to think of Gabe's hard body doing sizzling sexual things to me. God, I was a wreck. I needed sleep. Food. A normal life. *Focus!*

"Uh, should I tell Vance about the jump rope?"

He shook his head. "No, they have a lab running down the fibers and other scientific stuff. Instead, try to find out more about Faye. Follow Faye, and the clues we have, to the killer. Use the clues to make it fit: The brochure in Faye's hand, the newspaper articles, Faye getting interested in the play Dominic told you about and the cars that were spotted in the motel parking lot—those will lead you to who Faye might have let in that night." He reached out his hand, his long fingers curling around my bare arm. His eyes darkened to serious black coal and hardened on me. "Just don't try anything dangerous yourself. Got it?"

That was a little insulting. Sometimes I got the impression Gabe thought I was a danger to myself. "You

know I took down two thugs last night?" I described the
two men working on the truck at Dominic's apartment.
". . . So I sprayed them both and Grandpa and I took
off. That was when we crashed into Vance's car."

"You hit a homicide detective's car?" He said each
word carefully as if he might choke.

I glared at him. "Don't you dare laugh. The point is
that I can take care of myself."

His mouth twitched, but he didn't laugh. At least, not
out loud. "And take out a homicide detective at the
same time. You are scary-lucky sometimes."

"Yeah?" I stuck my chin up. I put one hand on the
door handle. Gabe still had his hand wrapped around
my upper arm. "Some of it's skill. I'm getting better at
investigating."

Ali turned to regard at me with her liquid brown eyes.
From behind her, Gabe stared at me with the same intensity. "What exactly is the reason you are honing these
skills, Sam?"

"To be capable. Strong." He knew this about me.
Most of it.

"To do what?"

I looked away. "Do you know what this town thought
of me, Gabe? The stupid, fatherless girl that married
the town skirt-chaser. They assumed I was so damned
grateful just to be married that I accepted it."

"You changed that."

"Damn right I did."

"Except for being fatherless. I'm wondering if you
might be polishing your investigating skills to search for
your father."

God, how did he do that? How could he see in me
what I tried so hard to hide from myself? Looking for
my bio-dad would be hurling myself into a pit of pain
and rejection. I knew it, accepted it and yet. . . . "I'm in

my thirties, Gabe, I don't need a father. Besides, I have Grandpa." I ignored the clenched muscles in my stomach that tightened my chest and changed the subject. "What about you, Gabe? Thinking you might want to take a turn in front of the camera? Or maybe write scripts for shows?" Apparently he'd been working on some scripts for a while. Was I going to lose him to Hollywood while I stayed in my little blue-collar town and matched up lonely hearts? The sense of loss sneaked up on me. I lifted my chin to look him dead in the eyes. "Maybe a career in Tinsel Town?"

Silence hung for long seconds until Ali broke the moment by jumping down on the floor by my feet and whining. I opened the door and let her out. She ran around, then found a place to relieve herself.

I turned back to Gabe. Leaning across the seat, he put his mouth less than an inch from mine. "Give me a reason to stay here, Babe."

Shit. Damn. "Gabe—"

He sighed. "I have to go, Sam. But we're not done with this conversation, and we sure as hell aren't done with you being naked for my pleasure."

A shiver ran through me. "I have kids. I can't just do that whenever . . ." I lost the words in his hot kiss.

Breaking the kiss, he looked into my eyes. "Be ready, Sam."

"For what? When?" With Gabe, anything was possible.

His grin spread sin. "Just be ready."

Blaine looked up from his chorizo-and-egg burrito as I came into Heart Mates. The kitten lifted her tiny black nose over the edge of the box in my arms and sniffed at the thick sausage smell. "Jeeze, Blaine, you ever eat anything green?" I set the box down on the folding chairs in the cramped reception area.

"Guacamole. What are you, half virgin, half biker chick?"

I looked down at my white pleated skirt short enough to require built-in panties that I had paired with a black leather halter. I finished the outfit off with black stilettos that had a thin, sexy ankle strap. The heels and short skirt lengthened my normally stubby legs to the red zone. To draw attention to my best feature, I had put on a long silver necklace that dipped into the deep V of my cleavage. Going to the coffeemaker, I poured myself a cup. "I was a little down this morning. Thought I'd dress up."

"Man trouble?"

I winced. Oh, yeah, man trouble. Hollywood was seducing my boyfriend. How the hell did I compete with that? "Who, me?" I lifted my chin. "Romance is my profession."

"That outfit screams *professional*. Works on you, though, especially in the bird. That black leather halter"—he gestured toward me with his hand holding the end of the burrito—"would look fine against the red seats and white paint job. Did you have the top off this morning?" He popped the rest of the burrito in his mouth.

"Uh, thanks, I think." Frowning into my coffee cup, I said, "Did you just say I look like a hooker, but it works on me because of my car?" Which would Blaine choose? A decadent sports car or a decadent woman? As a romance professional, I should know the answer. I didn't.

Wiping his hands on a paper napkin, he ignored me. "What about the kitten?"

I sighed. "I don't know. I'm out of ideas. Got to find a home for her." Taking a sip of hot coffee, I glanced at my watch. "I have a couple of phone calls to make, then I'll be ready to go over the computer matches from yesterday. Any messages?"

He wrapped his greasy napkins up in the wax paper the burrito came in, then arced it toward the trash can by his desk. A direct hit. "Nothing that can't wait until you're done with the phone calls."

Nodding, I glanced at the kitten to see that she was quiet. I went into my office. After dumping my purse in the bottom drawer and putting my coffee out of spill-all-over-me range, I reached for the phone just as it rang.

I stared at it. Given the way my day had gone so far, I was expecting a disaster. Or my mother.

"Sam, line one for you. Linda Simpkins," Blaine called over the cubical wall.

Good or bad? Linda was the president of the PTA. Visions of getting roped into chairing a committee or doing a fundraiser made my bare arms itch with the threat of hives. Then I remembered I had run into Linda at Smash Coffee. She'd been there when I'd gone to talk to Dom and ended up dealing with that tattletale mannequin, Tristan. She'd said she'd ask around about Faye for me.

Taking a quick sip of coffee to wash down my PTA panic, I picked up the phone. "Hi, Linda."

"Sam, I did what you asked and called around. But I think you're going to have to follow up on this yourself."

Linda's voice was hushed to a tone I knew well. *Gossip.* "Why, Linda? What did you find out?"

"I don't want to speak ill of the dead. . . ." She trailed off.

I picked up my cue. "Of course not. But if you have any information that can help me figure out what happened to Faye, that's not gossip."

"Well, no one was willing to let me use their names or to call you themselves, but two of the women I had talked to had heard a rumor that Faye left her husband for another man."

"Another man? But—" Faye was having an affair? I already knew Faye hadn't been coming to Heart Mates to find love. Adam never said anything about another man. Maybe he didn't know. Maybe it wasn't true. Just who was Faye Miller? "Linda, did they say who the man was? He could be Faye's killer." Which meant my list of suspects was growing. Adam—who I didn't consider a serious suspect, Dominic Danger, Jim Ponn and now a mystery lover.

"No. That's all I got, Sam. I swear. Neither wanted to talk about it and both said they hadn't seen proof firsthand. More like . . . uh . . . they surmised from what they saw kind of thing."

Great, a third-person clue handed to me in a word puzzle. Just friggin' perfect. Obviously, Linda was trying to give me a hint of at least one of the women with this information. How did I track this down? I pulled the sharpened pencils out of my heart-shaped pencil holder TJ had gotten me for Christmas and balanced six of them across the top of my steaming coffee cup. Not a single pencil leaped off the cup and wrote down the answer to my dilemma of tracking down the clue. But Linda had tried. "Thanks, Linda. I'll try to track this down." I should buy a crystal ball.

"Sure, Sam. I'll let you know if I hear anything else." She hung up.

Faye having an affair—what did that tell me? If true, it had to have been a very secret affair if only two people had even heard the rumor. In a small town like Lake Elsinore, word got around. Everyone in town knew when Trent had been screwing around on me—well, everyone except me. But that was because of my natural head-in-the-sand talent. Trent hadn't made any real effort to keep it a secret.

Staring at my white coffee cup stamped with pink

hearts and topped with sharpened pencils, I tried to picture myself having a clandestine affair. What evidence would I leave? Phone records? Maybe I could get those, or Grandpa could through his connections, but the police would already have those. I needed another path to run down this affair rumor.

What do secret lovers do? I hadn't had a secret lover, but I had read a ton of romance novels. I knew the answer. *Gifts*. Lovers give each other gifts. I had to think about this, but I bet I could track this rumor down that way. If it were true, I'd find out.

If Faye was having an affair, did Adam know? Mindy had been Faye's best friend, and she hadn't seemed to know. Or she didn't want to tell me.

I reached for the phone and dialed Angel. While the phone rang, I started looking through my drawers for a diet bar. I was starving.

The answering machine clicked on and Angel's sexy voice purred in my ear.

I was having none of it. "I know you're there, Angel. Pick up the phone now. If you don't pick up in ten seconds, I'm going to call a certain homicide detective and the two of us are going to take a ride over to your—"

"Sam! I just ran in the door. How are you?"

"Great!" I matched her perky voice. "Let's see, my best friend's been avoiding me and lying about her new investment. I have two days to solve a murder. My week has been filled with dead bodies, vomit and public nakedness. How are you?" My drawers were filled with yellow pads, pens, pencils, staples but no diet bars so far. My stomach growled.

"Figured you'd puzzle it out. I wanted to tell you, but—"

I jumped in. "Don't tell me anything! If I am asked directly, I want to say that I don't know where Adam

Miller is hiding." I reached my hand way in the back of
the drawer that I kept my emergency makeup, hair gel
and blow dryer in. Bingo! I pulled out a slightly smashed
diet bar. Triple Mocha Fudge flavor. Yummy.

"Sure. That's why we didn't want to tell you. Anyway,
these creative nerd types are high-strung and paranoid."

My hand froze in the process of trying to tear the
plastic wrapping off my diet bar. *"High-strung?* As in the
kind of high-strung that could snap and, say, kill someone?" Had I been wrong about Adam? Given the information that Faye might have been having an affair . . .

"God, no! Adam couldn't kill a bug. High-strung like
not caring about putting the finishing touches on the
computer game because he's so broken up over Faye.
Paranoid that if the police find him, they won't listen to
him. He's desperate for you to find who killed her."

Relief flooded through me. Angel had experience
with men. She also had experience stalking men. Stalking
her ex-husband was her hobby. But that wasn't what I
needed to talk to Angel about. "Listen, I need to set up
a meeting with Adam."

"Mindy told Adam that she'd handle all of that with
you."

I redoubled my attack on unwrapping the diet bar. "I
don't want Mindy in on this. Just him."

"Why?"

The damn plastic wrap on the bar wouldn't tear. Frustrated, I clawed at it with my nails. "Because I'm hearing rumors. He didn't level with me. I don't want Mindy
talking for him. I want the truth from Adam. If he wants
to get to his wife's funeral in two days' time without
being fitted for silver bracelets, you get him to a meeting place and tell him he'd better tell the truth and all
the truth." A tiny hole opened in the wrapping. I stuck
my fingernail in and yanked the wrapping off the bar.

"What did you hear, Sam? Do you know who killed Faye? Are you okay?"

"No, I don't know who killed Faye. But whoever it was might be trying to destroy Heart Mates too. So, yeah, I'm okay, and I'm going to stay that way by having a chat with Adam to see what he knows." The world that I had so carefully built around my sons, Grandpa and me was threatened. But so far, I was pretty sure that TJ, Joel and Grandpa were safe. Still, I meant to find out exactly what was going on. "I'll explain the rest when I see you. I think Lookout Point up in the Ortega Mountains is a safe place. How soon can you and Adam get there?" Lookout Point is a beautiful spot that overlooks Lake Elsinore. I doubted that there'd be any cops there in the middle of the day.

"Uh, how about eleven-thirty?"

"Fine. Oh, Angel, if you had a secret lover, what kind of gifts might you exchange?"

"Secret lover? Well, flowers can usually be explained if the card's not signed. I don't know, Sam, what does this have to do with Adam?"

"I'm not sure. I'll see you and Adam at Lookout Point at eleven-thirty."

Hanging up, I thought about flowers. Hm, that might be it. Frank and Molly owned Frank's Flowers. They were on my phone tree from soccer and Linda knew them. Maybe she had talked to one of them, and they had told her about the affair rumor. Possible.

Right now, I had a couple of hours to get some work done before I ran home to get Ali and meet Adam and Angel. I meant to follow Gabe's advice about being careful, and Ali had proved herself as a guard dog. Picking up my coffee, I went through the reception area to the interview room. Blaine had already run copies of the contact sheet for each client the computer matched. The thickest pile was for Leslie Lee.

Spreading the sheets out on the round oak table, I stared at the possibilities. The computer did the job of cross-checking interests and preferences, then I went through every match myself, looking for the ones that I thought might have chemistry or real companionship.

Romance was a combination of art and science. I loved this part of it. That was why I liked to do the initial interview with clients myself. I could get a feel for them, and then, hopefully, come up with some good matches. The fact that I had been unable to do this in my own life made me try even harder with my clients.

The work helped me focus.

"Boss, what are you going to do about the newspaper articles? Two female clients called this morning and wanted us to take them out of our files."

Bent over the table, I looked up. "Those must have been the messages that you mentioned could wait." At his nod, I went on, "We have to emphasize that Heart Mates is safe. I was thinking of asking some of our clients to call the paper and give quotes about that. But this two-part exposé seems a little too focused on us. The public has not been told about the brochure found in Faye's hand, so that's not the reason." Brochure, jump rope, Heart Mates—those were the clues. And possibly a mystery lover. Who killed Faye? And why? The kitten Adam meant to give Faye, and Adam himself, convinced me he didn't do it.

Blaine worked on the stacks of matched clients, compiling a list of them to call and see if they were interested in meeting each other. " 'Cause it sells papers. Tawdry dating service gets client killed."

I made a face at him. "Heart Mates is not tawdry. Well, not anymore since I bought it." The old owner had teamed up with my husband, the panty-collecting condom salesman, to peddle drugs.

Blaine stopped fiddling with the papers and held up a contact sheet. "What about Leslie Lee? She asked the most questions, took a lot of time researching our service. Maybe you could ask her to call the paper and give her comments on her progress as she uses our service."

"Hey, not a bad idea. Good publicity." My mind went right to work on that while Blaine and I spent the next hour figuring out the best matches.

When everything was ready for the client phone calls, I said, "I'll call Leslie Lee about her matches and ask her about calling the newspaper with some positive quotes." I looked down at my watch to see it was ten-thirty. That gave me an hour to get home and then to Lookout Point. It was a winding, somewhat treacherous drive up the Ortega Mountains. "It'll have to be later. I have to run out to meet with . . . a client. Will you contact the other clients about their matches?"

"Sure, Boss."

Getting my purse from my office, I came back out and saw the kitten rummaging around in her box for some food. "Uh, Blaine"—I opened my purse and pulled out a small can of Anchovies Delight—"do you think you could watch the kitten?"

He pulled himself up to his full height. More brawn than height, Blaine was probably about five-foot-nine, but his thick build made him scary just the same. Running his blunt-fingered hand over his brown hair and automatically checking the ponytail in the back, he said, "No. And have you noticed this place is starting to smell like a pet shop?"

I sniffed. *Ugh.* Now what did I do? "All right, I'll take her home and leave her in my bathroom." I wrinkled my nose. My bathroom smelled like a barn. Picking up the kitten box, I headed for the door. "I'll either be back around one or two, or I'll call you."

Getting the kitten settled in the passenger seat, I started the car and headed home.

"Meow."

Looking over, I had to smile. The little kitten had her tiny gray paws up on the edge of the box, and her curious slate-blue eyes stared at me. "It's not fair, you know. Faye would have adored you." I couldn't keep her. Driving by the lake, I tried to think who might want her. I couldn't have my office and home smelling like a pet shop.

Hm, pet shop. Eddie! Eddie might have an idea. I could swing by Eddie's pet shop and ask him. At Riverside Drive, I turned left, heading toward the campground on the north end of the lake. Hooking a right, I went into a strip mall across from the campground. Seeing Frank's Flowers reminded me that I needed to talk to them about the affair rumor. But first I wanted to talk to Adam. I needed straight answers. He might even know the identity of Faye's mystery lover, if she had one, and save me the trouble.

Right, like I had that kind of luck.

I parked the car in front of Eddie's pet shop. Cute bunnies, gerbils and kittens lined the front window. Picking the kitten up, I got out of the car and headed inside.

It smelled like a pet shop, a combination of litter boxes, sawdust and wet fur. The shop was set up with the fish tanks gurgling along the left wall, rows of pet merchandise in the center and the larger animal cages on the right wall. Birds were up front and squawking away.

I spotted Eddie working at the fish tanks, but the kitten in my arms started hissing at the birds. They, in turn, began flapping and scolding in their cages. It was all I could do to hold on to the gray ball of hissing fur.

In my mind's eye, I saw a repeat of the incident on

Mindy's front porch when I fell off and the kitten peed all over me.

"Sam." Eddie came to my rescue. He rushed up and took the kitten from me. "Shh, kitty." Cuddling her to his chest, he stroked her behind her ears and she calmed right down.

Then he looked up at me. "What brings you here?"

His bloodshot, faded blue gaze looked worried. Eddie still had a pale, sick appearance, but nothing like this morning. "Are you feeling better, Eddie?"

He nodded. "Yeah." Looking around the empty shop, he added, "Sam, I don't want Jan to know I hired you. No one can know!"

"I remember. I came by to see if you know of anyone who might want the kitten." I inclined my head toward the scrap of fur in his arms.

He looked down. "She's a great little kitten. Faye would have loved her."

Startled, I stared at him. But then it dawned on me. Adam had to get the kitten from somewhere. Or rather, Mindy had, since she actually bought the kitten. "The kitten's from your shop?"

"Sure. This is the best pet shop in town. Mindy came in and said she was buying Faye a kitten that was supposed to be a surprise from her husband."

"So you knew Faye?"

He looked up at me. I could clearly see the shadows under his eyes. "Sure. She loved animals. Came in here sometimes. Jan and I saw both Faye and Mindy at the BBQ Shack."

I felt like an idiot. A tired, paranoid idiot. "Of course. Faye did love animals. She would have loved the kitten." And I had to get going. "Listen, Eddie, I've been trying to take care of the kitten and find a home, but I'm not having any luck."

He grinned. "Yeah, your grandpa and sons were in here buying stuff for the kitten. Judging by all the stuff they bought, I got the impression they were hoping to keep her."

"We're not." That was final.

Eddie looked down at the kitten. She had gone to sleep. "Okay, we can put a sign up for a free kitten or something."

"That would help." I glanced at my watch. "I have to run, Eddie."

He nodded. "You're not going to forget about my little problem, are you? I don't know how much more of this I can take. I need to know how she's making me sick."

Taking a breath, I told myself I had plenty of time. "Uh, Eddie, this could be serious, you know? Maybe Jan needs a little help?"

Gently petting the sleeping kitten, he shook his head. "No, she's not crazy. Just . . . controlling. She won't kill me. But if you can figure out how she's making me sick, I can fix this."

I still had trouble believing it. The town children loved Jan. Why in God's name would she poison Eddie? She was proud of marrying him. A guy like Eddie, a popular football player, never looked at her in high school. It didn't make sense. Trying to still my impatience, I looked for the right questions. "Eddie, when do you usually get sick?"

"In the mornings. Just like today."

"Okay." Rummaging through my purse, I yanked out my yellow tablet and made a note. "Do you eat the same thing for breakfast?"

"Whatever she makes me. It's never the same thing. Some mornings it's just cold cereal and milk that she sets out."

"Uh-huh." I noted that. If this was true, one thing

Eddie had been right about was that Jan was smart. Too smart to make it easy to catch her. Looking up, I said, "Is there any pattern to getting sick? You know, like every Tuesday and Thursday morning?"

He shook his head. "No, and I don't get sick after eating just one type of food. I can't figure it out!"

I stopped writing and looked him dead in the eye. "Eddie, do you know why she's doing this?"

He gaze skittered away. "Maybe. The why doesn't matter. All I want to know is how she's doing it. Then I can handle it. I have an idea."

And I had to be somewhere. "What?"

"Tonight Jan's getting a Chamber of Commerce award. We'll be out of the house from six-thirty until at least ten. Can you maybe just go in and take a look?"

"Break into your house?"

"I'll give you a key." He shifted the sleeping kitten to one arm. He went over to the cash register and picked up a set of keys next to his large silver travel coffee mug. Balancing the kitten, he managed to work one key off the ring. "Look through the kitchen and stuff and see if you can find what she might be using. Whatever it is has to work pretty fast. It makes me nauseous, sweaty and my heart races." He held the house key out to me.

I stared at the key. There was something really weird about this. "Eddie, what are you going to do if you find out how she's poisoning you? What do you really want?"

His soft jaw clenched. "I love her, Sam. She's smart and organized and special. If I know how she's doing it and tell her, she'll know I'm as smart as her and stop punishing me this way."

I believed him. It was weird, but I believed him. "Okay, I'll give it a shot." Tearing off a piece of paper from my yellow tablet, I jotted down my cell phone number. "Keep this with you. If anything goes wrong, call me and I'll get out of the house."

Relief sagged his thick shoulders. "Thank you, Sam." He gave me the key and put my number in his pocket. "How's the search for Faye's killer going?"

"That's what I'm late for right now. I've got a lead I need to follow up."

"I'll keep the kitten here for a while if you want, Sam. She'll be fine. What kind of lead?"

A break! What do you know? "Eddie that'd be great! The lead is about Faye. Uh, do you know, or have you heard, if Faye was involved with anyone?"

"Involved? But I thought she went to your dating service. Why would she do that if she was involved?"

To use me. "Just wondered if you heard anything. I have to run, Eddie. Thanks for watching the kitten." I turned and hurried out.

Home was about ten minutes away. I made it in seven. It was eleven o'clock. Grandpa wasn't home yet from his morning coffee thing. I unlocked the front door and meant to turn down the hallway to grab my stun gun in my closet.

But I caught site of Ali sitting outside the sliding glass window in the dining room. She was sitting very still and watching me.

With something in her mouth. Something bright blue and poppy.

I froze halfway across the living room and met Ali's liquid brown eyes. Slowly, I forced myself to walk across the old brown shag carpet on to the yellowed linoleum floor to the sliding glass door.

My heart crashed against my rib cage. Sweat popped out beneath my leather halter top. My scalp prickled. I knew what I was seeing in Ali's mouth.

The brochure. The one Faye had designed for Heart

Mates. Almost unaware of my movements, I unlocked the slider and moved it back along its tracks.

Ali stood up. The ends of the brochure hung out of both sides of her slim muzzle. Without actually thinking it, I held my hand out.

Ali gently set the brochure into my hand.

I looked down. The front was glossy and beautiful, the blue as bright as the sky. The writing was a clean, beautiful white and it said: *Get Hot With Heart Mates.*

Except that someone had taken a red marker and crossed out *Hot* and rewritten it so that it read:

Get Dead With Heart Mates.

11

I stared down at the brochure and shivered in the bright sunlight pouring through the sliding glass door.

Get Dead With Heart Mates.

A threat. In my own house. The icy shock cracked. The boys were at school, but where was Grandpa? What did I do? Turning around to the kitchen and the living room I had just come through, I wondered if someone was in the house. How did Ali get this brochure?

Should I get out of the house? God, I didn't know. Call the police? Find Grandpa? Make sure the boys were safely in school?

Wait. I made myself slow my racing thoughts and think. Gabe had seen Grandpa while I hid in the bathroom at his house this morning. Grandpa had told Gabe he took the boys to school.

Okay, the boys were safe. My heart thumped in my ears. I stood by the opened sliding glass door in the dining room. The refrigerator hummed.

A threat. A death threat? Dead meant death. Oh, God. Ali whined and used her cool, wet nose to nudge my arm. I looked down at her. "You'd know if someone was in the house, right, girl?"

She barked.

I forced my brain into gear. I had to think past the terror building in my veins.

The house was locked. I'd had to unlock the front door with my key to get in, and I'd had to unlock the sliding door to get to Ali. I turned back toward the kitchen, looking past the counter with the sink to the door that also led to the back yard. It was closed and didn't look jimmied.

And there was Ali, calm Ali. "How'd you get this?" I held up the brochure.

She cocked her head and stared at me.

I didn't really understand dog language, but I understood the threat. Someone left it for me. Leaning toward the opened slider, I glanced out into the backyard. A patio with a redwood picnic table, Bermuda grass and a big round trampoline for the boys. I doubted anyone actually came in the backyard. One look at Ali would change their mind.

Did someone throw the brochure over the fence and run? The coincidence of my dog getting hold of this brochure, a brochure that Faye had designed for Heart Mates and that had the original writing changed . . .

Gabe's words from this morning echoed in my head. *There's something about the brochure the police are holding back.*

Blood-red fury exploded behind my eyes. "Goddamn Vance!" This was what the police were holding back about the brochure found in Faye's hand. It had been changed to read *Get Dead With Heart Mates*. And Vance never warned me. Never told me.

I looked down at my watch. Two minutes after eleven. The boys were in school until after two. Plenty of time to hunt down Detective Vance. Vance and I were done playing games. He was going to tell me the truth, all of it, and we were going to solve Faye's murder.

Before someone else gets hurt. Or dead. "Come on, Ali." I grabbed my keys when the front door sprang open.

Whirling around, I opened my mouth to scream, but it was only Grandpa.

"Hey, Sam, what are you doing home?" He shuffled in and stopped in front of me. "What's wrong?"

Grabbing the back of a kitchen chair, I fought to calm down. No doubt about it, I was spooked.

And pissed.

Silently, I showed Grandpa the brochure.

He squinted at the print, then lifted his fading blue eyes to me. "Where'd you get that?"

My mind raced over the answer. "Ali had it in her mouth when I walked in just a couple of minutes ago. Right now, I'm going to the sheriff's station and kick some detective butt. You better come with me. I don't want you here alone." I tucked the brochure into my purse.

"Sam, you go on. I'll be fine here. I got some work to do on the Internet. I've been saying it all along. There's something off about your detective." He slow-stepped into the kitchen, got a mug down, poured out some coffee left from the morning and put it in the microwave.

Watching him, a lump filled my throat. I'd spent much of my childhood with Grandpa and Grandma while my mom chased down her career or men. I missed Grandma, but Grandpa had always made me feel special and loved. He'd done the same for TJ and Joel. I couldn't risk leaving him here in case the killer came back. "Grandpa, it's not safe. Please, I—"

A click.

Grandpa turned from the microwave holding an opened switchblade. The same switchblade Gabe had taken from him and Grandpa had pickpocketed back. The same switchblade he'd pulled on the thugs at Dominic's apartment. I hadn't even seen his hand move.

The microwave beeped. His coffee was done. He calmly folded the blade and stuck it back in his pants pocket, then hiked his pants back up his bony hips. He opened the microwave and took out his coffee. "Go on, Sam. I'll be fine and I'll pick the boys up from school." He passed me to set his coffee down at his desk and fired up his computer.

Grandpa and a switchblade. It boggled my mind. Hell, it scared me to death, but what was I going to do? How could I take it away from him? And I felt guilty about my sons. I should pick them up from school, not Grandpa. Going to him, I leaned down and kissed his cheek. "You be careful, and I'll be home for dinner with the boys. I have to spend more time with them."

Grandpa grabbed my hand. "You're doing a fine job with TJ and Joel, Sammy. Now you go on and be sure to take Ali."

That lump in my throat grew painful. Swallowing it, I whispered, "Thank you." While still holding his hand, I cleared my throat, "About that switchblade—"

Grandpa let go of my hand and turned his attention to the computer screen. "Ah, just what I've been waiting for. You run along and I'll see you later."

Dismissed, Ali and I headed out. She loved riding in my T-bird and since the top was off, she leaped over the door and planted herself in the front seat.

In spite of everything, I had to laugh. Getting in, I started the car and said, "Okay, Ali, let's go get 'em."

She barked her agreement.

We drove past the lake to midtown and came to a fork in the road. Staying left, the road turn into Graham and would lead down to Main Street. We veered right on Lakeshore, which took us by a launching dock for the lake.

An odd assortment of homes dotted the lakefront, ranging from nicely livable to boarded up and condemned. We passed Swick & Matich Park that hosted Little League games. The new Lake Elsinore sheriff's station was on the left. Ali and I turned in there.

Now was probably not the time to wonder how they'd feel about a dog in their building. But Ali was a police dog dropout. Maybe they'd cut her some slack.

Check that. Detective Vance would cut Ali some slack. We were here to demand information, not ask permission. After parking the car in one of the allotted spaces in front of the station, I opened the car door and got out. "Come on, Ali," I called.

She leaped over the seat and got out. Her nose went into the air. She sniffed, looked around, sniffed some more. I wondered what she was thinking. Did this remind her of her time training? I walked to the glass front doors set in a red-brick building trimmed with green paint. Ali followed, her head whipping around to see everything.

Inside the sheriff's station it looked like a corporate lobby. It was quiet, with only the occasional burr of a telephone. Straight ahead was a tasteful glass-fronted case with awards and pictures of local sports teams for children that the sheriff's station sponsored. The walls had photos of police and dignitaries.

"May I help you?"

Turning to the desk built into the wall on the left, I said, "Yes, I'm Samantha Shaw and I need to see Detective Vance immediately."

The woman behind the desk was fiftyish, had her brown hair styled in beauty parlor wash-n-set and wore thin black-framed glasses and a black headset that connected her to the phone. An organized and calm expression guided her smooth movements. I doubted if a massive earthquake would rattle her. "I'll see if he's in.

What shall I tell him this is about?" Her gaze dropped to Ali. "Is this in regard to your dog?"

I was pissed off at Vance, but I wasn't going to take it out on this receptionist. "No. But Ali here is a trained police dog. She'll be no trouble."

The receptionist made no comment and dialed. She asked some three-digit number to call her back. She went right back to moving files around. No one else was in the lobby.

A discreet ringing sounded and the receptionist pushed a button. "Yes. Samantha Shaw. She's here with her dog, a German shepherd that she explains is K-9 trained. Uh-huh. I'll tell her.

"Ma'am. Detective Vance is tied up at the moment. He'll get back to you as soon as he can."

A red haze blurred my vision and it was a monumental effort to remember that this lady was not at fault. "Please call back and tell Vance that I found a brochure for Heart Mates at my house with the word *hot* crossed out and *dead* written in with red pen. Then tell him if he doesn't get out here right now, I'm going to tell the newspaper how my two sons' lives were threatened and he did nothing."

She had hazel eyes that appeared to take hysterical threats in stride. She reached over and dialed the phone again with the request for a three-digit number to call her back.

It only took about twenty seconds for the ringing response. I assumed that an annoyed Vance was on the other end. The receptionist stated my message word for word. I hoped the sheriff's department valued this woman.

The door on the right side of the desk opened. Satisfied, I turned, ready to let Vance have it. The words died in my throat.

Vance was dressed in gray sweatpants and athletic shoes. It looked like he'd pulled on a blue T-shirt over his sweaty body, because it stuck to his shoulders and chest. With the civility of his suit gone, I now faced a hot, sweaty, irritated man.

Good-looking man. Not the street-dangerous, daring-all-women-to-try-and-tame-him look of Gabe. No, Vance had the I-was-a-sports-god-and-campus-pretty-boy-in-high-school look. That look had matured into a handsome man. And wouldn't you know it, all sweaty and teed-off, he still looked good. Life wasn't fair sometimes. Ali nudged me with her nose. I snapped out of my surprise. "Uh, do you have a gym back there?"

"Get in here." He held the door open.

Lifting my chin, I headed for the door with my hand on Ali's head. Vance smelled of thick sweat and tangy anger. I passed him and paused. Right in front of me was a set of cubicles staffed with what appeared to be clerks. Soft voices mixed with the hum of computers. Lake Elsinore was still considered a small town, but the sheriff's station was part of the Riverside sheriff's department and state of the art.

Not a donut in sight.

Vance strode past the clerical area. We went down another hallway. On the right was a row of doors. The left side held an area of more cubicles. Inside the cubicles were built-in desks topped with phones and computers. Most were empty.

An uniformed officer passing by looked at me and stopped. Grinning, he turned to Vance and said, "You gonna need a CSO for this one?"

"Nah." Vance turned into the second cubicle.

The uniform laughed and went on.

My female radar kicked in. It was like I had just walked by a construction site full of testosterone-laden men issuing wolf whistles. Putting my hands on my hips, I stared down at him. "What's a CSO?"

He leaned back in his chair and regarded me with his brown eyes. "Community Service Officer."

"What's that? Why would you need one?"

His gaze rolled down my black-leather halter top and short white skirt. "Most of the women who come through here dressed like that end up being hauled to Temecula to be booked on prostitution. We don't usually book prisoners here in this facility, but call a Community Service Officer, or CSO, to escort the prisoner for us. Now, what the hell got you all lathered up?"

Damn, I'd been going for sexy and desirable, not twenty-bucks-a-pop doable. This outfit was going in the trash when I got home. But right now, I had more important things to worry about than my lack of dress. "Ali, sit down." While she did that, I reached in my purse and fished out the brochure. Silently I handed it to him.

He read it. "Where'd you get this?"

He left me standing. It made me feel like a schoolgirl in trouble. "I found it in my dog's mouth when I got home. I came right here."

"I see."

"It's the same as the brochure you found in Faye's hand, isn't it?"

"We're not releasing that information."

"Fine." Vance needed to understand that I was not going to be ignored. "I'll just call the newspaper and give them the quote from me they've been begging for. Let's see, something like, 'Detective Vance of the Lake Elsinore sheriff's station had information that clearly endangered my family and refused to tell me or help me.' " I stuck my hands on my hips and glared at him. "How does that sound, Vance?"

He rolled up to his full height. "You threatening me, Shaw?"

"I heard her threaten you." A snicker.

I whirled around and saw two sweat-clad men with their arms draped on the cubicle wall watching us. They had to have just come from the same gym as Vance.

"Yeah, Vance, I heard it too. Want us to protect you?"

"Go play with yourselves. I have work to do." Vance's voice thundered over my shoulder.

I had sons. I recognized this. Oh, yeah, I got Vance now. TJ and Joel were starting this aggressive male thing, the all-important tough-guy image. Turning back to Vance, I saw the high school star who had also been a pretty boy. Oh, yeah, bet he fought hard to establish himself as more than a pretty boy with a good set of pecs in the cop world. I'd reviewed plenty of romance novels with cop heroes, and I knew cops had their way of culling out those who couldn't be trusted to watch the back of a fellow officer out on the streets.

Detective Vance protected the image he had built for himself. Did I threaten that image somehow? Little tremors of power helped to soothe my vanity over the hooker thing. Now I needed to get this situation in hand. "Are these nice men detectives? Maybe they can find Faye's killer."

Conscious of the two now very silent men hanging over the cubicle wall, I watched Vance. He didn't take the bait. "Those two couldn't find their own service weapons if their mommies didn't strap it on for them."

The two men snorted and melted away. I didn't actually see them leave, I just felt the decrease in testosterone. How did the female cops deal with this? My admiration for them rose a notch.

Vance's gaze returned to me. "When you got home, was your dog"—he glanced down at Ali—"inside or outside?"

"She was outside. My house did not appear to be broken into. I doubt that anyone got in the backyard. My best guess is that someone threw the brochure over the fence."

He was still looking at Ali. "Would your dog attack someone she didn't know?"

I shrugged. "If she thought they were a danger to her family."

"I heard Rossi shot her, that he was aiming at you."

Wincing, I automatically reached out to pet Ali's head. I didn't want to remember being trapped in Detective Rossi's house with Gabe handcuffed to the gas pipe in the garage. I'd attacked Rossi physically and run. If Ali hadn't come barreling in from the garage and leaped . . .

I'd be dead.

Stuffing the thought down, I looked up. "Are you making a point?"

He sighed. "Yes. You got a warning from the killer. Heed it and stay out of this investigation."

"It's gone too far for that, Vance. Besides, you need me."

"Like a migraine. It might surprise you to learn that I know what I'm doing, Shaw. I've investigated murders and have a good clearance rate. Now go home and read a book."

I narrowed my eyes. "You're convinced it's Adam?"

"We want to talk to him."

Shaking my head, I said, "He didn't do it."

"Have you forgotten that you thought it was Adam Miller who changed Faye's profile at Heart Mates? Adam Miller was there at the motel the night Faye was murdered. She left him and he didn't like it, nor did he like her going to your dating service. It all fits. Changing the profile on the Heart Mates computer, then changing the wording on the Heart Mates brochure fits the pattern. You were never in any real danger."

He believed that. Or he wanted to. "Except for one thing, Vance."

He tilted his head. "What's that?"

"Adam Miller brought the divorce papers to Faye that night. He was willing to let her go if that's what she wanted. But she decided not to sign them. She was thinking of going back to Adam."

His full lips flattened. "Ah. I suppose Adam Miller, whom none of the Lake Elsinore police or sheriff's personal can find, told you that? And being a romance expert, you just know he's telling the truth."

"You're not listening to me!" God, I wanted to smack him. "Did you find the divorce papers? Had Faye signed them?"

"He killed her before she could sign them."

His arrogance fueled my frustration. Adam Miller was not a killer. He didn't have the passionate anger of a killer. The man used oven cleaner to kidnap me, for the love of mercy! I struggled to reason with Vance. "He's been in hiding. Do you really think he'd drive up to my house and leave that brochure, a brochure that would link him to Faye's murder if he were caught with it, at my house? Does that make sense to you?" It didn't make sense to me. Especially as I knew that Adam was with my friend Angel. She had told me this morning on the phone that she was trying to get him to put the finishing touches on his computer game. Knowing Angel, I'm certain that Adam hadn't left her sight.

Vance looked down at me like I was a child. "He might if he felt threatened enough by you. Those who murder, especially impulse murder, begin doing stupid and desperate things to cover it up. Real life isn't like a book. We don't get a string of clues like breadcrumbs that lead us to the culprit. Very often, the culprit trips over his own feet and falls right in our path."

Desperate and stupid. I was very familiar with both, but what Vance said made sense. And scared me. What if the killer got desperate enough to hurt one of my kids?

"You have to find him, Vance. You can't just assume it's Adam to make your job easy!" A panic that felt like broken glass rose in my chest. "Have you even bothered to check anyone else out? How about Jim Ponn? Did you know he was angry at Faye? He thought she was stealing clients from him and that she used him! And Dominic Danger had jump ropes in his bedroom!"

Stillness enveloped Vance. "Jump rope? You know about the murder weapon? That's being kept quiet."

I blinked and tried to gauge exactly what I had done. Could I get Gabe in trouble for tracking down that information and telling me? Detective Vance had a square face with flat temples. Right now, I saw a vein throb on the left side of his temple. *Uh-oh.* "I remembered the jump rope. Faye jumped rope for exercise. It was white with blue threads in it and it hung off her mirror. You told me Faye was strangled and I figured that—"

"Save it." Vance lifted a hand like he was stopping traffic. "I'm not a stupid man, Ms. Shaw. Much as I'm beginning to see that, despite your blond-streaked hair, boob job and slut clothes, you are not a stupid woman. You've gathered quite a bit of information, but as a civilian you are clueless as to what to do with it."

He leaned in and I caught a whiff of spearmint gum mixed with the sweaty aftershave or whatever it was he wore. "I—"

He cut me off. "So I'm going to tell you what you're going to do. You are going to get the hell out of my investigation before you or someone else gets hurt. Your PI boyfriend was a cop, a dime-a-dozen street cop, not a detective."

Before I thought, I practically yelled, "Gabe's a hero! He saved lives in that bank robbery!" I'd seen the scars on Gabe's knee from the bullet he'd taken.

Vance snorted. "He did his job, nothing more. His

job was to protect civilians and he did it. Cops all over this country do it every day and they don't get their pictures in the paper and special awards. Your PI probably could have stayed with the department once he'd recovered from his gunshot wound, but he chose to bail. Got a little scared, maybe couldn't do the job anymore. Hollywood is more his speed—they don't have the real thing in Hollywood. So don't be sending him in to do a real cop's job, and sure as hell not to do mine."

I curled my fingers into fists and dug my nails into my palms. I had underestimated Vance as a detective. Clearly they had figured out that Faye was strangled with the jump rope. And he knew about Gabe's consulting on the script. But he had also underestimated me. "Gabe wouldn't have to do your job, Vance, if you'd do it. You didn't answer me about Jim Ponn or Dominic Danger. Dominic is the one who gave Faye the idea to jump rope for exercise."

"They both have alibis. Jim was bowling and Dominic was at the community center for karate lessons and then went out to kareoke at the Don Jose restaurant. That is what real police work is—tracking down the facts, not fantasy."

I tried to sort out this latest information. "What about Faye? Have you investigated her? Who she was with those last days, if she was having an affair with someone—"

"Give it up, Shaw. Adam Miller did it. His car was there. He was there. His fingerprints were there. We'll find the jump rope and we'll nail him." He paused, took a breath and lowered his head until he was nose to nose with me. "And if you know where Adam Miller is, Ms. Shaw, you'd better tell me now. Otherwise, if I find out you know, I'll arrest you as an accessory after the fact."

Think. Okay, Jim and Dominic were out as suspects. I believed Vance when he said he checked them out. After all, he'd known more about what Gabe was up to than I had. But Vance was missing something. I could almost . . . I grit my teeth trying to think what it was.

"God, you're a scary woman."

Blinking, I looked up at him. "Huh?" I kept sorting this out. All right, Vance was following the facts, the murder weapon, fingerprints . . . but he was missing the main component. The human component—Faye herself.

"You just won't stop. From the squeezed expression on your face, I can see your brain scheming and meddling."

I decided to ignore his comments. "You know what, Vance. I believe you. You're a good detective, good at going where the evidence takes you, except for one thing. The thing you need me for."

The corners of his full mouth kicked up. Crossing his arms over his swimmer's chest, he looked me over in a slow display of machismo. "This oughta be good. What do I need you for, Ms. Shaw? I mean, sure, you have your, ah"—his gaze slid down the V of my leather halter—"charms, but my taste runs a little more upscale."

I didn't take this crap from anyone. "Then you should meet my mother, Vance. You'd be the perfect boy toy for her. But what I meant is that while you're sifting through the facts, you are missing the human factor. The stuff I've learned about Faye wasn't all that hard, Vance. I've lived in the town all my life. People talk to me. Do they talk to you, Vance?"

He laughed. "Boy toy? Jeez, Shaw, you are something else."

I think I hit a nerve. Suppressing a smile, I said, "Try to focus here, Vance. Do the folks around town talk to you?"

His laugher died and his face went all cop. "Of course they do. I'm investigating a murder."

I pointed out how small towns work. "But you're not

one of us. You're not part of the soccer league, PTA, or business folks. You're an outsider. I have a phone tree from my years on the PTA and doing team-mom duties. I can get information and gossip faster than you can run one of your fancy fingerprint computer search thingies."

"Gee, Shaw, your mastery of the technical language impresses the hell out of me."

Oh, well, that explained the tight jaw and angry specks of yellow floating in his brown eyes. My cell phone rang, making me jump. Ali shifted next to me, clearly restless. Thinking of Grandpa alone at the house, I grabbed the phone out of my purse. "Hello."

"Sam, where are you?"

"Angel!" Damn, I'd forgotten. "Uh, listen, I'm on my way. Can you . . . uh"—cripes, I'd almost said "and Adam"—"wait for me? I'm finishing up something here at the sheriff's station."

A second of silence. Then, "Yes."

I put the phone away and looked at Vance. "You need me, Detective. Once you get over your macho pride and realize that, you know how to reach me. In the meantime, you'd better pray nothing happens to my family or employee." I turned to leave his cubicle.

"Hey, Shaw."

I stopped and looked back.

His gaze rolled all the way down my body to my stilettos and back up to my face. "Why are you dressed like a streetwalker?"

Forcing myself not to look down at my short white skirt and leather halter top, I smiled. "To make your day, Vance. It's probably the closest you get to sex."

12

Lookout Point was actually a turnout in the winding mountain road that wove over the Ortega Mountains, through the Cleveland National Forest to the beach communities of San Clemente and Dana Point. I pulled my T-bird into the turnout and parked next to Angel's blood-red Trans Am. Getting out, I glanced at the little roadside café, then decided I didn't want to leave Ali in the car alone. "Come on, Ali."

She jumped across the seat and out my driver's-side door, then ran up to the line of boulders that acted as a guardrail on the edge of the mountain. "Be careful!" I slammed the door, hurried over as fast as my high heels allowed on the dirt and grabbed Ali's black metal-studded collar that Joel had bought for her. It was a sheer drop to the valley below, and I felt kind of dumb thinking I'd be able to hold back eighty pounds of German shepherd if she took it into her head to leap over the line of boulders. On the other hand, in the car, I threw out my right arm to save my boys whenever I came to a sudden stop. They always laughed at me.

Ali didn't ever laugh at me. Smiling, I looked down at Lake Elsinore spread out in postcard beauty. An occasional boat broke the still blue waters.

Of course, up close the lake was shallow and green. But up here in the clean mountain air, it looked blue and pristine.

The sound of jangling keys disturbed the serenity.

I turned. Angel and Adam were walking across the dirt from the café. The sight of them together was a walking oxymoron. Angel Crimson could make a Paris runway model weep in jealousy. She had waist-length red hair, green eyes, and a long, graceful body. Wearing an emerald-green T-shirt, black cropped pants and clunky shoes that would have made me look like Humpty Dumpty, Angel looked hip enough to be the new Estée Lauder model.

Beside her, Adam loped along like a goofy puppy in Velcro tennis shoes. With his hands stuffed into his wrinkled tan Dockers, he clanked his keys to some nervous rhythm in his head.

My teeth ached and I wondered if Adam's coppery hair that looked like a porcupine accident was really some kind of self-defense mechanism against the grating sound of those damned keys.

But once Adam was close enough for me to see his face, I forgot about the annoying clatter. His wire-framed glasses magnified the anguish in his round blue eyes rimmed by red-tipped lashes. Those pools of agony fixed on me as if I could save him from drowning. It was impossible to look away, to notice the abundant freckles scattered over his milk-white skin, or the oversized white T-shirt, or the metallic noise radiating from his pockets.

It took my breath away.

I had to fight down a feeling a panic, of smallness in

the face of Adam's pain. Faye was dead. Murdered. And somehow I was supposed to make it better.

"Who killed her, Samantha?"

The flat tone of the question reminded me of whom I was dealing with. I glanced at Angel.

She reached out and touched Adam's shoulder. "We're trying to find that out. You have to answer Sam's questions."

He looked past me, over the hip-high boulders to the valley below. "I'm not proficient at talking. There are meanings and shadows behind words. There are . . . layers. I don't understand the layers. That's why Mindy was helping me. That's why she talked to you. Faye always understood the layers. She understood me."

Ali whined deep in her throat.

I knew how she felt—we were wading around in this man's sharp pain and it hurt. But I had a job to do. "Did you understand her, Adam?"

He turned back to me, opened his mouth and sneezed. He pulled out a white handkerchief and blew his nose. "Sorry, dog hair." He glanced at Ali, then back to me. "I understood her. I knew she was happy when she was needed. It made her feel loved, I guess. But when I got busy in my game, I forgot about her. And now she's dead."

Romance did not beat loudly in this man's heart. But that's not a sin, nor did that make him a murderer. "What about Faye's profile at Heart Mates? Are you the one who changed that?"

The tips of his ears reddened. "Yes."

"Why?"

"Because she wouldn't listen to me! I didn't know how to reach her anymore. While I hacked away on what I thought I loved, Faye left me. She told me, she cried, she pleaded, but I just went away to my computer. I didn't get it until Faye was gone and living in that motel."

I leaned forward. "Didn't get what? What were you trying to do by changing her profile?"

He looked to his left where Angel stood. "Tell her, Adam."

His bony shoulders sagged. "I loved Faye more than any game. And I lost her. But worse . . . Jimminy Cricket!"

Flattening my mouth to keep from smiling at Adam's idea of swearing, I urged him on, "What was worse, Adam?"

The jangling noise rose. His eyes slid left and his mouth tightened. Finally, he looked back at me. "Faye was doing wrong. Not criminal wrong, but wrong to herself. *He* was influencing her."

My heart skipped a beat. "He?"

"He." Adam nodded.

"Adam." I didn't realize I'd stepped forward until I touched his arm. "Who is he? Was Faye having an affair?"

A tremor of emotion ran through his arm. "Yes. But I don't know who it was. Faye was desperate, Samantha. I know that now. She had found my investor"—he glanced again over at Angel—"and then she wasn't needed anymore. My investor found a public relations firm to package my game and me. Faye . . . didn't feel loved. She needed to feel loved and she found it."

"How did you find out?"

He dropped his eyes to the ground. "Mindy told me. And Faye moved out. She was done. Tired of being second to my game. Tired of supporting my dream. Tired of not being noticed." He lifted his pleading gaze to me. "She was taking advertising and design classes at the community college. I never even realized . . . she was doing it to learn to help me market the game. And we cut her out."

Guilt and remorse had eaten away at him. And now I knew why Angel had been guarding him, keeping him from the police. Adam's guilt was so thick, and his communication skills so poor that had he been arrested, he would have been indicted, tried and convicted and probably not even care.

Adam Miller did not kill Faye. Maybe he failed her as a husband, but a worse thing had happened to her. Based on what I knew of Faye, and what I'd heard from everyone else, I began to have a pretty good idea what happened.

Some man had used Faye's hunger to be needed and influenced her to do things she wouldn't have done on her own.

It pissed me off. It angered me to my core.

"Adam, didn't you ever try and find out who she was having an affair with?"

He closed his eyes. "I hid from it."

That smacked so close to home that I had to remember to breathe. I had woken up from my marital delusions as brutally and painfully as Adam had.

If Adam had the ability, if he wasn't wanted by the police in connection with Faye's murder, he would be out on the streets looking for the bastard that killed her.

But Adam couldn't, so I would.

"Adam, tell me what you can. All about the changes in Faye, and between the two of you."

"She began chasing her dream. It was a good dream for her, you know? She wanted to design advertising publications and print them. Faye, with her bubbly, live-in-the-moment personality could do it. You might not believe this, but I wanted her to succeed."

I dropped my hand from his arm to get some distance and to think. "I do believe you." I did because Faye had told me that. Knowing what I did about Adam, I understood that he could be completely clueless, but deceit wasn't in him. Nor did he have the ability to play with words to make a person believe one thing when something else was the truth.

Adam told the truth as he saw it.

"Well, at first she didn't ask me for much. She started getting these ideas. One was to go to Heart Mates. From there, she could connect with other business owners, make connections and get clients." He paused to see what I would say.

I just nodded, trying to keep the same blank expression on my face that I used when TJ and Joel explained themselves.

"I warned her not to. But she didn't listen to me. I think she was listening to *him,* her . . . other man. And that's why I tried to sabotage her. Boy, was she mad."

I had to smile. More like exasperated. And it was a dumb thing to do. Invented by the mind of a nine-year-old. "Go on."

"This went on for a while. But the good thing that came out of it was her new friend, Dom something— the actor guy."

"Dominic Danger."

"Right." Adam waved his hand. "He seemed to have some kind of influence on her. Faye started getting stronger, exercising, and thinking for herself. And then she got upset."

"When did she get upset? What did she say?"

"The week or so before she died. I'd been helping her do her website and we were getting closer again. Like we used to be. Rediscovering what we saw in each other. Helping Faye . . ." His eyes slid shut and his red-tipped lashes moistened. "I'd never really helped her before. She'd always helped me. Our marriage had been about me. This was new and I . . . it was exciting."

I smiled at him.

"Anyway, she said she had done things she hated. That

she was going to fix them. All of them. That's how she said it. She was upset. She needed me again. I . . . we . . ."

Angel cleared her throat. "They boinked each other."

I laughed and Adam's ears burned red, but he went on. "So later I left, and that's when Faye was trying to fix things. Then I brought the divorce papers the night she was killed. I was trying to support her with the divorce papers."

"You mean"—I decided to help him out—"that you would give her the divorce if that's what she wanted? You were okay with that?"

"Yeah, because you know, she was happy. Well, not exactly happy, but trying to be happy. Besides, that night we decided to put the divorce on hold. But Faye wasn't ready to move back in. She said she had to get strong on her own first."

Oh, Faye. That was the woman I knew. Trying so very hard. Thinking I had some magic answer. I didn't. I just keep trying. And Faye should be here and alive to keep trying too. "Adam, any clues who the man is that she had an affair with? Anything you can think of?"

"You might ask Mindy."

"I'm asking you, Adam."

He shook his head. "No. Except that, you know, it was all so secret. He had to be married."

That made sense. A sad kind of sense. It would explain the secrecy and why Linda couldn't get anyone to tell her a name. "Okay, Adam, you go back to your computer and stay there."

"But what about Faye? Her memorial service is Saturday, the day after tomorrow. I have to go."

Angel put her hand on his shoulder. "They'll arrest you if you go, Adam."

His blue eyes were wide and childish in his pale, freckled face. "Not if Samantha can find the real killer first."

A bubble of hysterical laughter filled my chest. The idea was absurd, except that Adam needed me. He believed I could do it.

That made me want to do it. Need to do it.

"Adam, I'm going to try. Tell me, did Faye ever get any flowers that weren't from you?"

His nose wrinkled. "Well, yeah. Once when she was still working at the BBQ Shack right before she left me. She brought them home and I had an allergy attack. Then just last week there were flowers in her room. I asked her who they were from and she said, 'my past.' Is it important?"

"Maybe. I'm going to try and track down her mystery lover."

Ali and I turned off the Ortega Mountain Road onto Grand, then hooked a right on Riverside Drive. Passing the campground on the right, Ali leaned her head out over the passenger door and worked the smells. Must be a myriad of scents since the campground was at the north shore of the lake. I made a left turn into the strip mall where both the pet and flower shops were so I could investigate Faye's lover and pick up the kitten. I parked in front of the cheerful little florist next to a donut shop. "You stay here, Ali."

She barked her agreement and went back to twitching her nose. Lots of sniffing to be done.

Smiling, I glanced at the pet shop across the parking lot and decided the kitten could wait. I went into the florist shop through a glass door that had bells hung on it to announce a customer's arrival. The thick funeral smell common to all florists stuffed up my nose. Passing the refrigerated flowers in white buckets, I went to the green counter. Behind the counter was the workroom. I spotted Frank back there attaching a helium balloon to a festive bouquet of flowers tucked into a colorful reusable basket. What a deal.

Frank looked up and smiled. "Be right there, Sam." He tied off the balloon, then wiped his hands on his blue apron and walked out. "What can I do for you?"

"Uh . . ." Probably on that twenty-minute drive down the mountain, I should have thought out my approach. I hadn't so I stalled for inspiration to strike. "Is Molly here?" My only inspiration was that Molly might be easier to get gossip out of than Frank.

"Sure. She's uhhh—" He looked around, apparently having misplaced his wife. "Molly!"

"What?" A disembodied voice called back.

"Sam Shaw's out here! Wants to talk to you!"

"Thanks, Frank."

He turned back to me. "This about the murder, Sam? We heard you are investigating that. You giving up the dating business?"

"No." I shook my head. "I'm just helping out a friend." Frank and Molly were part of the PTA and soccer parents, which gave them a prominent place on my phone tree. "No, I'm not giving up Heart Mates. The Internet and personal ads have burned people. They are ready for real person-to-person contact. Heart Mates is the place for that." Or would be soon. I was determined to make Heart Mates successful, and that meant changing the town's perception of the dating service.

Frank's eyes skidded away. "But one of your clients was killed."

"All the more reason for me to find out who killed her, Frank."

"Yeah, I guess so. I've been hearing that you're getting pretty heavy into the PI thing. I sort of wondered."

He rubbed his green-stained hands up and down on his blue apron.

"Wondered what?"

"If you were interested in the PI stuff because of Trent. You know, like you could offer to find cheating spouses for other women, kind of a sideline of Heart Mates, I guess."

I blinked. "No, that's not it." Even I wasn't that cynical. A dating service with its own catch-a-cheater-if-things-go-wrong warranty?

He shook his head. "Guess I just don't get it then."

Maybe not, but his wife, Molly, had come to me fast enough when some videotapes of their bedroom activities turned up missing. It turned out that Lake Elsinore had a pair of porn thieves hawking their smut on the Internet. Molly saved me from answering as she walked out from the back. "Hi, Sam." Then she turned to Frank. "Can you finish loading the van for me? I need to deliver the flowers for the funeral this evening."

"Sure." Frank lifted a hand in a silent wave to me and hurried out.

Molly looked at me. "He's embarrassed, Sam. You saw those tapes when you found them being sold on the Internet."

I had seen them and spent a considerable amount of energy since then trying to forget. But Gabe, Grandpa and I had solved that case and gotten those tapes off the Internet. Now I needed a favor from Molly. Although she had paid me for my work, I was sure she'd help me now. "Molly, I need to know who ordered the flowers for Faye. The ones that were delivered to her at the BBQ Shack a few months back, and the ones delivered to the motel room last week."

Molly nodded her head, her brown bob bouncing around her face. "I guessed you'd come here after talking to Linda. Frank and I have a strict policy not to gossip about our clients." She stopped talking and looked past me.

I had a business to run, so I understood, but this was too important. "Molly, you know I kept your secrets"—I referred to the naked tapes—"but whoever Faye was dating might know something."

She brought her gaze back to me. "He might also have a life that could be destroyed."

So the mystery lover was married. "Molly, please. Faye's dead—how much more destroyed could his life get compared to hers?"

She sighed. "You're right. All I can tell you is that both flowers were ordered by Eddie Flynn."

I felt like I'd been smacked with a dinner plate. My ears rang. "Eddie? Of Eddie's Critters? Jan's Eddie? Are you sure, Molly?" The Eddie who had been chasing me in his white Suburban? Another thought crossed my mind. Gabe had said there had been three cars at the motel the night Faye was killed. One was a white truck with a camper shell or an SUV.

That could have been Eddie's Suburban, since I knew now it wasn't Jim Ponn's white truck. Jim had been bowling the night of Faye's murder, so his truck had been at the bowling alley.

Molly cut into my thoughts. "I'm sure Eddie ordered the flowers. I'm not sure about anything else, but . . ."

Molly had this annoying habit. As she got nervous, she stopped using full sentences. So far, she was just mildly tense. "But what?"

"Been doing flowers forever. One gets to know things."

Okay, more nervous. "What things?" I struggled for patience.

"The last order, it was make-up flowers. Most of the men try it. The woman breaks up with them and they come in or call, asking for flowers to make the woman come back."

"That's what Eddie did? He came in here and ordered flowers?"

"He ordered on the phone and gave his company credit card. Made it sound like business since once in a while Faye would help him out in the pet store if he was short-handed. But he said he'd made her mad and wanted to make up for it."

Faye had worked for Eddie? "But you think it was something more than employee relations?"

She looked at me. "Don't you? How many male bosses send a temp employee flowers?"

Damn few.

I had more questions than answers. I thanked Molly and left. Getting Ali out of the car, we walked across the parking lot to Eddie's Critters Pet Shop. My head was swirling. Eddie had been Faye's lover? But I thought he and Jan were so happy.

Were all men tail-chasers?

I didn't want to think so. My grandparents had a good marriage. A long, happy marriage. It didn't take a session with a shrink for me to figure out that I was trying to duplicate that with Heart Mates. I wanted to find out if there really was the everlasting love I read about in romance novels.

Apparently, Eddie and Jan didn't have the happily-ever-after that I envisioned. That was depressing.

Ali decided she knew where we were going and ran ahead. Balancing on my high-heeled shoes, I struggled across the blacktop and got to the pet shop to find Ali with her nose buried in the seam of the front door. "Want to go in, huh?"

She didn't move. Ali could be determined. I reached out to open the door.

It was locked. Lifting my gaze, I saw the sign on the door. It was a clock design. Over the face of the clock, it read *Sorry to miss you. Come back* . . . and the hands on the clock pointed to *tomorrow.*

I stared at the glass door. Putting my face against the panes, I could see inside. No movement. The lights were off. No animals were in the petting cages. Everyone was locked up for the night. Where was my kitten? And where was Eddie?

What the hell was going on?

My cell phone rang. Ali took her nose out of the door seam to look at my purse.

I dug the phone out. "Hello?"

"Sam! I got it!"

"Grandpa? What do you have?" Things were getting odder by the second. No telling what Grandpa had.

"Your detective. Detective Vance. I know why he's trying to keep you out of his way."

Oh, boy! Grandpa had something, I could tell by the excitement in his voice. Being an expert snoop and gossip, his information could be anything. A dark thought crossed my mind. Could Vance be the murderer? Could he be the man Faye had the affair with?

I dismissed that as fast as I thought it. That was my hangover from Rossi. I'd seen Vance in his cop environment. He'd been tough and macho, but he also meant to find Faye's killer. Too bad he was so fixated on Adam. But I wasn't, and Eddie Flynn looked like an interesting possibility.

"Sam? You there? These confounded cell phones." Click.

"Grandpa! I'm here!"

A dial tone answered me. Frustration tightened my stomach and I looked up to see myself in the glass window of Eddie's Critters. "Damn, Vance was right, I do look like a slut." I wanted to know what Grandpa had on Vance. I had to know. Now. Dropping my gaze back to the phone, I said, "Ring!" I knew better than to try to call Grandpa back. I'd get a busy signal, he'd get a busy signal . . .

The phone rang. "Grandpa! What did you find out about Vance!" Eagerness had me bouncing on my heels. Catching sight of myself in the window again, I stopped. Quickly I looked around, but the sidewalk in front of the buildings was empty.

"Sam, glad I got you back. I lost you there. You should check your battery. Maybe it needs to be charged."

"Grandpa!"

He chuckled in my ear. "Hold your girdle, Myrtle. It's worth the wait."

If he didn't tell me, I was going to pee in my pants on the sidewalk in front of Eddie's pet shop. "What?" It came out a gossipy whisper.

"Detective Vance's full name is Logan Reed Vance."

My excitement crashed. "That's it?" I tried not to sound too disappointed.

"No, but it's important. Now, you know how Vance digs at you about reading and reviewing romances?"

"Yeah. He's threatened by the heroes in those books." It felt good to say that. I hated his attitude about romance novels.

"Nope, that's not it."

"It's not? Come on, Grandpa!" I rocked on the balls of my feet and damn near fell through the window. Throwing out my hand, I caught the frame of the door and stopped myself.

"Sam?"

"I'm here!" If he hung up on me again, I'd throw myself through the window. "Please, Grandpa, tell me!"

"Detective Logan Reed Vance isn't just a homicide detective. He's R.V. Logan—the romance novelist!"

13

I dropped Ali off at home, took one look at TJ and Joel's hungry faces, and headed back out with TJ to go grocery shopping.

Extramarital affairs, murders and detectives who moonlight as romance authors take a back seat to two hungry sons. Grandpa and Joel were going to work on a science project. I just hoped they didn't blow up the house before TJ and I got back from the store.

I had just pulled into the Stater Bros. parking lot when TJ said, "Grandpa said to remind you to buy oven cleaner. But if you're afraid of oven cleaner now that you know . . . you've been a victim of an oven-cleaner crime, I can get it for you."

Turning off my car, I glanced over at my smirking son. "Well, gee, TJ, now that you mention it, I'm probably too afraid to clean the oven too. How about you spend Saturday morning doing that?"

His grin widened. "You gotta get over your fear, Mom. You know, tough it out." He hopped out of the car.

Laughing, I got out and followed him. "TJ, grab a cart, will you?" I asked as we headed into the store.

He pushed the squeaky cart alongside me. "Mom, what are you going to do about the kitten? Are you just going to leave her with Eddie?"

Picking up some beer out of the cooler, I set it in the cart and looked at TJ. His blue eyes were as intense as his father's had been. Sometimes, I looked in my oldest son's eyes and remembered the man I fell in love with.

Too bad that man had only existed in my head.

But TJ, he was special. Strong willed, with a firm sense of justice and smarter than I could ever hope to be. The boy understood algebra. I, on the other hand, believed that calculators were made to wipe out the plague of algebra. "I'll check with Eddie tomorrow, TJ. I'm sure the kitten is fine. But she needs a good home, TJ. We can't keep her."

Brushing his sandy hair off his forehead, he nodded solemnly. "Yeah, but you know what a baby Joel is. He's gonna complain."

Heading toward the fruit, I hid a smile from him. At barely fourteen, TJ wasn't about to cop to feelings for a kitten, but he'd happily use his brother for the job. Tossing in an insult to his brother was a bonus. Choosing some apples, I said, "Ali's all we can handle right now, TJ. Joel loves her." All of us did.

"Yeah. Can we have ice cream?"

Growing boys. "Sure."

Gathering up some salad fixings, I watched TJ with his head bent over the waist-high freezer, scanning the choices of ice cream. I was sticking to salad and dumping this hooker outfit first chance I got. TJ selected a flavor and came back.

"Mom, I was wondering."

"Hmm?" We left the produce to go down the cold frozen-food aisle.

"Faye being killed like that. Do you think someone will try to kill you too?" He walked ahead of me, his head down. "Rossi tried to."

I stopped the cart. "Oh, TJ." TJ and Joel's whole life had been turned upside down when their dad died. We'd been left broke. Trent's Beemer was repossessed, and I'd sold the family van and Trent's other classic car, a fully restored 1964 Mustang convertible. We'd been forced to sell the house and move in with Grandpa. Then, just when we were getting our lives together, some thug came into my dating service, stun-gunned me and left a demand for a half-million dollars of drug money that Trent stole from them.

Once more, our lives were shattered. But we'd faced that disaster and survived. Yet every once in a while, TJ showed the somber, apprehensive side that came from his young life being disrupted. My heart squeezed with the need to reassure him. "TJ, Gabe's helping me, you know that."

He lifted his head and turned around. "Where is Gabe?"

My sharp son probably sensed my tension. I debated lying and then tossed it aside. "Gabe went into Hollywood today to work on a script for a sitcom. He'll be back this evening."

Goosebumps bubbled on his thin arms from the freezers blowing out a cold fog on both sides of us. "Hollywood? Is Gabe going to work in TV?"

He voiced my own fears. I had never meant to bring any man into the boys' life. My mother had had an endless series of boyfriends, each one creating desperation in her to keep the man. I never quite understood what drove her. Maybe it had something to do with my bio-dad abandoning her when she was pregnant with me. At least, I guessed that he abandoned her. I hadn't wanted that for my own sons. Yet somehow, Gabe just wove his way into our lives. And if he left now, it would not only hurt me, but TJ and Joel too. "I'm not sure how to answer you, TJ. The truth is that Gabe is capable of doing whatever he wants to do. I think he's happy living here in Lake Elsinore doing his PI work and he's doing this script stuff on the side."

He thought about that for a few seconds, rubbing his hands over his cold arms. "Kind of like you do the PI stuff on the side, Mom?"

God, I loved this kid. "Exactly like that, TJ. If Gabe comes by the house tonight, you can talk to him about it, okay?"

TJ nodded and went off to study frozen possibilities.

While I wondered just when Gabe was going to show up. And if he'd keep his promise. He'd told me we weren't finished with . . . In spite of the freezers, my whole body heated at the memory of posing naked for Gabe.

And that he wasn't alone when I shouted *Surprise!*

Just to make sure I thawed all the food within a ten-foot radius, I remembered his admonition to "be ready."

A heat shiver rolled over me, but a cart rattling down the aisle chilled my lust. Looking up, I groaned.

Tristan Rogers stopped his cart and glared at me. "Get out of my way."

I saw TJ turn from the frozen waffles to watch. Sweeping a glance over Tristan's carefully organized cart, I met his gaze. "How nice to see you too, Tristan. I don't think my cart is blocking you." He had plenty of room to pass by.

His skinny nose was perfect for sneering. "You think I don't know how you got that detective to drop the harassment charges?" His wide-set eyes took in my black-leather halter top and short white skirt.

Tall and thin, he wore his polo shirt with the collar starched and tucked into pressed pants. I was pretty sure a smile would crack his mannequin face. "I wasn't harassing you, Rogers. I was looking for Dom. Can't you get into trouble for filing false police reports?"

"Harassing Dom is more accurate. Maybe even stalking. I saw you and that old man at my apartment last night. If I catch you anywhere near Dom again, I'll have you arrested. Stalking is taken seriously in California. You can't *suck* your way out of that one, Shaw." With that, he shoved his cart by mine and headed for the produce.

"Slip on a banana peel and die," I muttered. He had to be spying on us from somewhere last night. Dom had said Tristan went to a friend's apartment. Obviously the creep was watching from that apartment. And that suck-your-way-out comment made my ears burn and simmered my temper dangerously close to boiling over.

"Sam? Are you all right?"

I looked up. It was Rosy Malone, one of Grandpa's senior friends. She had her gray hair done in a tight chin-length perm with bangs and wore a pink jogging suit. "Hi, Rosy. I'm just irritated at Tristan." I tilted my head in the direction that Tristan had disappeared around the corner.

Rosy put her hand on my bare arm. "Don't take it personal, Sam. I knew his mother back when I taught literature at UCR. She was a janitor there and mean as they come. Used to make fun of Tristan, calling him a pansy because he always had his nose in a book and wanted to be a writer."

Well, that was a surprise. "In front of you, Rosy? She knew you taught literature at the university, right?"

Rosy nodded, her tight curls bouncing. "Sure, that's why she'd say it. Tristan would be moping around the campus if his mother couldn't dump him off on his grandmother. In the beginning, I'd felt sorry for him and gave him books to read, talked about some of the classics with him since he enjoyed it. He'd hang out in my room if I didn't have a class. Tristan's mother didn't like that. Didn't want Tristan thinking he was better than she was by associating with the educated. She was a hard-scrabble, mean woman. By the time Tristan was a teen-ager, he'd developed into a surly loner and I stopped feeling sorry for him. When he turned up here and opened Smash Coffee, I'd hoped he'd changed. Espe-cially after meeting Dominic. Now, he's a charmer." Her skin pinkened to match her jogging suit.

"Hi, Mrs. Malone," TJ said to Rosy, then asked me, "Mom, who was that man talking to you like that?"

I forced my face to relax. "That, TJ, is a prime exam-ple of a jerk."

Rosy smiled at me. "You don't let him bother you, dear. I have to run. Be sure to tell Barney hello for me. Bye, TJ." She shuffled down the freezer aisle.

I glanced at TJ. "Come on, let's finish shopping so we can get home and fix dinner."

Dinner was out on the back patio. Grandpa and the boys grilled hot dogs, tossing one or two to Ali in the process, while I boiled corn on the cob. Then we gath-ered around the redwood picnic table.

Who needed a boyfriend? I had everything I wanted at this table, including Ali sitting at the end of the table, patiently waiting for what she considered her due: any food.

"Mom, can Gabe get me some autographs? The stars of *Buffy the Vampire Slayer* or *Dark Angel* would be awe-some." Joel stuffed half a hot dog oozing relish into his mouth.

"Where'd you watch those shows?"

Joel glanced at Grandpa, who was right next to him and across from me.

"Grandpa." I sighed. "You know I don't want them watching too much of that stuff."

He winked at me. "I forgot."

I tried not to smile at him. He was incorrigible—and the best thing that could have happened to my sons or me.

"Sam, what are you going to do now that you know about Vance's secret life?"

Joel swallowed down his hot dog. "What secret life? Who's Vance?" His blue eyes glittered.

"Detective Vance, who is working on Faye's murder," I explained and sipped some iced tea. "Grandpa found out that he is a romance writer." This time I did smile.

"Ugh!" Joel said.

"No way," TJ said. "A cop wouldn't write that soppy chick-flick stuff."

"Oh, yes, he does. Not only that, I've written reviews on his work. He's good. He captures the . . ." I almost choked with laughter. ". . . delicate and deep emotion!"

"Cops are not romance writers." TJ finished his milk and picked up his plate. "Hurry up, Joel. I need to get the dishes done. I have homework."

"Then go do them," Joel suggested.

"You have to help. Mom said we both have to do them."

Joel shrugged his shoulders. "I'm not the one in a hurry." He turned to feed Ali the end of his bun.

I shot my hand out and caught TJ's arm before he threw a corn-on-the-cob husk at his brother. "Joel, you and TJ clear up and get the dishes done. Then homework." I held up my hand to silence the well of protest forming on Joel's full lips. "After that you can have some of the Chocolate Death ice cream."

Joel's twin dimples appeared. "You never buy Chocolate Death."

"I did this time." I wondered how much of it was going to plaster itself to my hips and thighs while I innocently slept, dreaming of carrot sticks and diet soda. When TJ and I returned home from the store, I'd taken off the short skirt and pulled on a pair of old, faded jeans. They were suspiciously tight. No Chocolate Death for me.

"All right!" Joel got up and started stacking dirty dishes.

"You'd better," TJ muttered.

I did a quick mom-gauge and determined that the two boys probably would only mouth off at each other and not make sudden use of any stray kitchen utensil. The testosterone levels in those two were rising by the minute, but mostly they got along with each other.

Mostly.

"Sam—" Grandpa leaned his elbows on the table. "What now?"

"First I have to call Leslie Lee. She's a new client this week at Heart Mates. I thought that since she asked so many questions about our system, I'd ask her to talk to the newspaper. You know, sort of balance out that stupid exposé article. We had two female clients today call and demand they be taken off all our records."

"Why don't you go do that, and I'll start some coffee." Grandpa stood up.

"Don't you help TJ and Joel," I warned.

"Wouldn't dream of it, Sammy. Just want some coffee." He shuffled off with Ali on his heels.

Pushing myself up, I went in the back door and waded through TJ and Joel's bickering and Grandpa's refereeing to get to the phone. My purse was on the kitchen table. I dug through it to find Leslie Lee's number. I found it on a phone message paper.

I'd been in such a hurry to get dinner on that I'd

only changed out of my skirt, but I still had the leather halter top on. Picking up the phone and dialing, I decided to change that after I talked to Leslie Lee. After three rings, voice mail picked up. "A-1 Laundromat. Our hours are from . . ."

I hung up. Must have dialed wrong. Glancing into the kitchen, I saw Grandpa leaning against the counter talking to the boys, but he wasn't doing their work. I redialed.

"A-1 Laundromat . . ." I hung up and stared at the phone number in my hand. I wanted to believe that I had written the wrong number down. But I knew that I hadn't. Instead I had been helping the very woman writing those articles in the newspaper. God, I was stupid. I should have paid more attention at work. I had thought Leslie Lee was excessively interested, to the point of downright annoying, in the workings of Heart Mates. But I'd been so focused on Faye's murder that I ignored my instincts. I hadn't put together the obvious connection of someone writing those articles and her excessive interest.

But why? What reason would she have for doing those articles?

"What's wrong, Sam?" Grandpa asked.

Fury pumped through me and made it impossible to stand still. I slammed the message paper down on the table and paced to the coffeemaker. Taking down two mugs I smacked them on the counter.

"Mom?" Joel looked up at me from his bent position over the opened dishwasher.

Seeing my unfailingly cheerful son's worried expression, I stopped myself. "It's okay, Joel, I'm just mad."

Grandpa slipped up beside me, lifted the coffeepot and filled the two cups I'd pulled out. "What is it, Sam?" He set the coffeepot back on the warmer.

"I know who wrote that article. Or at least who did the research. Leslie Lee."

Grandpa handed me a cup, his fading eyes thoughtful. "Who'd you get when you dialed?"

"A-1 Laundromat."

He shuffled toward his computer. "So she used a phone number that looks legitimate. She knew what she was doing."

Cripes, I hadn't thought of that.

"Do you have the address she used?" Sitting down in his chair, he set his coffee mug down on the built-in holder on his desk and bent his balding head over the keyboard. "What's the whole name this Leslie Lee used? A Social Security number would be pay dirt."

I didn't understand a lot about computers. One day I was going to learn. Computer fear is stupid.

Okay, so computers hated me and made me feel stupid.

Going through my purse again, I pulled out the message slip. "Leslie Lee is her whole name. I assumed that Lee was her last name. Here's her address." I squinted at Blaine's writing and read it off.

"The address is for A-1 Laundromat too," Grandpa announced.

"So how do we find her?" I pulled out a chair and sat down. It was time to stop running after each little scrap of information and look at the whole package.

Turning his chair, Grandpa picked up his coffee and said, "I'll work on that, but first, how do you think this is connected to Faye's murder?"

"I wish I knew. Gabe thought that maybe it was a little misdirection. The articles cast suspicion on Heart Mates and away from the real killer. But I don't know, that seems too iffy to me."

"Unless the killer had a real connection to the newspaper. Knew he could get the articles in the paper somehow."

"Maybe. That would mean the killer knows or has

some kind of connection to Leslie Lee. But how does Eddie fit into this? Where is he? Why'd he close up the shop and take off?" Getting up, I had an idea. "I'll call the Chamber of Commerce and find out if Jan really is getting an award tonight."

"Why?"

While getting the phone book out of the kitchen cupboard, I explained about Eddie asking me to search his house for possible poisons while he and Jan were at the award ceremony.

His gray eyebrows shot up. "The beloved town librarian poisoning her husband?"

"Yeah, and now I know why. Eddie was having an affair with Faye. In fact, she sometimes worked in his pet shop." Flipping through the pages of the phone book, I remembered how much Faye loved animals.

The perfect hook. It would have been so easy for Eddie to use that to get Faye's attention. While she was feeling unneeded and unloved, Eddie, who was older than Faye by at least ten years, could have played her without breaking a sweat.

Getting the phone number, I dialed the Chamber of Commerce. A machine picked up and told me they were closed. Of course, it was five minutes to six. I thought of my phone tree. "I'll be right back," I told Grandpa and raced into my bedroom, snatched up my Rolodex off the cluttered desk and ran back out to the kitchen. Flipping through the cards, I pulled out Barbara Rickles. Turning over the card, I said, "Ah-ha." There on the back was my careful notation of Barbara going back to work at the Lake Elsinore Chamber of Commerce. I dialed her home number and quickly confirmed that Jan Flynn was indeed being honored with an award dinner at the Sizzler. It began at six-thirty.

Hanging up the phone, I glanced at Grandpa.

"Sam? What are you thinking?"

Putting the phone book away, I left my Rolodex on the counter and sat down. "Why did Eddie really come to me about the poisoning thing? Yeah, he looked pretty bad this morning." I wrinkled my nose at the rancid memory of my puke shower. Ugh! "When the boys were little and likely to eat anything, I kept Syrup of Ipecac to induce vomiting in the house."

"You think he made himself sick?"

I thought for a moment, then shook my head. "That's not Eddie. He and Jan don't have kids, so he's not even likely to know about that stuff. Eddie doesn't do research." He told me that himself. "Eddie likes to see his enemy. I can see him using me to keep tabs on Faye's murder investigation, but I don't think he made himself sick."

"So Jan's really poisoning him? Lots of us go to the library, Sam. Jan's always nice and helpful."

I glanced up. "Yeah, but we're not always what we seem. No one in town ever thought I had it in me to step outside my PTA life and run a business." Especially a dating service that I was just barely keeping out of the red.

"I did."

I smiled at him. "Yes, you did."

"Sam, do you think Eddie killed Faye?"

My stomach cringed at the thought. "I don't know, Grandpa. Someone killed her with her own jump rope. That jump rope is missing."

"You're not thinking of going into Eddie's and looking for that jump rope." He stood up and fixed a serious stare on me. "Of course you are. I'm going with you."

I shook my head. "You have to stay here with the boys. You could work on the newspaper angle. Learning more about Leslie Lee might lead us to the killer if the articles are being planted by the killer as some kind of diversion.

"Besides, I really don't know if Eddie's involved. From what I got out of Molly, it was her impression that Eddie was sending Faye make-up flowers." Thinking back over my conversation with Adam, I added, "I think Faye broke up with him. Eddie led her into some shady business practices. Signing up at Heart Mates to find men who knew how to start a business, stealing clients, and worse . . . She was sleeping with a married man. Faye's own father left her and her mother for another woman."

"So Eddie killed her?"

I couldn't quite believe it, yet it made a kind of sad sense. "Faye was young and beautiful. Eddie is an aging football star turned pet store owner. His wife is well regarded in town, and smarter than him. To have a woman like Faye hang on his every word, then suddenly have her break it off. . . ."

Grandpa set his coffee cup down. "Men have killed for less, Sam. You have a point."

"And, in his high school days, Eddie had been brutal out on the football field." Something slipped around in my mind. I tried to put it all together. Mindy had gotten the kitten from Eddie for Faye as a gift from Adam. So Eddie probably took that as a sign that Faye and Adam were reconciling.

That fit. A white truck or SUV was at the motel the night of Faye's murder. Had Eddie rushed over there to talk Faye out of reconciling with Adam?

But what about the brochure? "Grandpa, why would Eddie change the brochure and leave it in Faye's hand?"

He looked at me. "Who was Faye's mentor, Sam?"

I winced. That made a sick sense too. All my *suggestions* to Faye about building her own business, being

strong and thinking for herself—had that led her away
from Eddie and to her death? And perhaps Eddie's
anger lingered enough to threaten me by leaving a second altered brochure at my house. Or scare me away if
he thought I was getting too close. Which meant he
took some brochures home with him. Another thing to
look for in his house. I still wasn't sure why he chased
me in his SUV, but he really could be hiding the fact
that he hired me from Jan.

The jump rope. Eddie was strong enough to strangle
Faye with it. Faye would have let him in the motel and
trusted him. He could have picked the jump rope up off
the mirror and it probably wouldn't have alarmed Faye.

After all, this was Eddie, who loved animals.

But . . . "I'm missing something." I cupped my hands
around my cup of coffee and tried to force my brain to
sift through what I knew. Something nagged at me.
About Eddie? The clues? Faye?

"Call Gabe. He's experienced, Sam. He might be able to
see this from another angle. You two work well together."

I wanted to. But I wasn't sure about where Gabe and
I were going. What if he went to Hollywood? I had to be
able to do this on my own. I made a decision. "I have
Eddie's key. He's sure to be with Jan at the award dinner. I'm going to look through his house for the jump
rope and see if he has any of the brochures that Faye
made. She probably ran off several test copies." And
maybe the thing, the piece of the puzzle I was missing,
would jump out at me.

"Sam, it's too dangerous for you to go to Eddie's
house. He could be waiting for you. What about your
detective? You could talk to him."

Vance the romance writer? "Oh, I'm going to call
Detective Vance. Just as soon as I get more information

on Eddie. And this time, Vance is going to listen to me."
I'd seen just how macho and tough Vance acted at
work. He was not going to want his cop buddies to know
he wrote romance novels. From now on, Detective Logan
Vance, a.k.a. R. V. Logan, was going to cooperate with
me every chance he got. But to reassure Grandpa, I
said, "Jan and Eddie will be at the dinner. You can even
check if you want, Grandpa. I'm sure a lot of your
friends are there, and they all have cell phones. Call
them and double-check if you like. I'll have my cell
phone with me." I got up and picked up my purse.

I was being smart now. Gathering my facts. If I found
anything linking Eddie Flynn to Faye's murder, I was
going to walk out of the house and track down Lake
Elsinore's very own romance-writing homicide detective.

Eddie and Jan lived in a one-story ranch home in an
unincorporated part of town. That meant no street-
lights or sidewalks. That was both good and bad news.
Fewer neighbors were likely to see me skulking around
the house.

And fewer neighbors were likely to notice anyone
sneaking up on me with a jump rope.

I shivered and got out of my car where I'd parked it
at the end of the street. Having put on my old soccer-
mom vest now packed with a flashlight, stun gun, cell
phone and defense spray, I started up the street.

Eddie's house was on the corner of a small cul-de-sac
that opened off the through street I had parked on. I
passed a wall of shrub blooming with white flowers that
shielded the side of Eddie's house and backyard. This
tract of homes had large yards, some as big as an acre.
Turning the corner, I saw the blue-with-white-trim house.

The shrub stopped at the edge of the house, leaving the front lawn, driveway and porch exposed. A bright porch light glowed over the front door.

Look confident, I told myself. If I looked like I knew what I was doing, any stray neighbors looking out wouldn't question why I was going into Eddie and Jan's house. I held my head high, strode up the empty two-car driveway and followed the sidewalk up to the porch.

My pounding heart drowned out all other sounds. Pausing on the porch, I quickly looked over my shoulder.

I didn't see anyone, but it wouldn't be wise to stand around under the porch light advertising my presence to the neighbors. Quickly, I slipped the key Eddie gave me out of my jean pocket, opened the screen door and nearly died of fright when it squeaked. I dropped the key and heard it skip along the cement by my feet.

"Get a grip," I muttered, looking down. Spotting the key, I leaned over and picked it up while keeping the screen door open with my hip. Standing back up, I looked at the lock. A single deadbolt. I took a steadying breath, inserted the key and turned.

Easy as that, the front door opened. Okay, I was in. Carefully, I eased the screen shut and gently closed the front door.

To my right, the living room spread out with a single lamp left on. There was a coat closet to my left, and beyond that a hallway leading to the three bedrooms. If I walked straight, I'd end up in the spacious country kitchen. Jan and Eddie hosted a few library functions here where everyone gathered in the big kitchen or out in the half acre or so backyard.

I decided to head for the bedrooms. I doubted Eddie would leave evidence in the living room or kitchen. He'd be likely to hide it somewhere Jan wouldn't look.

Hmm. Suddenly I wondered if that would be the pet shop? Had Eddie sent me on a wild-goose chase?

Or worse? I checked my cell phone. Grandpa was going to make sure that Eddie and Jan were at the award dinner. He'd call me if Eddie was missing. Certain the cell phone was on and functioning, I slipped it back into my vest pocket and turned left down the hallway.

The first bedroom on my left had the look of an office. It was dark in there, so I took my flashlight out and aimed it around the room. Bookshelves lined two walls and bulged with books. Quickly, I glanced at the titles. *Wuthering Heights, Grapes of Wrath, Of Mice and Men, The Handmaid's Tale* and many more by Shakespeare, Hemingway and Hawthorne. A librarian's paradise.

I wrinkled my nose, much preferring contemporary work. *The Handmaid's Tale* was by a living author, and a pretty good read, actually. The rest were a sleeping pill.

I went to the computer desk. The top held the monitor and a single red rose. Sitting in the chair, I ran the flashlight beam into each drawer. The first one held pens, pencils, stamps, the usual assorted desk junk all neatly arranged. Bored, I moved on to the second drawer. In there, I found a stack of bills still in envelopes, and a stack that appeared to be paid and organized by dates. I flipped through them and stopped at the Visa bill.

Pulling it out of the envelope, I scanned the list of charges. Some were obviously business related and a few were to restaurants. Quickly, I found the charge for Frank's Flowers. I sat back in the chair and looked around.

Jan's fingerprints were all over this office. The books. The single perfect red rose on the desk, probably from her backyard rose garden. The floral prints on the walls. The pink chair cushion I sat on. The smell of Jergens hand lotion in the air. So why would Eddie charge something on this card if Jan would see it?

I looked at the bill. It was addressed to the pet shop address.

So Eddie handled his own bills for work? Or maybe just this work charge card? Setting the flashlight on the edge of the desk, I flipped through more of the bills in the beam of light. There were utility bills, both for the Flynns and the pet shop, all addressed to the home address.

Okay, Eddie had gotten his own business credit card, had the bills sent to work, and Jan found it. And found the Frank's Flowers charge. She figured out Eddie was on the prowl—then what? How would she find out Faye was the other woman? And then what would she do?

I thought about Jan. Intelligent and very well organized. Did not like chaos. What did Eddie say? *Jan's a little . . . high-strung. She likes things perfect. If I screw up, she has a way of making me pay for that.* Okay, I could buy that. After all, she had a treasure chest to reward children who read, so if she believed in rewards, then by the same token, why not believe in punishment? Following that logic, she found out about Eddie's dalliance and punished him by poisoning? Brutal and dangerous.

But what about Faye—would Jan feel the need to punish her? By strangling her? It didn't add up—poisoning was hands off, while strangling was, literally, hands-on murder. Putting the bill away, I grabbed the flashlight, got up and scanned the books again. Leaving the classic section, I found myself in mysteries. Mostly older mysteries. She had several by Dorothy L. Sayers, including one titled *Strong Poison*. Browsing more titles, I stumbled on *Arsenic and Old Lace* and *The Piano Bird*. All mysteries about poisoning. Hmm, *The Piano Bird*. I'd read that . . . I think. The trouble with having read so much was keeping the books, plots and characters straight.

Leaving the fiction section, I saw some books on botany. The study of plants. Yawn. There was a limit to my attention span. The books told me only that Jan might have read some murder mysteries.

Didn't make her a poisoness. Conscious of the time, I quickly looked through the rest of the desk drawers and took a peek in the closet. No sign of Faye's jump rope or any brochures for Heart Mates. Nor did I find notes on how to poison Eddie. Time to move on.

I went into the guest bathroom and found expensive guest soaps and hand lotion. Next I tried the guest bedroom. Frills and lace dominated the room, but no hidden murder weapon or any other evidence. The master bedroom was at the end of the hall.

I hesitated. Frankly, Eddie would have to be a special kind of stupid to hide anything there. I tried to think.

His shaving stuff! That might be a safe place to hide something. Quickly I bypassed the bedroom and went into the bathroom. It was done up in greens. There were two medicine cabinets. The first one was clearly Jan's, including birth control pills. I closed that and went to the second one.

Toothbrush, razor, deodorant, asprin, BenGay, Rogaine ... more than I wanted to know. Nothing there, so I dropped to my knees and looked under the sink. There was a black bag typical of a traveling shaving kit. Pulling it out, I opened it up and shined the light in it.

It was full of little cards and notes. I could make out Faye's signature. My heart leaped into high gear. Bingo! I'd found something. The shaving kit was filled with notes and cards written to Eddie by Faye. God, what these could tell me! I was reaching my hand into the shaving kit when I heard the noise.

Ohmigod! Someone else was in the house!

14

Frozen on my knees in the master bathroom of Eddie's house, with my hand stuck into the black shaving kit, I turned off my flashlight and listened.

The noise came from the front of the house. The slow push of a door closing into a tight frame. Not shut firmly, but pushed slow and quiet into its wood frame.

A sneaky sound.

Shit. Closing my hand around a handful of the notes and cards, I stuffed them into one of my vest pockets, rezipped the shaving kit and tossed it back into the cupboard. Standing up, I tried to think what to do. I was all the way back in the master bathroom, and in the dark with my flashlight turned off. I didn't dare turn it on now.

Who was in the house? Eddie? Had Eddie come to kill me? Maybe that was why he sent me here in the first place, to set me up to kill me.

I was trapped in the bathroom, but I did have some weapons. I pulled out my pepper spray. But pepper spray didn't work the same on everyone. It took seconds to get into the victim's eyes and debilitate them.

And there's always the chance I'd spray myself instead of my attacker. Slipping the spray back into my vest pocket, I got the stun gun out and turned it on. A low pop sizzled. A zap with this should drop a grown man to the ground.

Armed, I had to try to get out of the closed area of the master bathroom. Slowly, I eased my way across the carpet and passed the mirrored closets to the bedroom. Stopping, I peered around the end of the closet to the hallway door. Since the hallway dead-ended into the door of the master bedroom, I had an unobstructed view of the long hall and into the living room. I couldn't see anyone, only the light coming from the living room. No moving beam of a flashlight. No shadows of a killer.

Stop that! The stun gun shook in my trembling hand. I had to get control. On the other side of the bedroom was a set of French doors that led out to a patio. It was black out there, and I knew the yard was huge. A thick wall of shrub surrounded it. Jan had lots of green grass, a lovely rose garden, a beautiful white gazebo and end-less places for a killer to hide.

But out there was better than in the house where I could get trapped in a corner. I heard another noise. It sounded like someone sliding a hand along a wall. A whisper.

A damn scary whisper.

Sweat ran down my back beneath my leather halter. My mouth dried to a desert. Thoughts pounded at my brain, flashing pictures of TJ and Joel. TJ as a newborn, Joel at four and a half when he kicked the soccer ball into the opposing team's goal and beamed with apple-cheeked pride. TJ on his first day of kindergarten, a lit-tle man in a five-year-old body.

I gritted my teeth and focused. Maybe only a second had passed.

A light thump. I guessed it came from the kitchen.

Looking in my memory, I pictured the wide rectangle of the kitchen. Wood floors—that was the whisper I had heard, the sound of feet moving across parquet. French doors led to the back. A big trestle table sat in the middle. On the far end was an entertainment center with a TV and stereo. The left side had standard kitchen appliances, cupboards and tiled counters.

Someone was making his or her way through the kitchen. I had to hurry. I needed to run past the opened door before the intruder made it to the hallway where he could catch sight of me. Then I'd be free to escape through the French doors.

Holding my breath, I promised God, *Get me out of this and I'll stick to my dating service from now on. No more sleuthing for me.* Done praying, I darted across the doorway. Once across, I froze to listen. Had he heard me? Who was it out there?

Don't think about it! Just get out!

Quickly, I made my way between the king-sized bed and the dresser to the French doors, trying to be quiet. My vomit-soaked running shoes were in the trash, so I had on little white tennies from Payless Shoe Store. They were flimsy but silent. The fingers of my right hand had a death grip on the stun gun. If anyone caught me, I'd zap first and ask questions later.

Once at the door, I studied the white frame in the darkness. I put my hand out, feeling for the handle. It was one of those long, push-down kind. I pushed.

Locked.

Panic built in the back of my dry throat. I no longer heard whispering noises from the hardwood kitchen floor. He was on the carpet now. I was sure of it. And headed this way. It would only take seconds to walk down the hallway and into the bedroom.

Terror poked me hard in the middle of my back. The pressure at the back of my throat was building to a scream. I fumbled my free hand over the surface of the door, looking for the lock. The stun gun stayed clutched in my right hand.

There! I found the lock. Beneath my fingers it felt like a simple dead bolt with a turn latch.

Just as I turned the lock, a breath of air moved my hair. Oh God! Someone was behind me! My brain numbed with sheer terror. Instinct took over. I lifted the stun gun, pivoted left, and brought up my right hand. The shadow of a big man stood there.

Before my eyes and brain communicated, I slammed the end of the stun gun to some part of him—his head? His neck? Don't know.

Squeeze!

My finger obeyed and I squeezed the trigger.

"Sam. . . ."

The man went silent and crumpled to the ground.

Uh-oh. I stared down at the heap on the ground as his voice echoed in my head. Trembling, I carefully turned off and put the stun gun away. Next, I pulled out my flashlight. Turning it on, I aimed the beam of light at the man on the floor.

Gabe. He had on black jeans and a black T-shirt. He'd fallen on his back, his left arm splayed outward and his right thrown over his chest, reaching toward me. With his Italian temper unconscious, I figured I had about three minutes to make a run for it. Before he woke up and choked me with the hand reaching toward me.

I'd accidentally sprayed Gabe with pepper spray once. I didn't think I could get away with assaulting him a second time.

But I couldn't leave him. What if I'd really hurt him? What if he stopped breathing? My heart squeezed into a painful lump. Sinking into a knee bend, I laid the flashlight on the ground with the beam aimed at his face. His dark, straight hair fell over his forehead. I reached out my hand to see if he was breathing.

Gabe's arm resting on his chest shot out and clamped around my left wrist.

I screamed.

"Shhh!" His closed eyes scrunched in pain. "God, what did you hit me with?"

"Stun gun."

"Christ."

That about summed it up. "Uh, yeah, well, sorry about that. But you sneaked up on me." My defense mechanism decided to make this his fault. "I thought you were the killer! Why didn't you call out and let me know it was you?"

One eye slid open. It was a pool of black fury.

"Uh, what are you doing here, Gabe? How'd you know I was here?" I hoped to distract him from any plots of revenge swirling in his brain.

"TJ called me, Babe."

"He did?"

"You were gone when I got to the house. Barney filled me in."

"You mean Grandpa sent you after me? I had this under control."

The second eye opened. "Right. That's why I'm lying on the ground with six or seven jackhammers working overtime in my head."

I tugged on my wrist. "Your reflexes look fine." When I'd been stun-gunned, I'd had trouble making my tongue work, letting alone my arms and legs.

He tugged me closer. "You're going to pay for this, Sam."

I believed him. "Look, Gabe, you can't sneak up on someone and—"

He arched a single brow. "And yell *surprise?*"

I closed my mouth. I would never live down my naked show this morning. It'd be a cold day in hell before I tried that again.

Gabe let go of my wrist and sat up. He appeared to steady himself, grabbed the flashlight off the ground and then rolled up to his feet.

I scrambled to my feet.

"I gotta find some aspirin." He turned away and stalked out of the bedroom with the beam of the flashlight aimed to the floor.

"Gabe!" Running, I followed him down the hallway and into the kitchen.

He stood at the sink on the left side of the room, prying open a bottle of Advil. I had a ton of questions. TJ calling Gabe worried me, but right now I had to finish what I came here to do.

Which meant I had to continue my search for the jump rope that strangled Faye, any spare copies of the Heart Mates brochure and maybe a clue to how Jan was poisoning Eddie. If she was poisoning him.

Going to the sink, I picked up the flashlight. Since we were at the back of the house, and thick shrubs shielded the backyard, I steered the beam around the large room. The usual cupboards, stove and microwave and refrigerator lived in the kitchen end of the room. The middle had the big trestle table with a glass vase and some white flowers. I recognized those from the shrub I had passed on my way in. The other end had the entertainment center with the large-screen TV, stereo and two easy chairs. Where in here might Eddie hide the murder weapon?

Jan would find it. If she found the receipt for his company Visa card, she would find a murder weapon hidden in the house.

I swung the light around again. Only the coffeemaker and a set of four flowered canisters sat on the counters. Jan didn't drink coffee. Guess that was her concession to Eddie—a coffeemaker. Jan drank tea.

"Sam? What are you doing?"

While running the beam of light around, I told Gabe what I was looking for and what I had found, including the Visa receipt with the charges of flowers. "Flowers," I repeated, thinking . . . something.

It hit me then. What seemed odd? I whipped the flashlight back to the flowers in the center of the table. "Jan has a beautiful rose garden in the backyard."

"Yeah, and I have the scratches to prove it."

Okay, now I knew Gabe had come through the backyard. He wasn't dumb enough to stand at the front door and pick the lock. From past experience, I surmised he picked the lock on the French doors here in the kitchen to get in. "But Jan has these flowers off a shrub on her table. The big white ones." Come on! Something about the books nagged at me. The botany books? No. . . .

"So? They're pretty enough. Kind of a tropical look, a flower that birds would like."

Birds. *The Piano Bird!* I whirled around, looking at Gabe. "Oleanders! Oleander is used in the book *The Piano Bird.* The killer skews a hot dog on the branch of an oleander to cook it. The victim eats the hot dog and dies."

Gabe stared at the flowers. "No shit? You think Jan's poisoning Eddie with oleander? But how?"

Excitement bubbled in my chest. "How?" I looked around. "I doubt she gets him to eat a hot dog on a stick. All parts of the oleander are poisonous. This morning it had been early when Eddie got sick, too early for hot dogs—" I trailed off as my flashlight hit the coffeemaker. Immediately, I thought of Eddie and his always-present silver travel coffee mug.

"Ohmigod!" I whipped the light back to the glass vase. It was only half full of water. "She's using the water from the vase of flowers to make Eddie's coffee!"

Gabe put the Advil back where he found it and strode over to stand next to me. "That would do it? Just the water the flowers were put in?"

"I think so. And it makes sense from Jan's point of view. She's not trying to kill Eddie, just punish him. It'd be hard to prove, and Lord knows she could claim it was a mistake."

In the dim light, Gabe turned and looked down at me.

"What?"

"I'm thinking your dead husband got off easy. If you'd ever yanked your head out of the sand and seen what he was doing while he was alive—"

I winced. "But I didn't, did I? And my two sons might have died for it. That will never happen again." I had wanted so badly for Trent and my life together to be a romance novel come true that I constantly rewrote the truth into fiction inside my head. That kind of desperation is difficult to explain to someone who hasn't lived it. My mother's man-chasing had left me with the impression that an intact family was the best thing for my two sons. Determined not to have a parade of men marching through their lives, I ended up subjecting them to a weak, panty-chasing, drug-smuggling one.

I would never fail my boys that way again. Or myself.

He touched my face. "I know that, Sam. And so do your sons."

"But TJ called you." Dang it, I had work to do. I couldn't afford to whine about my son not believing I could handle things myself.

His dark brow arched. "Is that so bad? TJ trusting me to help you out?"

"I don't know."

He said nothing, his fingers light on my face. Then finally, "You'd better figure it out soon." He dropped his touch from my face and grabbed my hand. "Let's go. Barney dropped me off here, so we'll both take your car."

"Wait! I want to look for—" I stumbled toward the back doors.

"The jump rope's not here, Sam. You've already looked in the likely places. Besides, it's getting late and they could be home soon." We melted out the doors and into the dark night.

Halfway across the dark backyard, another thought occurred to me. "You said Grandpa dropped you off? Where are the boys? Where was Grandpa going?"

"Your mom is with the boys, and Barney said he had something to do."

Something to do? Uh-oh.

Gabe and I arrived home to find my mother and the boys playing Monopoly. Mom looked up and frowned at me. "Samantha, tell me you didn't go to the Chamber of Commerce Awards Night looking like that!"

I swallowed a groan and guessed that Grandpa had lied to my mom. "Okay, I didn't. Gabe and I went to a movie." To head off more lectures, I turned to my sons. "Clean up, boys. It's time for bed. You have school tomorrow." They got up with a minimum of complaining.

Gabe passed me by and headed for the kitchen. "Hi, Kathryn."

"Hello, Gabe. Don't you think Samantha should dress more her age? She's a mother, after all. Of course, you are younger than she."

"Want a beer, Kathryn?" Gabe asked and headed around the corner into the kitchen.

My mom wrinkled her nose. "No, thank you. I'm going home and having a glass of wine."

Gabe was not quite the man my mother wanted for me. She didn't think a PI was respectable enough. Gabe didn't care, which only made him more intriguing to me. God, I was in my thirties and acted like a teenager. I tried to yank my mind out of adolescence into adulthood. "Mom, did Grandpa say where he was going?" I was a bit worried about him.

"To visit a sick friend, and he didn't want to call you home from the awards dinner at Sizzler. Why'd you lie to your grandfather, Samantha? You should have just told him you were going to the movies. Or better yet, you should have dressed like a lady and gone to the awards banquet."

My right eye started to twitch. "My lady clothes are in the laundry."

Gabe came out of the kitchen with two opened beers. Handing me one, he gestured to my black-leather halter peeking out beneath my vest and tight jeans. "So these are your *babe* clothes?"

Swear to God, I could actually see blue arcs of electricity sizzling between us.

Joel's voice interrupted the electric flow of sensual energy. "Mom, you gotta sign my science project. I get extra credit."

Ripping my gaze from Gabe, I remembered I was a mom. I had two sons. I looked at Joel standing by my mom waving a packet of papers at me. "Leave them on the table, Joel, and I'll sign them."

He grinned. "Gramps and me did a cool project. I'm gonna get an A and win the district competition."

I smiled at him. "I bet you will."

He hugged my mom, then sauntered off to bed, probably planning to take over the world after he mastered the world of science.

"Samantha, I couldn't help but notice your Rolodex."

I drank half my beer, then looked at my mother. "I used that when I did volunteer work, Mom."

"Very clever. It will be useful to build clients once you get your real estate license." She walked a couple steps to pick her purse up off the love seat and headed for the door. "I have to run. Got an early meeting with a client tomorrow. Oh, and if you and your grandfather are snooping into Faye's murder—"

I stared at her, preparing myself for the lecture. After all, real estate agents must uphold certain standards. The fact that I would never become a real estate agent did not factor into my mom's world. "Mom, Faye was my client, I'm just—"

"Save it, Samantha."

Automatically, I shut my mouth while flushing under the rebuke. I didn't dare look at Gabe. I might not be able to back-talk my mother, but I'd have no trouble slugging the smirk off Gabe's face. Instead, I looked at Mom.

Her face shed the carefully cultivated sophistication and flashed a glimpse of her trailer-trash roots. "If you insist on doing this, Samantha, then find the bastard that murdered Faye. No woman deserves to be killed for trying to better her life. Oh, and one of you better track down your grandfather. He left with binoculars and that Sonic Ear toy of Joel's." She turned and left.

Dumbfounded, I watched the front door close.

"Cool. Sort of reminds me of you."

I whirled around and faced Gabe. "I am not like my mother!"

He laughed and dropped his gaze to my breasts. "I

like your upgrades. But I'd say that behind that sophisticated shell, your mom has a sharp and devious mind
just like her daughter."

Hell. "She didn't get to be the Real Estate Queen of
Lake Elsinore and the surrounding areas by being stupid, Gabe. But I don't live with my head in the sand like
she does."

He arched a single eyebrow at me and lifted his bottle of beer to his mouth.

Damn. "Okay, I don't live with my head in the sand
anymore." So maybe there was a slight resemblance between my mother and me. But at least I wasn't trying to
force my sons into a career they didn't want. On the
other hand, I knew that my mom wanted me to have
the safe, married-in-suburbia life that she never had.
Which was why Gabe didn't quite make the cut in my
mom's opinion. Safe in suburbia he was not. Turning
this back on him, I said, "What about you? Are you like
your mother? Or your father?"

He shrugged. "Hard to know about my dad. He's been
dead for years. Probably my brothers are more like him
than me. I'm the rebel."

"No shit." Curiosity bubbled into a roiling boil. "How
are your brothers more like your dad?"

He tipped back another quarter of his beer. "They're
firefighters. I had to be different and become a cop. A
rebel."

So his dad had been a firefighter? How did he die?
Brothers who were firemen? Any sisters? How many
brothers? Why didn't I know any of this stuff? Why hadn't
I met them? God, I wanted to sit down with him and ask
a zillion questions. Hell, I wanted to drive to Los Angeles
and track down his mom to ask her a zillion questions.
But Grandpa was out there somewhere, and he was armed
with snooping equipment. My worry for Grandpa out-

weighed my curiosity. Just barely. "As much as I really
want the scoop on your family tree, one of us has to go
look for Grandpa."

The barest gleam of silver lights danced in his dark
eyes. "Go ahead. I'll kick back here and catch some basket-
ball on TV and keep an eye on TJ and Joel."

"I have a better idea. You go, and I'll kick back here
in a bubble bath."

Gabe set his bottle of beer on the TV. "Bubble bath?
Naked and wet?" He walked to me.

I backed away. "Gabe, the boys—" *Be ready,* he had said.
Oh, Lord, I was ready. Physically. The emotional stuff always tripped me up.

A bad-boy grin tweaked his mouth. "I'll don my cape
and hunt down your grandfather."

He knew I remembered his admonition to *be ready.* It
sat there between us. My belly quivered with tension.
And needs.

Then Gabe turned, strode to the door and slipped out.

Holding my beer bottle, I fought the rush of sheer
lust that made me want to race after him and tackle him
on the front porch.

I headed for the kitchen. Maybe I could stick my head
in the freezer and cool off. Throwing my beer bottle
away, I decided instead to take a bath. I wanted to read
the cards that I'd snatched from Eddie's house and
reading in the tub would keep my mind off Gabe.

Maybe.

A knock on the front door surprised me. I went back
into the living room to find Ali at the front door. She
had gone with the boys into their room, but a knock on
the door required her guard-dog attention. Stopping by
her, I caught her fleeting glances toward Gabe's quarter-
full beer bottle that he had left on the TV. I opened the
door and forgot about Ali and the beer bottle.

"Eddie!" That was all my brain could come up with. So much for sharp and devious. Eddie stood on the doorstep dressed in a pair of dark gray slacks and a white dress shirt with the tails hanging out. GQ he was not.

"Sam, I only have a couple of minutes. I told Jan I was going to the store for a bottle of wine to celebrate her award. Did you do it? Look in my house?"

"Uhhh . . ." I was really hoping my brain would kick into gear. The note cards in my zippered vest suddenly felt heavy. Obviously Eddie didn't know I'd taken them. Not yet anyway.

Eddie rocked back and forth, then looked at his watch beneath the porch light. "Do you know how she's making me sick? I have to know, Sam."

Finally, I started thinking. Eddie had hired me to find that out, so telling him was something I should do. "I think so, Eddie. It's your coffee. You know those white flowers Jan has on the kitchen table from your oleander shrub?"

He nodded, leaning slightly forward.

What if Eddie killed Faye? Would he try to kill me? But he didn't know I knew about their affair. "Well, they are poisonous. I think Jan is using the water from the vase of oleander flowers to make your coffee." I had less trouble believing that Jan would poison Eddie now that I knew he was a cheating pig. But even so, it was dangerous. "What you need to do, Eddie, is tell the police." If he didn't kill Faye, then he would go to the police.

"No! No police. I don't want Jan to get into trouble."

"Eddie, she could kill you!"

He shook his head. "No, don't you see? This is exactly what I need to make her respect me."

"Huh?"

"Yeah. If Jan sees that I can figure this out, that I can be book-smart, then she'll stop trying to control me like this." Eddie nodded to himself, then looked at his watch again. "Sam, did you find anything else?"

I had to force myself not to touch the heavy lump of note cards in my vest pocket. "Like what?"

"Jan hiding anything maybe?"

Like the credit card bill she found at your work? "No."

"Okay. Thanks, Sam. Can you bring your bill by my work?"

I tried again. "Eddie, you should go to the police. They can test the coffeemaker or something."

"No. Jan's not a criminal. She's *not,*" he said more to himself as he looked down again at his watch. "She wouldn't kill someone; she wouldn't kill me. She's not a killer." He looked up at me. "I have to go. Bring me your bill." He turned and walked down the steps.

Was he the killer? And what exactly did I do with my suspicions? I didn't know, so I said to his retreating back, "I want my kitten back!"

Oh, yeah, that was clever. I shut the door and turned around to see that both my guard dog and Gabe's left-over beer bottle were gone.

Great, my kitten was missing and my dog was a lush-thief. I probably wasn't going to win an Ace Investigator award this week.

With the boys tucked in for the night, I poured some almond-scented bubbles into the tub of my tiny bathroom. I left the water running full strength and went into my bedroom. Taking off the black fleece vest, I pulled out the note cards Faye had written to Eddie. Methodically, I stacked them in a neat pile with the earliest ones on top and the last one on the bottom.

I kicked off my white tennies, stripped off my jeans, unzipped the leather halter, and pulled off my black thong underwear. Gathering up the note cards, I went into the bathroom.

The tub was full. Turning off the faucet, I stepped over the edge and sank down into the hot water. I trusted that Gabe would track down Grandpa and keep him out of trouble.

I was the one in trouble. My feelings for Gabe were in the danger zone. The place that made me want to build fantasies about love and happily-ever-after. Ruthlessly, I clamped down on those feelings and let the hot, scented water relax me. I had to read the notes and concentrate on Faye.

I picked up the stack from the side of the tub and started with the card dated right after Faye left Adam.

Adam didn't believe I'd leave him. Now he believes me. You were right, he couldn't just ignore me and expect me to sit by and wait for him to remember he has a wife. All the time I worked to help him market his game. I even took classes in advertising and design to learn how to help him, Eddie, but he just thought it was a hobby. I'm going to do it. Start my own business.

Thank you for loving me, Eddie. You are making me stronger. I feel needed and . . . how do I describe what it's like to be loved by you? Like I can do anything.

She signed her name and I set the card aside. I picked up the next one, until finally I was on the last card. It was like a series of snapshots in the incredible metamorphosis of Faye Miller. Starting with the weak, needy woman led into unethical behavior by an unprincipled older man. Eddie might not be a mental giant on an academic scale, but he had recognized Faye's insecurities and used those to manipulate her. But by the end of the notes, Faye had chosen to stop that behavior, was trying to make amends and get strong on her own. She dumped Eddie, and she attributed her change to Dominic and myself.

Staring at the last card, a simple postcard that she designed herself with her name and business on it, I read the words. Her last words.

Eddie, stop. I loved you once, but now I am learning to love myself. Or at the very least, respect myself. I wish you well in your life. Faye.

Lying back in the cooling tub, I whispered, "I respect you, Faye," through a tight throat. Probably more than anyone, I understood the struggle Faye had endured to strengthen herself and go on alone. For me, it had been easier because I had two sons to do it for. Faye had only herself, yet she chose, and was determined, to take the path of honesty and respect.

Did Eddie kill her for it?

A noise cut through my thoughts. Holding my breath, I turned my head to the closed bathroom door. My bedroom door was closed too. What had I heard? A shuffling sound of some kind? Was someone in my bedroom?

15

Tensing in the warm, scented water of the bath, I told myself that the day's excitement had made me paranoid. There was no one in my bedroom outside the tiny bathroom. The experience at Eddie's house had heightened my senses. Made me jumpy and prone to hearing things. I stared at the closed door.

Nothing.

Probably I'd just heard Ali prowling around, checking things out. Little sounds could echo in the small bathroom. It had a shower-tub combo, toilet, counter with a sink and door. Two full-grown people would have trouble turning around.

I did not want to get caught in here.

The doorknob rattled. That was not Ali! I lunged up to a sitting position, quickly looking for a weapon. Shampoo, conditioner, soap, bubble bath, washcloth and safety razor were the only things in my reach. Running my gaze over the sink and counter, I spotted a metal nail file.

My only chance. I'd grab the nail file to use as a

weapon. It had to be bad news at the door. Gramps and the boys would knock.

Putting my hands on the sides of the tub, I tried to rise as quietly as possible to grab the nail file.

The doorknob turned and clicked to open.

My heart stopped and I froze, staring at the door. Braced to rise from the warm water, my breasts were exposed and had rivers of soapy water running down them.

The door slid open.

Oh, God. Terror rolled over me in hot, shivering waves.

"Surprise."

"Gabe!" He was naked. The picture of male splendor. Nothing pretty or soft about Gabe. His face had hard lines that only a smile softened. The two hundred pounds were tightly packed into his six-foot-plus frame. Unclothed, he radiated powerful male.

Uh, make that powerful and *aroused* male.

With his sinful grin plastered over his face, he tossed a small square packet on the counter. "Are you surprised?"

Horny came to mind. So did stunned, excited, overwhelmed. My nerves stretched taut with humming desire. Even in the chilling water, with my hands on the cool porcelain sides of the tub, terror turned to gotta-have-it-now lust rushing through my veins. A thick liquid pooled in my belly and spread lower. "You could say that."

He strolled into the bathroom, filling up the space. His shoulders spanned from the edge of the counter to the metal towel rack. When he got to the tub, he looked down. "Told you to be ready, Babe." His eyes darkened to a sexy black, studying me in the thinning, cooling, bubbles. "You look ready."

"The boys . . . Grandpa . . ." Thoughts were not forming in complete sentences. I had a rule ... about ... something about no sex with the boys in the house. Dumb, dumb rule.

"Boys are asleep. Talked to Barney on my cell. He's on a stakeout. Says it's boring." Gabe bent over at the waist and cupped both my dripping breasts, then slid his hands under my arms. "Time to get out of the bath." He lifted me up.

"Wait!" I got my legs under me and stepped out of the tub.

"I'm done waiting." He pulled me into his arms.

"I'm wet!"

"Hope so." He brought his mouth down on mine. His naked dry skin was hot against my wet skin. His tongue in my mouth shivered down the back of my spine. He put a hand at the base of my neck, massaging and coaxing, while kissing me with a deep, hot passion.

His engorged penis pressed against my belly. The steamy bathroom heated with the scent of our bodies.

Without breaking the kiss, he put both hands on my butt. Then he lifted me and sat me on the counter between the sink and the toilet. Yanking my head back, I looked up into his eyes. "What are you doing?"

"Let's see if you are as wet as advertised." Both his hands landed on my thighs. He watched my face while he spread my legs and touched me. He made a groan deep in his chest and looked me in the eye. "Oh, yeah, you're wet."

My butt was spread out on the counter, exposed to the mirror behind me, and I didn't care. Gabe did this to me. He made me open myself to him and want hot, raw sex. With him. "God, you make me want you."

His mouth curved in pride. "Damn right, Babe."

The heavy, throbbing need between my legs boosted my pulse into the red zone. The world narrowed. Only naked Gabe covered in a sheen of bathroom steam and sporting a huge erection existed. Reaching out, I ran my finger along the underside of him. "How long you been carrying this around?"

His body jerked. "Since you posed in my office door. Hot, sexy and unpredictable, you make me need you, Babe. Drive me to craziness."

My breath caught into a sound deep in my throat. "Because I'm elusive?"

One of his rare soft smiles. "Because your . . ." He dropped his gaze over my breasts and hips. ". . . excellent package is wrapped around a bold and gutsy woman." He stopped talking. Reaching for the packet he'd tossed on the counter, he turned back to me and tore it open. "Now, Sam."

The words came out hoarse, desperate, and so thick with need that I felt them in my own chest. He put the condom on, then cupped my hips to slide me to the end of the counter.

Stepping forward, he lifted my thighs around him and looked into my face. "Later, I want to spread you out and have you slow and thorough." Sweat dotted his face; his breathing echoed in the small bathroom. "But now. . . ." He thrust inside of me, hard, deep and very possessive.

In the cooler bedroom, I pulled on my black thong underwear and zipped myself into the leather halter top. "I want to show you the notes Faye wrote Eddie. I took them from Eddie's house." Trying to concentrate on this case, and not the sex we'd just had, I dropped my jeans back onto the bed and picked up the note cards I'd brought out of the bathroom. Turning around, I took a few steps to where Gabe stood by my desk.

He ignored the cards and stared at me.

"Gabe?" My skin heated under his gaze. "Uh, let me grab my pants."

He caught my arm, pulling me back. "That's one sexy outfit."

I looked down. "It's just my underwear and top."

"Black thong and leather halter are not the ordinary woman's wardrobe."

I had my gaze fixed on his chest. He worked out regularly, but I suspected he was born with muscles like that.

I had been born with cellulite on my thighs, as my mother often pointed out. "Uh, I'm not ordinary, Gabe. I used to be ordinary and I hated it. Now I'm . . ." What? Different?

"Sexy." He tugged me closer and kissed me.

Again? My belly contracted with the hot, slow kiss that tangled our tongues. The recent memory of sex in the bathroom was burned on my brain and playing a rerun in my head. Cripes, I've turned into a sex addict.

The phone by my bed rang, dragging me out of sexland. Mom instincts kicked in, and I darted across the room to answer it before it woke the boys.

"Hello?"

Gabe came up behind me. Reaching around me, he traced the edge of my thong panties on my belly. Leaning back against him, I shivered and prayed it was a wrong number.

"Sam?"

I jerked up straight. "Grandpa? Where are you?"

"Now don't get upset, Sam."

Too late. "What's wrong?" Please, don't let him be in the hospital. Let him be okay. But he's talking to me so he must be okay. "Tell me, Grandpa."

"Sam, I'm in jail."

* * *

A sleepy TJ and Joel accompanied Gabe and me to the sheriff's station. I refused to leave them alone in the house, and Gabe refused to let me go to the sheriff's station alone.

He'd muttered something about getting myself arrested. Probably he was right. I knew who arrested Grandpa—a closet romance writer who thought he was a tough cop. He hadn't seen tough yet.

Cooling our heels in the foyer of the station, I watched the door to the right of the receptionist's desk. The boys sat on the stone bench, silent and wary. Gabe leaned up against the glass trophy case behind the bench, looking comfortable. And why not? He'd been a cop for several years before he'd been shot.

I paced back and forth.

The door opened. Detective Vance came out looking tired and harassed. Without his suit jacket, Vance's shoulder holster stood out against the green shirt. His sun-god face looked like it had seen too much sun and not enough sleep.

Tristan Rogers strode through the door behind Vance, looking as cool and sleek as he had in the grocery store hours ago. He even wore the same sneer when he looked at me.

"Sending an old man to spy on me, Samantha Shaw? I warned you I'd call the authorities." Turning to Vance, he added, "Arrest this woman, Detective. She is harassing me. She followed me to the grocery store this afternoon."

Vance's square jaw twitched. "Go home, Rogers."

Tristan turned his head and looked down his Michael Jackson nose at me. "Hope you brought your knee pads. It's going to take a lot of mouth work to get the charges dropped against your loser grandfather."

My sons heard that. Angry heat rushed into my face,

but before I could react, Gabe slipped past me like a street shadow. I caught a glimpse of his tight mouth, clenched jaw and narrowed eyes. Gabe grabbed Tristan by his polo shirt and yanked him forward as he drew back his right arm and slammed his fist into Tristan's face. All in a single swift motion.

We all watched in shock as Tristan went down hard, landing sprawled on his back. A slow trickle of blood seeped out of his nose and down his face.

Gabe looked down at him. "Watch how you talk to Sam."

The wide-open stunned expression on Tristan's face melted. He blinked rapidly and wiped the back of his hand across his nose. Then he held his blood-smeared hand in front of his face and sputtered, "I'm bleeding. My nose is bleeding. He actually hit me." With his other arm, he pushed off the floor to a sitting position and pointed his bloody hand at Gabe. "Arrest him! He assaulted me. My nose could be broken!" His finger moved to me. "She put him up to it!"

Shock made me silly. I damned near laughed out loud at the very idea that I could control Gabe. Taking stock, I turned to see both TJ's and Joel's huge eyes moving back and forth between Gabe and Tristan on the ground. The ever-present mom-voice in my head suggested that I tell them violence was never the answer.

I ignored the mom-voice and turned back to Tristan's shrill tone as he spewed out insults and threats while Vance helped him to his feet. "Your nose isn't broken, Rogers," Vance said in a tight voice. "And you brought that on yourself. Shut up, go home and put some ice on your nose."

"You keep that bitch away from me!"

Gabe had stepped back to stand beside me. At Tristan's insult, he moved again.

Vance whipped his head around while still hanging on to Tristan's arm. "Do it, Pulizzi, and I'll have your PI license."

Gabe visibly relaxed, dropping his powerful shoulders into a casual stance with his hands hanging loose at his sides.

I didn't for one second believe that Gabe was intimidated by Vance's threat. I wasn't sure what stopped him, but I guessed it might be my two sons sitting behind Gabe and me. Maybe.

"Go home, Tristan. I will call you in the morning and let you know what charges will be filed against anyone." Vance pushed Tristan toward the door.

Tristan turned around, his flat gaze sweeping over us to fix on Vance. Blood continued to trickle from his thin nose. "Keep her and the old man away from me and Dom. She's stalking Dom, trying to seduce him, just like that actress."

Actress? Did he mean Faye?

He fixed one last look on me. "You even know how many jump ropes Dom has in his bedroom, don't you?" Then he turned and stalked out of the sheriff's station.

I stared after Tristan, remembering what Rosy Malone had said in the grocery store about Tristan's mother. Had his mother turned him into a lunatic woman-hater? Please, God, I thought quickly, let me be a better mother to my sons.

"That went really well." Vance turned to glare at me with lines of tired frustration around his eyes. "What is it about you that drives men to violence, Shaw?"

"You're blaming me for this? Tristan's the one that verbally attacked me! I have no idea what that man has against me." I couldn't explain Gabe's reaction, or I was afraid to explain it. Afraid to believe it. Looking sideways at him, I wondered if his hand was okay. I saw him flex it once or twice, but no expression crossed his face.

"If you had stayed out of this investigation, you wouldn't have crossed paths with Rogers in the first place."

True, and since I could possibly come out on the losing side of that argument, I changed the subject. "Where's my grandfather? You let him go this second."

He crossed his arms over his chest. "Shaw, he was caught spying on Tristan and a woman friend. We have stalking laws in California. Given the binoculars and Sonic Ear we found on your grandfather, there's a good possibility the District Attorney will file charges." His eyes flicked toward Gabe, then back to me. "Then there's investigating without a license."

Sonic Ear? That was Joel's, a toy listening device that looked like a small satellite dish with a set of earphones hooked up to it. By aiming it toward a target, you could hear conversations in the next room. "That Sonic Ear belongs to my son. And everybody has binoculars. Your case won't stick."

"He had the headphones on from the Sonic Ear and was looking through the binoculars into the apartment window. That sure looks like investigating without a license to me, Shaw." Vance stared at me.

I knew exactly what he was up to. He'd arrested my grandfather to get me off his back. He figured he would force me to stay out of his investigation by dropping the charges against Grandpa. One step and I was nose-to-chin with him. My pulse double-timed, pumping the fury into a whooshing sound racing past my ear canals. "Tell me, Vance . . ."

I dragged it out. Savored it. I had him. Finally, I meant to smack the arrogance out of him. I dropped my voice and he must have sensed the importance because he leaned forward a fraction of an inch.

". . . Uh, I mean R. V. Logan. Do you need a license to write romance novels?"

His face blanched from sun god to shocked mortal. A vein in his neck throbbed. Straightening his back, he said, "Let's go in the interview room."

I didn't move. "Where's my grandfather?"

I swear he wanted to shoot me. "In the interview room." He said each word clearly.

I smiled. "Then we'll go to the interview room." We followed him through the maze of white walls and cubicles.

Gabe said into my ear, "He really writes romance novels?"

I nodded. "How's your hand?"

He ignored my question and instead said, "Good work, Babe."

I looked back and whispered, "Grandpa's work." His hand looked fine, maybe a little red around the knuckles.

Gabe grinned. "Figures."

Vance led us to the detective area I'd been in earlier today. He took out a set of keys and unlocked a door on the right-hand side across from the cubicles. He opened the door and went in. We all followed. The room was small and had a beat-up table with a phone on top of it and three chairs. Grandpa sat on the far side of the table facing the door. He was playing with a set of unlocked handcuffs.

"How the hell did you get those off?" Vance strode in and took the cuffs from Grandpa, looking them over. "You unlocked them?"

"Magic." Grandpa smiled at us. "Hey, Sam, TJ, Joel, Gabe. Left Ali home, huh?"

Joel shot past me. "Hey, Grandpa, you should have seen Gabe. He flattened some guy who insulted Mom! It was just like those wrestling shows!"

I heard Joel, but I had to smile at Vance. He was still examining the handcuffs. He even took his key ring out, checking to see if he had the little cuff key on it. Escaping handcuffs was a standard magic trick. Who was the schmuck now?

"Detective." Gabe spoke over my shoulder. "Maybe you have a break room where TJ and Joel could get some hot chocolate?"

"Ah, man," Joel said.

"Uh . . ." Vance looked up from the cuffs. "Yeah." He picked up the phone and called the receptionist. She quickly appeared in the doorway and led a bummed TJ and Joel away for a snack.

Vance went out of the room and returned with another chair. Then he shut the door. The four of us sat down. "All right, Shaw, spit it out."

I sat across from Grandpa. Ignoring Vance, I reached across and took his hand. "Are you all right? What happened?"

His blue eyes lit up. "I got a lead on the reporter— the one who came to Heart Mates posing as a client, then wrote that exposé."

I stifled a groan. "Leslie Lee?"

"Yep, but her name is Lee Page and she lives in the same apartment complex as Dominic and Tristan." He looked at Gabe. "Who'd you flatten?"

"Tristan Rogers," Gabe said.

I was trying to make sense of what Grandpa said and didn't want to get sidetracked away from who killed Faye. I remembered Dom saying Tristan was friends with another writer in the building. That must have been Leslie Lee, a.k.a. Lee Page. "So you went to her apartment? Why?"

"I wanted to make sure it was the same woman. I went into Heart Mates' computer files and pulled up her picture. Anyway, I was sitting there watching her apartment, getting bored, when I saw Tristan Rogers go in."

He'd had the Sonic Ear and binoculars. "What did you see? Could you hear anything?"

He glanced over at Vance.

I squeezed Grandpa's hand. "Vance is going to drop the charges." I turned my attention to Vance. "Aren't you?"

He glared at me.

I stared right back. "And help us figure out who killed Faye. Otherwise I'm going to tell all his macho cop buddies about his moonlighting as a romance writer. One who pens exceptional emotional depth and sizzling sex."

The vein in the side of his neck swelled. "Are you blackmailing me, Shaw?"

Smug satisfaction spread out all over me. "Yes."

His eyes narrowed. It took an obvious effort to get control of himself. Rocking his chair back on two legs, he said, "I did a little research on you. Reviewing romances is a hobby of yours. You didn't work your entire marriage. You bought Heart Mates on what appears to be a whim or nostalgia. You have a little community college, virtually no training, and barely make ends meet with your income."

"So?" I didn't like his summary of my life. "What you are missing are the nuances. That's the problem with you, Vance. You're all about the black-and-white facts. Years of raising my sons taught me to think ahead, to be one step ahead of those two to avert disaster. My years of volunteer work taught me about people, and how to get them to do the things they don't want to do. It also brought me in contact with a great many folks in Lake Elsinore. And I didn't need a CPA to tell me that Heart Mates was my dream job. I love going to work every day, Vance. How about you?"

The gold flecks iced in his brown gaze. "Not today."

"Too bad for you." Figuring I'd better quit gloating and move on, I leaned forward and put both my forearms on the table. "Here's the deal, Vance. You drop all the charges against my grandfather. Then you work with me to find Faye's killer."

He slammed the chair down on all four legs. "No wonder Rossi wanted to kill you."

I stared him down.

"Fine. Your grandfather's free to go."

"And you'll work with us to find Faye's killer?"

He toyed with the handcuffs. "Yes."

I was pretty sure he wanted to wrap the chain between the two handcuffs around my neck and pull real hard. "Great!" I flashed Vance my special smile—the smile my sons swore was a fake smile.

Then I turned back to Grandpa and gently squeezed his hand. "So what did you hear and see in Lee Page's apartment?"

With his blue eyes twinkling at my handling of Vance, he explained, "I heard them discussing the exposé that Lee Page was writing. Apparently the two of them worked on the first one that was in this morning's paper, and they were hard at work on the second one for tomorrow's paper."

Letting go of Grandpa, I leaned back. "But why?"

"They never said, exactly. But the theme of the articles was that Heart Mates' security would not prevent a determined killer. He could get through your security measures to find victims if he wanted to."

"But how does this connect to Faye? Tristan never even met her. Faye wanted to lose some weight before she auditioned for him." I looked at Vance.

"He doesn't like you, Shaw. You push his buttons. Tristan Rogers is a smart businessman. He's making

Smash Coffee into a financial success. He's also a writer. It hasn't been an easy process for him, given that he grew up being bounced between his minimum-wage mother and his welfare grandmother. You are messing with his hard-won life."

"You investigated him?" I asked, surprised.

"Preliminary. According to his bitter mother, Tristan has nothing to do with her, and his grandmother is dead. He put himself through community college to earn an AA degree in economics and took several classes in literature. He takes care of the business end of the coffee shop and they are in the black. Successful." He smiled at me.

I ignored his implication that he knew Heart Mates was not in such hot financial shape. "What else?"

"He's smart, Shaw. But he doesn't like interference, and he sees you as interference in his little empire. People who start with nothing and build a life for themselves can be a little protective."

Looking down at the grains of the laminated table, I thought about that. "But Dom sought Heart Mates out. We didn't solicit his business. So how does Tristan see me as a threat?"

"Rogers told me that Faye Miller wanted Dom to teach her about starting a business. Since your dating service connected Faye and Dom, Tristan doesn't care for either you or your underhanded tactics. He just wants you out of his life. But that's not the point. Rogers is your problem, not mine, since he doesn't appear to be connected to Faye's death."

Gabe spoke up. "Unless Dominic killed Faye and Tristan is covering it up."

Vance shook his head. "Won't wash. Dominic Danger's alibi checked out. He took his karate lesson, then went to Don Jose's for karaoke. He was seen there well past the possible time of death. His background check is clean, no arrests, no family problems. In fact, Dominic comes from a large family that appears to be quite fond of him."

Clearly, Vance did his fact checking, and his description of Dom matched my impressions. It was interesting that Tristan realized Faye was using Dom, but it didn't appear to have any relevance to her murder. So we were back to Eddie—although Gabe didn't seem convinced. I looked over at him. "I thought you agreed with me about Eddie."

"It's a credible theory, Sam, but never rule out other possibilities if the evidence leads you there. Then there's the coincidence of those articles appearing right when you are looking for Faye's killer. I'm not a believer in coincidence."

Vance watched Gabe with a guarded look. "You never made detective?"

"No."

"Hmm."

The tension notched up. Some kind of male-dog thing. I sighed. "Can we get back to Faye?" Turning my attention to Vance, I went on, "Faye was having an affair with Eddie Flynn of Eddie's Critters Pet Shop. His wife is Jan Flynn, the town librarian." While I did believe she was poisoning Eddie, I couldn't be sure. I left that out for now.

Vivid interest flared in Vance's brown eyes. "How'd you find that out?"

"People in this town will talk to me. I've lived here all my life, Vance. I went to school with most of them. Our kids played soccer together. I put out a call for information on my phone tree and I got it."

He slumped back. "Gossip."

"Actually"—I oozed smugness—"I have a stack of

notes from Faye to Eddie. They pretty much outline their affair."

Vance's mouth dropped. He recovered and said, "I'll need those. How did you get them?"

I didn't move, although I had the notes in my purse. "Can't tell you that."

His eyes narrowed. "Just what can you tell me?"

"Here's what I know. Faye worked part-time once in a while in Eddie's shop. Faye loved animals and her husband at home was ignoring her. Eddie pays attention to her, plays on her love of animals and boom he's in her pants. Eddie's wife is smart and successful. Eddie's getting older, a little paunch, hair's receding and he's no longer the star football player he was in high school. Faye's his ticket to youth. If she wants him, he's still hot."

I thought about Eddie insisting on not going to the police with the knowledge that Jan was poisoning him. Because he was afraid the police would find out that he killed Faye? Eddie's affair with Faye appeared to be Jan's motive for poisoning Eddie, and once the police knew Eddie had an affair with Faye, then he'd be a natural suspect.

"And?" Vance prompted me.

Seeing that he was impressed with my information, I pressed on. "In the meantime, Faye realizes that Eddie is pushing her to do things she doesn't want to. Like using my dating service to steal information and clients. She starts standing up to Eddie, tries to make amends where she can and finally breaks up with Eddie."

"Not bad." Vance stared at me as if I'd suddenly grown a brain. "On the other hand, Eddie in the picture is more motive for Adam Miller to have killed his wife."

"Dog with a bone," I muttered. Pushing my hair back off my face, I remembered Adam's painful desperation to find Faye's killer. "I know Adam didn't do it! He's not a murderer. His way of dealing with bad news is to escape into his computer, not strangle his wife. Can't you at least get a search warrant or something to look in Eddie's pet shop? If he killed Faye, maybe he hid the jump rope there. It's not at his house."

Vance's brown eyes zeroed in on me. "How do you know the murder weapon is not in his house?"

"Uh, Eddie gave me the key to look for something while he and Jan were at an awards dinner tonight."

He actually winced. "And while you were there, you stole notes that Faye wrote him?"

"I took them by accident." My hand had been in the shaving kit when I heard the noise. It'd been a reflex to grab the notes and stuff them in my pocket. A nosey reflex. Reaching in my purse, I pulled out the notes from Faye and slid them across the table.

Vance glanced down at them.

While he used a pen to move the cards around and take a look, I explained about the flowers Eddie had ordered for Faye on his company Visa, and how I came across the bill in his house.

"All circumstantial," he said as he studied the notes from Faye.

I had only one more shot. "Didn't the night clerk see a white truck with a camper shell or an SUV at the motel the night Faye was killed?"

He looked up from the cards straight at Gabe, most likely guessing that Gabe had gotten that information, then back at me. "One of them, yeah."

"Eddie drives a white Suburban."

Vance set his pen down and fixed a cold look on me. "Here's the deal, Shaw. I'll get the search warrant and check Eddie Flynn out. But"—he leaned forward, narrowing his gaze—"don't you ever try this blackmail shit on me again, got it?"

"Sure, Vance." Knowing when to leave was part of my charm. "Whatever you say. Come on, Grandpa." I turned to leave.

"Shaw."

Damn. Turning around, I looked past Gabe to Vance. "What?"

"Your threats won't stop me from finding and arresting Adam Miller if he turns out to be the one who murdered Faye. I'm not Rossi. I'm a damn good cop."

Yeah, a damn good cop with a juicy little secret life. "Deal."

I was dragged out of a restless sleep by the phone. Grabbing it, I glanced at the green digital numbers on my clock radio. One a.m. God. "Hello," I said into the phone.

"Shaw, it's Detective Vance. I have one question."

Oh, good, 'cause too much sleep makes me attractive. I was too tired be sarcastic verbally, so I just said, "What?"

"Did you or your PI boyfriend ever tell anyone that Faye Miller was strangled by a jump rope? I mean *anyone.*"

How the hell would I know that at one a.m.? "I don't think so. Maybe . . ." Had I told Grandpa? Or Adam? "Possibly my grandfather, but no one else. And he wouldn't tell anyone either. Why are you asking?"

"It's what detectives do, ask questions."

"At one a.m.?" I don't think that came out as a polite question.

"In special circumstances, and you, Shaw, are a special circumstance. Good night." He hung up.

I hung up the phone. What the hell was that about? What was Vance up to?

16

I woke up tense and cranky. TJ and Joel ate their cereal while I staggered into the kitchen following the scent of coffee. The pot was nearly full. I picked up the coffee carafe and thought about drinking it straight from there. But I tried to limit myself to one cup of coffee at home and a dozen more at work. That usually left the coffee-pot more than half full for Grandpa to warm up later while he was gossiping online.

I got a cup down and filled it. I didn't want Gramps to run out of caffeine energy right in the middle of juicy gossip. There was more than half a pot left to fuel him later on.

The phone rang on my first sip. Swallowing the hot coffee, I glanced over to the table. Grandpa had his nose in the newspaper, while TJ and Joel spooned in sugared cereal. Ali lifted her head to look at me.

Taking my coffee, I went to the phone. "Hello."

"Samantha Shaw, what have you done!"

I looked back at the pot of coffee. I should have drunk it straight from there. "Good morning, Mom."

"Good morning? How can you say good morning to me?"

I yanked the phone two inches from my ear.

"What's this about your grandfather getting arrested! He's an old man, Samantha, and he was arrested!"

I gulped down half the cup of coffee. Fortified, I struggled to make sense of the phone call. "Mom, Grandpa is fine. Where are you?"

"I'm in my car. I had a meeting at Smash Coffee with a client at six-thirty. We were discussing business when a detective came in and started talking to Tristan Rogers. The detective told Tristan that no charges were being filed against Barney Webb." Mom's voice rose. "Imagine my horror when I realized he was talking about my father! Didn't I tell you last night to go find him before he got into trouble?"

A shrill echo bounced around in my head. "Mom, it was a mistake."

"Really." Her voice dropped from hysterical to pissed. "And the bruise on Tristan's face? From his rantings at the detective, I gathered that your boyfriend hit him. Really, Samantha, that's uncivilized."

I sucked in a deep breath and squeezed my right eye shut to stop the twitching. "Gabe's uncivilized, Mother. And Tristan's a prick." Shit, I'd forgotten the kids.

"Samantha! I should think the word *unstable* would suffice. No need for sailor language."

I smiled in spite of everything. My mom could make a sailor blush if she got worked up enough. But in her rational moments, she denied it. "In any case, Grandpa is fine. There won't be any charges filed against him." The memory of blackmailing Detective Vance with his romance-writing secret life made the morning more bearable.

"Samantha, Tristan said you and Grandpa were stalking him, and that Gabe assaulted him. What's all this about?"

"Tristan is behind the article yesterday morning about Heart Mates and me. Grandpa found out he was working with some sleazy reporter."

"I see. Was he also behind the article this morning?"

I turned my gaze to Grandpa. "Another article?" Of course, Grandpa had seen Tristan and that reporter working on it. The same reporter who had posed as a client for Heart Mates.

Grandpa looked up and nodded, pointing to the newspaper.

Great. "I'll look at the article, Mom, but yeah, he's behind it."

"He was nuts this morning, Samantha. Really mad. Claimed the police were not doing their job. When the detective left, Tristan grabbed up the phone and yelled at Dom to get over to Smash Coffee right away. My client and I left."

"Mom, where are you headed now?" *Please,* I begged silently, *not here!*

"To the office. I have to put together a list of properties for my new client."

Thank you, Lord! "Grandpa's fine, Mom, so don't worry."

"He should move into a senior citizen complex. These things wouldn't happen then."

I saw Joel waving the paper he'd wanted me to sign last night. "Gotta go, Mom. Joel needs me. Bye." I hung up before my mom could launch into Grandpa's moving and me getting a decent job in real estate.

Going to the table, I took the pen from Joel and signed the paper. Then TJ and Joel turned their attention to fighting over the last bowl of cereal left in the Cap'n Crunch box.

I moved to stand behind Grandpa's shoulder. "Is that the article?"

He nodded.

I leaned in to read it.

This reporter found that Ms. Shaw and her assistant were happy to show me files that included names and addresses of clients. Furthermore, while she does a standard background check, she had not completed mine when she showed me these things. The office is strictly a two-man operation that is focused more on Ms. Shaw's side career of nosy investigations than a professional dating service.

"Idiots. If Vance finds that jump rope at Eddie's pet shop once he gets the search warrant, that'll mean Heart Mates had nothing to do with Faye's death. Our security is good." I closed my eyes and thought about Eddie. I remembered him back in high school after the Friday night football games hanging out with the latest cheerleader of his choice at the pizza place. A womanizer even then, but a murderer?

Grandpa touched my arm. His unwavering and wise blue eyes searched my face. "You did the right thing, Sam. It really looks like Eddie killed Faye."

"Yeah. I'm just tired. Vance called in the middle of the night to ask a question that could have waited until morning." The phone rang. Both Grandpa and I looked at it.

"Think he's calling again?" Grandpa asked.

I sighed and went to find out. "Hello."

"Sam," Gabe said, "I got a call. Vance has the warrant to search Eddie's shop. They are going to his house to pick him up, then go to the shop. I'm going to head over there now and see what goes down."

My stomach bubbled. Setting my coffee down, I took a breath to calm my nerves. "Vance called you?"

"A *source* called me. Vance won't like that I'm there, but if I stay out of the way, he'll cooperate."

"He probably wouldn't like me there."

Gabe snorted. "Not likely after your performance last night."

I laughed. "Vance didn't like me blackmailing him much."

Gabe's voice shifted into the hot zone. "I thought it was sexy. You were something to watch, wearing your black leather halter and thong while bending the local homicide detective to your will."

"I had on pants!" Realizing what I said, I looked over to see TJ and Joel pretending to be interested in their cereal. Grandpa's mouth twitched, but he kept his gaze on the paper. I pressed my lips together.

"But I knew what you had on under those tight-fitting jeans."

The needle went from hot to blazing. And here my two sons were sitting a couple of feet away, eating their cereal. I needed to be hosed down. Changing the subject, I asked, "So you'll let me know?"

"First chance I get. Go to work, Sam. And call Adam. Tell him it looks like he will be able to go to Faye's funeral tomorrow."

"All right. And Gabe, thanks."

"Sure thing, Babe. We're a team." He hung up.

A team, huh? I still wasn't sure this team wouldn't be broken up by the lure of Hollywood.

"Mom, do you know you left the oven cleaner out?"

Forcing my mind away from Gabe, I looked at TJ standing by the kitchen sink and pointing at the yellow-and-red can by the coffeepot. "Yeah, I need to spray the oven before I go to work."

Grandpa got up. "I'll do that, Sam, then I'll take the boys to school. You go get a shower." He kissed my cheek on his way to pick up the can of cleaner.

"Thanks, Grandpa." Guess now I'd really have to clean the oven when I got home from work. That was depressing.

After Grandpa left with the boys, I tamed my hair with gobs of straightening gel and slicked on some shiner stuff. Now my hair looked smooth and frizz-free. My makeup routine took me another six minutes. I went out of my bathroom to my closet in my red thong panties and bra. I'd purposely chosen red to cheer myself up.

Now would be a fine time for Gabe to sneak into my bedroom. Staring at the innards of my closet, I wondered how he'd like my red underwear. Good grief, I must be hormonal today. I pulled my sleeveless red dress off the hanger and slipped it on. It took a little wiggling to get the dress over my hips. Had it been this tight in the store? I shrugged. It didn't matter if the dress was a little tight since I wasn't going to be doing any high kicks. Stretching up on my bare toes, I reached to the top of my closet for the shoebox.

New shoes. The perfect way to polish off my cheering-up outfit. They were strappy red sandals with the new slim wedge heel. Very sexy. Setting them down on the floor, I stepped into them and did a little test walk on the old brown shag carpet. Short of a strong wind, I was reasonably certain I could stay upright on the heels.

I added a pair of gold hoop earrings, a wide gold bracelet and my watch. "All set." I looked around and found my mind wandering to Eddie. Had the cops picked him up yet? Were they at his pet shop? Did he kill Faye?

The night clerk had seen an SUV at the motel that night that could easily be Eddie's Suburban. Faye had wanted to break if off with him and he appeared resistant. He had been adamant about not going to the police over Jan poisoning him.

But why would Eddie give me the key to his house if he killed Faye? That was it, the thing that had been bothering me. Had he been that desperate to stop Jan from making him sick?

I shook my head. Second-guessing at this stage was pointless. Something was scratching my foot in my new shoes. Wiggling my foot in the shoe seemed to fix it, so I left my room and headed down the hallway. My purse and keys were in the living room on the love seat, and Ali was already in the backyard. All I had to do was pick up my purse and keys and set the alarm on the way out.

My mind went right back to Eddie. Would Vance tell Eddie that I convinced him to search the pet shop? And what was that strange phone call about last night? Didn't Vance sleep? Why did he ask if I had told anyone about the murder weapon? I knew the police held some evidence back from public knowledge.

Damn, my right foot hurt. Something in the shoe was poking me. Reaching the living room, I half limped around the back of the brown plaid love seat. My purse and keys were right there on the cushion waiting for me. But first, I lifted my right leg and rested my new red shoe on the arm of the couch. I couldn't see anything, so I pulled the shoe off and looked at it. The white nylon strap that held the price tag had been biting into my foot.

White nylon. Something tickled at my memory. Vance calling about the jump rope. I'd only told Grandpa about the jump rope used to strangle Faye. Frowning at the nylon strap in the shoe, I struggled to think. Who was Vance really asking me if I had told? He figured out that Gabe told me, so he wasn't asking about him. Vance hadn't seen Adam. Jim Ponn and Dom had alibis. *Dom.*

Ohmigod, Tristan! He'd said something about me looking for jump ropes in Dom's room. Did he know about the murder weapon? How? It couldn't be because Dom murdered Faye since his alibi checked out.

I looked up from the shoe, and a cold chill went down my back. Something was wrong. I saw the love seat with my purse and keys resting on the cushions. Then the side table, lamp and living room wall. I turned and looked to my right.

What was wrong? I stared at the front door for a second and then it hit me. The door—it wasn't closed tight into the frame. As if it had been closed only as far as it would go without making noise.

Something stirred behind me. The skin on my back prickled and I knew.

Oh, shit—someone was behind me!

A sudden dump of adrenaline burned my gut. I had to get out of the house! Realizing I still had my leg up on the couch and the shoe in my hand, I tried to jam the shoe on my foot.

At the same second, I felt distinct movement behind me. With my head down, something flew over my head and caught me on the chin.

A rope. Oh, God, it was a rope! Tightening and biting deep into the skin of my chin. Terror ripped through me like a streak of sizzling lightning. With my left hand, I reached up to grab the rope digging into my chin.

Whoever was behind me tried to yank the rope lower to get it around my neck. Like Faye. So I would die like Faye. No! I wouldn't die. The rope forced my chin down to my neck. The rope was so tight, I couldn't get my fingers under it.

Don't panic! I couldn't think if I panicked.

How did I fight? Darting my gaze around, I saw my shoe still in my right hand. I didn't think, but just aimed the heel backward and swung hard over my right shoulder.

"Oomph."

The rope slackened. No time. I had to hit him again and run. Dragging my leg off the couch and throwing the rope over my head, I pivoted left and swung the shoe heel hard.

It caught Tristan Rogers on the side of his head. He stumbled sideways, holding on to the white-and-blue jump rope. Faye's jump rope.

Fury rushed through me. "You!" His face had a bruise on the left side from Gabe's fist. Blood poured out of a wound over his right eye where I had hit him when he was behind me. The second swing didn't have the same effect. I must have turned the shoe so that the flat side, instead of the heel, caught him on his temple.

Tristan brought his free hand up and wiped the blood out of his eye. In spite of the pain, a weird smile moved his mouth. "Of course it was me. Dom's too soft-hearted to deal with you man-eating bitches. But I've dealt with women like you all my life."

God, he was insane. He was also between the front door and me. The dining room was behind my right shoulder. Maybe I could get out by the sliding glass door. Ali was out there. Between the two of us, we'd escape Tristan. I tried to think past the terror humming in my ears.

Only seconds had passed. Tristan wiped more blood out of his right eye, then picked up the dangling end of the rope. "I gave you a warning when I left the brochure." He took a step forward. "You should have paid attention."

Out of time, I turned on my bare foot, tried to run and tripped over the high heel I still had on. Shit!

Laughter swelled behind me. Horrible laughter that sounded like one of those laugh tracks on old TV shows. Panting with pounding fear, I got to my hands and knees. Using my bare foot to try and scrape the remaining shoe off my foot, I crawled toward the slider.

Where was Ali? Why was she so quiet?

"That's where you belong. On your knees."

Shivers of horror exploded up my back. But I got my shoe off. *Get up and get out,* I told myself. The damn dress was so tight it was hard to get my leg up.

His hand caught my left ankle. I screamed in frustration and struggled to free my foot. Clawing at the floor, I fought to get away from him, to get to the sliding door. Where the hell was Ali? I dug my fingers into the yellowed linoleum floor, trying to get to the door. A sob ratcheted up my throat.

He was strong. Damn strong.

Tristan yanked me back, dragging me on my belly. Two fingernails tore. I looked on helplessly as blood welled up on the raw nail beds.

My mistake was going to get me killed. I had believed Eddie killed Faye. A thick dread weighed down on me with each inch that Tristan pulled me backward, closer and closer to him.

To death.

Another fingernail tore. The sudden ripping pain stung my eyes with tears and snapped through my thoughts.

I would not die! TJ's and Joel's faces popped into my head. They had lost their dad. No way in hell would I let them lose their mom too. A sudden surge of adrenaline fed my muscles. My heart went into full gear.

He stopped dragging me. Before I could react, he grabbed me and flipped me over.

Face-to-face with me, he raised the rope up in both

his hands and said, "Thing is, Samantha, all that dick-sucking didn't save you after all."

Think! I had to get him off balance, confused so that I could figure a way to strike fast and escape. Swiftly, I took stock of his mannequin face. Bruised and cut. Cut over his right eye. I focused on that cut and cast about for a comment to distract him. From my subconscious came, "You must have real mother issues to be such a twisted prick." I'd read a lot of romantic suspense novels that had serial killers in them and mothers were a favorite person to blame. So I added, "Does Mommy know you've turned into a murdering monster?"

Color rushed into his waxy face. He let go of the rope with his right hand and backhanded me across the face.

The hot blow twisted my head and slammed my left cheek into the floor. It stunned me and my ears rang. Pain bloomed horribly inside my head, but I had to go for the cut.

"I'm going to enjoy shutting up that mouth of yours."

Now, before he strangled me. I turned my head back to focus on the cut and drove the heel of my hand into the bleeding wound.

"Ouch, you bitch!" He didn't reach for the cut or move off me like I expected. Instead, with the rope stretched between both his hands, he dropped his full weight behind the rope onto my neck.

The rope hit my throat. I gagged. My reflexes tried to force out a cough, but the rope pressed into my windpipe. Immediate panic shot through me. I arched my back off the floor. I struggled, fighting for air and clawing at the rope.

He grinned, leaning over me. Blood dripped from his waxy face to land on my cheek. "I don't have mother issues, I have bitch-stalker-slut issues." His eyes watched me. "Ah, not so mouthy now."

He turned my insides to liquid. Fear, panic and pain rolled around inside me. *Think!* I had to think. I had to hurt him, get him off of me. Struggling, I tried to get the leverage to swing my knee into his balls. But I didn't have enough room to swing my leg and the damned dress was too tight.

Sucking for air, spots danced in front of my eyes. My muscles weakened so that my fingers slipped off the rope pressed into my neck. Tristan's face looked far away, like it was sliding away from me. I saw his mouth move, heard cracks of that canned laughter. Then he yelled, "Get dead with Heart Mates!"

Fury exploded from the deepest part of my heart. Kneeing him didn't work. My fingers were going numb, but I reached down with both hands, grabbed his balls and squeezed.

His face contorted. He arched up and screamed a high and tortured howl. With the rope off my neck, I kept squeezing while I dragged in painful gulps of air. It burned, but it was air.

My mind leaped from sluggish to spinning. I had to get out, get away. And where was Ali? The first time she heard me scream, she would have hurled herself through the sliding glass window.

Oh, God, not Ali.

Letting go, I shoved Tristan off me. He curled up into a ball on his side.

I struggled to get to my feet. We were between the living room and the dining room. Everything spun and I couldn't get my balance. My ears rang from him hitting me. On my hands and knees, I looked over at Tristan. "What did you do to my dog?" It came out in a croak. Hurt my throat.

"Dying." He was half crying, half groaning, his hands cupping his balls.

I knee-walked a couple feet to the dining room table and looked back. Shit. Tristan had gotten to his knees. But Ali—what had he done to her? "Dying?" God, that hurt. *No talking,* I told myself.

He gagged and coughed, then lifted his head, his eyes flat and doll-like. "Poisoned her. Now you." He started getting to his feet.

I pulled myself up on the kitchen chair. The slider door just ahead of me was locked. I had locked it this morning. I wouldn't be able to unlock it before Tristan got to me. Quickly, I looked into the long kitchen.

I needed a weapon. Knife? I pushed off the chair and made it to the wall separating the kitchen and dining room. Looking back, I saw Tristan was almost to his feet.

I forced my bare feet to hold me and searched the kitchen. There was my Rolodex on the counter across from me. Great for gossip but not for self-defense. No knives on the counter. I swept my eyes down to the sink.

Then back. There! Next to the half-filled coffeepot. Oven cleaner! Adam's gory description of what that would do to a person's eyes whipped around in my head. The can was just across the width of the kitchen from me. I heard Tristan. He was on his feet.

I ran across to the counter, grabbed the oven cleaner and tore off the lid.

"Die, bitch!" he yelled from behind me.

I whirled around. He came at me with the jump rope. Just seeing it made me gag. I fought the reflex and hoisted up the yellow can of oven cleaner.

His gaze fastened on the can.

I depressed the nozzle.

A hissing sound shot out, then sputtered. It sounded like farts. A few tiny drops spat out and then nothing.

It was empty.

No! Quickly, I threw the can at his injured eye.

He howled and sank to his knees, clutching the injured cut. I wasted no time, but turned to find something else. Anything! I moved to the sink. Maybe there was a knife in there. I didn't think I could get out the door on the other end of the sink before Tristan recovered and caught me. I had to hurt him or knock him unconscious and find Ali. He'd poisoned my dog. My hero dog. I had to save her. Tears welled up in my eyes and choked my already hurting throat. At the sink, I glanced out through the backyard window to find Ali. I couldn't see her anywhere. So I looked down in the sink for a weapon.

Shit, only my dirty coffee cup. Now what? I panted in fear, each sharp breath searing my throat. I didn't want to die. But I couldn't save myself with a coffee mug. I searched both sides of the sink.

Then I saw it. The coffeepot.

Some instinct had me look up in the window.

Tristan's reflection loomed up behind me. Raising the rope to wrap it around my neck. He bellowed, "Dom is mine! Smash Coffee is mine! The play is mine! Die, you ball-bustin' whore!"

Sanity sure as hell wasn't his. In a millisecond, the world spun away, and it was only the two of us in my kitchen.

One of us was going down.

And it sure as hell wasn't going to be me.

Summoning the last of my reserves, I reached across my body and grabbed the half-filled coffeepot. Wrapping my hand around the white handle, I yanked that pot off the warmer and swung, just like a tennis backhand. Turning as I swung, I croaked out, "One Smash Coffee!"

The carafe hit him on the right cheekbone, shattered and exploded hot coffee over us both.

Tristan's face froze in a mask of surprise before the

façade cracked. He screamed once, then slumped to the ground.

I stood there, shivering. He didn't move. Bits of glass twinkled in his skin, and bright spots of blood welled up. The cut over his right eye gaped open like a split melon. Tristan was either unconscious or dead. I'd beaten coffee boy with a coffeepot. Looking down at his unmoving form, I thought, *Gosh, would you have rather had decaf?*

Oh, God, I was losing it. I didn't care. I could slide away into the insanity. . . .

Ali! I tried to push myself off the counter. My knees buckled. No, I had to help Ali. I used a hand-over-hand method, holding on to the counter and shuffling toward the back door on the other side of the sink.

A loud noise exploded from the living room. "Sam! Where are you!"

Gabe. "Here." It came out a painful croak.

Cops with guns poured into my kitchen. I stood halfway between the sink and the back door. I watched with some weird detachment as the police surrounded Tristan. He didn't move. I heard someone say he was alive.

Was Ali alive?

Hadn't I heard Gabe's voice?

Then I saw him. He appeared in front of me. He reached out his warm hands to my shivering shoulders. His black gaze ran over me. "Babe, Jesus, you need an ambulance."

My eyes filled with tears. I shook my head. Wincing from the pain, I tried to make him understand. "Ali! Dying."

His black eyes snapped back to my face. "Ali? She's hurt?"

I nodded. Everything hurt. "Backyard."

Gabe helped me to the door. We both went outside. I saw the trampoline out in the grass. The picnic table on the patio. But no Ali. Where was she? Swallowing, I said, "Ali?" It came out little more than a hiss.

"Ali!" Gabe's voice roared next to me.

Nothing. Then I heard a whimper and looked down. She was against the wall by the door, sprawled on the patio. From the marks in the dust on the cement, it looked like she had tried to drag herself to the door.

To save me.

My eyes filled with tears and burned my injured throat. Her eyes looked foggy; her mouth hung open. Tristan hadn't been lying; he really did poison her. "Oh, Ali." Shrugging off Gabe's hands, I dropped to my knees and cradled her head on my red dress. She was breathing. Barely. I looked up at Gabe. "Please. He poisoned her." It was all I could get out.

Gabe knelt down and looked her over. "I'll get her in a police car and to a vet." His gaze turned to me. "Okay?"

I dipped my head slightly.

Gabe lifted Ali in his strong arms and strode back through the house. I heard him shouting orders, commandeering one of the cops. I wondered how Vance felt about that.

Like I cared.

Sitting on my butt, I leaned back against the side of the house. Tristan Rogers. Not Eddie. I tried to put it together. Tristan wanted Dom, Smash Coffee and the play he wrote all to himself. Or control over them. Faye threatened that in his warped mind. I don't think Tristan had any lost love for women on his best day.

What had Gabe told me? Find out about Faye and I'd figure out who she let in to murder her. I'd thought it was Eddie.

But Faye would have let Tristan in. She would have

thought she was letting in her dream to act in a community theater play. Instead she'd let in her nightmare. It would have been so easy for Tristan to call her and say he wanted to meet with her. Or maybe just drop by. Faye would have let him in.

"Hey, Shaw."

I opened my eyes. Detective Vance stood against the bright morning sky. He really was a beautiful man. "I was wrong."

He smiled and hunkered down so that he was eye level with me. "Yep." Reaching out a hand, he touched my throat gently. "Don't talk anymore. An ambulance is on the way."

Gloating cops. I sighed and said, "How'd you know?" Obviously Vance, Gabe and the cops had shown up here with weapons drawn for a reason.

He sat back on his haunches and looked at me. "Couple things. Tristan mentioned the jump rope last night at the station. That you knew how many jump ropes Dom had. That told me he knew what the murder weapon was and that you were looking for it. Then there was the whole thing with Eddie. I don't know why he gave you a key to his house, but he wouldn't have done that if he had murdered Faye. That would have been plain stupid."

"Your call." I meant the phone call in the middle of the night.

"Yeah, I had a hunch. I had to make sure you hadn't told Tristan about the jump rope. Once you so charmingly assured me you hadn't, I went and had a little chat with him this morning."

I stared at him. It came together in my mind with a cold click. The pain in my neck didn't stop me from saying, "You set me up."

He shrugged. "You blackmailed me. Besides, I had

every intention of getting here before he could hurt you too bad." His gaze searched me then, and his mouth tightened. "I miscalculated."

I really didn't have the energy to be too mad at him. Tristan was the murderer, not Vance. Besides, I had blackmailed him. And catching Faye's killer made it worth it. I'd recover. But Faye wouldn't.

I closed my eyes in sadness for Faye.

"You're one hell of a tough broad, Shaw. I've never seen self-defense with a coffeepot before."

I snapped my eyes open. Was that a compliment? From Detective hates-me-a-lot? All I could manage was a small smile.

"I hear the ambulance." He reached out and lifted me up in his arms, then rolled up to his feet. He walked through the house to the front porch and down the steps.

"Thanks," I whispered.

Vance looked down into my face and grinned. "Yeah, well, I still don't like you."

"Ditto."

17

I missed Faye's memorial service. Instead, I was spending Saturday in my living room, lying back on the couch with my feet up on the coffee table and Ali curled beside me.

Tristan Rogers had tossed four raw meatballs laced with poison over the fence. Ali had only eaten one and turned her slim nose up at the rest. God, was she smart or what? If she'd eaten all four, she would have been dead when Gabe and I found her by the back door.

Ali and I were alone. TJ, Joel and Grandpa had gone to the store to pick up some cold cuts and salads since we were expecting a few people to stop by after Faye's service. The boys promised to bring some ice cream and yogurt home for me. Swallowing hurt. I could talk, although the doctors suggested I stay quiet for a few days.

Gabe had arrived at the emergency room to tell me that he'd called Grandpa to pick up the boys from school and that Ali was going to be okay. Once the doctors were done picking glass out of my face and clucking over my throat and mild concussion, they let Gabe take me home. He had left late last night. I didn't know where he was today.

Ali lifted her head and growled a warning. Then I heard the knock at the door. "It's okay, Ali," I assured her and heaved myself off the couch. My entire head, neck and shoulders throbbed. My body screamed. Tristan had slammed me around pretty good. I opened the door.

Eddie Flynn stood on my front porch in a Rams football jersey. He had on a baseball cap over his receding hairline. "Sam, I brought your kitten back."

The little gray fur ball looked like she had grown in the two days since I'd seen her. Looking back up at Eddie, I figured I might as well be blunt. "I guess you know that I found the notes from Faye and gave them to the cops."

He nodded. "Yeah, they had a search warrant for the pet shop. But then Vance got a call and everyone took off. Now I know it probably had something to do with Tristan going after you."

Probably. I was still a little sketchy on information. But I had a question for Eddie. "What did you hire me for, Eddie? The truth." Ali padded up behind me and stuck her head out. She tilted her nose up to the kitten.

"I did tell you the truth. I needed to find out how Jan was poisoning me. After you told me how she did it Thursday night, I went home and confronted her. I held up the vase of oleanders and told her she'd better stop making me sick with the water in there. She was impressed, Sam." He looked down at Ali and stopped talking.

I thought about Jan. Betrayed by the football-hero husband she'd managed to snag after years of being ignored by him in high school. Okay, I kind of got Jan. It was sick, poisoning him like that, sure. But Eddie having an affair with Faye wasn't a shining example of marital bliss either. So that wasn't giving me much trouble. "Eddie"—I fixed my tired stare on him—"what did you mean when you told me Jan's not a killer?" Thursday night at my door, he'd seemed to be trying to convince himself of that. And he'd asked me if I'd found anything else Jan was hiding at their house.

He looked up at me. "I figured that Jan had found out about Faye. That was why she made me sick. To punish me. But I had to make sure that she wasn't . . . you know . . . trying to make Faye pay."

"Good Lord, Eddie, you thought Jan killed Faye? That's why you sent me there? To find out if Jan had killed Faye?" Ali slid her head beneath my left hand. I rubbed her head and said to Eddie, "You two need professional help." Or a divorce. Was any marriage worth this?

Eddie shifted the kitten and reached into his pocket. He pulled out a check. "Here." He held out the check and kitten to me.

I hadn't given Eddie any kind of bill yet, so I stared at the piece of paper in his hand. "What's the check for?"

"Gabe Pulizzi brought by a bill for your services this morning."

I took the kitten and the check. Now I had some idea of what Gabe had been up to today. "Oh, well." I looked down at the amount. *Not bad.*

"I never meant to hurt Faye. I loved her." Eddie turned around to leave. When he got to the porch steps, he turned back. "Oh, I have a gardener coming on Monday to rip out all the oleander surrounding our property."

A gardener? That was not exactly the sort of professional help I had in mind for Eddie and Jan. A psychiatrist was more like it. "That's a good start, Eddie. But you might think about some marriage counseling." Right, like I was an authority on the perfect marriage. Cripes.

He lifted one hand in a parting gesture and left.

I shut the door and looked down at the kitten. She was watching me with her big slate-blue eyes. "What do I do with you?"

Another knock startled me. Glancing at the clock on the VCR, I wondered if the memorial service for Faye was over. Ali watched me turn around and answer the door.

Vance stood there looking like he'd just stepped off a yacht. He had on tan casual slacks and a dark green, long-sleeved pullover that molded to his nicely muscled chest. I knew how muscled that chest was from when Vance picked me up in his arms to take me to the ambulance.

Which reminded me of my number-one rule: Good-looking men were trouble.

I forced my gaze up to his face.

Vance reached up and pulled his sunglasses off. His gaze studied my air-dried and slept-on hair, traveled over my T-shirt, down my old jeans to my bare feet, then back up. "You look like hell." He leaned over and picked up a big bulky box wrapped in blue paper.

I thought about slamming the door in his face, but the gift-wrapped box distracted me. "And here I thought we were gonna be friends."

He ignored that and invited himself in, walking by me. I caught a faint whiff of coconut oil. Made me think of lying on a warm, sandy beach and what Vance looked like in swimming trunks. No doubt about it, I had a concussion. I shut the door.

Vance set the box on the coffee table, went over to the couch and made himself comfortable. Ali thought that was a great idea and followed him up onto the couch. "Brought you something." He turned his attention to petting Ali.

I settled on the love seat, set the kitten down next to me on the brown plaid cushion and tore open the blue paper. Then I looked up. "A coffeemaker?"

Vance grinned. "Thought maybe you could use a new one. This one will grind the beans or you can use ground crystals."

"Jesus, Vance, I almost think you like me."

"Nah. You irritate me, Shaw. You're a nosy, demanding, blackmailing pest." His gold-flecked brown eyes gazed at me with a slow heat. "But I have to admire the fact that you took down Tristan in your own kitchen with a coffeepot." He took a breath. "In a short red dress."

Uh-oh. Vance and I, we had the perfect relationship. We hated each other. He didn't like my style and I didn't like his arrogant, good-looking charm. I stood up with the kitten. "I dress for success, Vance. You want a beer or something?"

"Beer's good."

Hiding my surprise that uptight Vance would have a beer, I went to the kitchen and snagged the beer for him. I got a bottle of iced tea for me, then, juggling two bottles and a kitten, returned to the living room.

Ali popped her head up when I handed the beer to Vance. "No beer, Ali." I tried to make my voice stern. After just being poisoned yesterday, I was pretty sure a beer today would not be wise. Maybe tomorrow.

Sitting on the love seat, I set the kitten on my lap and opened the tea. Glancing at the coffeemaker, I said, "Why are you here? I mean, thanks for the coffeemaker, but I doubt that's the only reason you came by." Vance was a careful, factual guy.

After twisting off the top and taking a long drink of his beer, Vance answered, "Tristan's under arrest for Faye's murder, and attempted murder of you. He's still in the hospital. But as soon as he's well enough, he'll be in jail."

"Good." I hoped Faye could rest in peace and Adam could get on with his life. "So how did you put it together? You still went to Eddie's to search his pet shop."

"I didn't rule Eddie out completely, just thought it unlikely. As soon as Tristan mentioned the jump rope at the police station, I started getting suspicious. Plus all his talk about stalkers, and he told me Faye had been using Dom—like confessing a motive." He stopped petting Ali and looked at me. "He might have gotten away with killing Faye if you hadn't come along. You drove him crazy. Just nuts. Aside from his hating women, he was smart and rational."

"Oh, yeah, what's not rational about killing off women because Smash Coffee, Dom and the play all belonged to him?" Talking bothered my throat, so I sipped the cool tea. It felt pretty good.

Vance smiled. "Rational enough to keep from getting caught. Anyway, I talked to Dom. I believe that he genuinely didn't know how obsessive Tristan was. Dom claims they were not lovers. But"—Vance shook his head and went back to petting Ali—"Dom said everyone loves him. He's a bit self-centered."

I had to smile. Yeah, that was Dom. I wondered if Dom was gay? Tristan sure as hell was. Oh, well, it didn't matter.

"Everything fit. Tristan didn't have an alibi that I knew of, and his black Accura fit the description of the dark-colored Accura or Honda Accord at the motel the night of Faye's murder. And according to what you and Dominic told me about Faye wanting to be in Tristan's play, Faye would have let Tristan in."

I winced at that. If only Faye hadn't let him in. I forced myself not to think about it. Instead I concentrated on Vance. "So you decided to go have a chat with Tristan and use me as bait? You figured that if you told him all the charges against my grandfather were dropped, he would believe the only way to get me out of his life was to kill me?"

Vance didn't flinch. "Tristan liked to think and plan, so I thought I'd have more time to make sure you were safe. But in a way, he did plan. He'd been here the day that he left the brochure and probably checked you out a bit. He must have known your grandpa drove the boys to school in the morning, giving him the time window he needed to get in here and kill you before you went to work. And"—he turned to look at Ali—"he knew about your dog."

It gave me the creeps to think of Tristan sneaking around my house. Vance using me as bait without my knowledge didn't thrill me a whole hell of a lot either. "Did you at least have Tristan followed or something?"

Vance shrugged. "I had a cop driving by Smash Coffee to keep an eye on Tristan's car. I didn't want Tristan to get suspicious by having a cop hanging around. Once the officer discovered Tristan's car missing, he called me."

That was the call Eddie had mentioned. I made a face at him, then regretted it. God, I was sore. "You could have warned me."

He was studying the beer bottle in his right hand while petting my dog with his left hand. "Warned you of what, Shaw? You're a private citizen, not a cop, so I certainly would not include you in a police investigation." He stopped petting Ali and leaned forward to fix his official look on me. "Even though I am a cop, and a damn good one, there's no way I could have guessed that Rogers would go after you once I dropped the charges against your grandfather."

I didn't move, just kept stroking the little kitten's soft gray fur. Vance was trying to imply that I was in way over my head with him. He wanted me to stay out of his way from now on. But I didn't scare as easily as I once did. Though I tended to live a little dangerously on the learning curve, I did learn. "Private citizen? Actually, I do work part-time for a private investigator, Detective Vance. It's all quite legitimate." Maybe. "Just like you write romance novels part-time, I might add. Hmm, I wonder how many of your colleagues know that?"

His brown eyes hardened. "I could make trouble for you, Shaw, and for that private investigator boyfriend of yours."

"Possibly. But then I could make trouble for you, Vance. I'm pretty sure that using me as bait is a little outside the cop rules, and God knows I would enjoy telling all the cops I can find about your moonlighting as a romance writer."

The kitten purred in the strained silence that followed. I refused to look away. Vance and I were deadlocked in our mutual threats. I believed he meant his, and I knew I meant mine.

Finally, his shoulders relaxed and he took a sip of his beer. Then he reached over and set the beer down on the table between the couch and the love seat. Looking at me, he said, "I swear you make a man think of only two things."

"Which are?"

Vance pushed Ali off his lap and stood up. Walking to the front door, he looked back at me. "Murder and sex." Then he pulled open the front door.

Stunned, I thought, *In that order? Why not sex first and murder second?* Then I realized Vance had not actually left but stood at the front door.

"Pulizzi," Vance said.

"Vance," Gabe said.

Shit. The two of them had gone into their wide-legged

cop stance with their chests stuck out, chins up and deep suspicion shooting out of their glares.

Ali lifted her head off the couch and whined.

Finally, Gabe said, "You could have gotten Sam killed."

Okay, now I got it. Gabe knew Vance had more or less set me up with Tristan. Setting the kitten on the couch, I stood. "Gabe, Vance couldn't know what Tristan would do." I lied because Vance had a gun, and there was a good chance Gabe had one as well. Both of them looked a little gun-happy to me.

Gabe didn't bother looking at me. "He knew. If he'd told me, I'd have been here with you instead of watching him go through the motions at the pet shop."

His words were rock hard. Gabe was pissed. Really pissed. I wasn't sure what to do.

"Get out of my way, Pulizzi," Vance ordered.

The temperature in the living room dropped ten degrees. My head throbbed, my throat ached and my muscles complained. I did not feel up to a pissing match. Glancing over at Ali, who had a sharp-eyed stare fixed on the kitten, I said, "You leave her alone." Then I stalked over to the men. "Cut it out."

They both turned to look at me.

Fury built up inside of me. "Vance." I glared at him. "Go home." Turning to Gabe, I said, "And you, get in here and stop acting like my father. If I have a problem with Vance using me as bait to catch a killer, I will tell him."

Gabe's winged brows shot up over his dark, annoyed eyes. Humor and anger shifted across his Italian features. Finally, he walked past Vance as if he didn't exist.

Vance stood there watching us.

I said, "Good-bye, Vance."

The detective hesitated another second, then left, closing the door behind him.

I turned back to Gabe.

He had his dark gaze fixed on me. *"Your father?"*

"What?" Now that I had a moment to study Gabe, I noticed how good he looked. Black jeans, long-sleeved oatmeal-colored shirt with the sleeves pushed up over his forearms. All stretched nicely over his long, lean and powerful body.

His lips twitched. "You accused me of acting like your father. That hurt, Babe." He crossed his arms over his chest and towered over me.

"Okay." I took a second to check out Ali. She was lying on the couch watching the kitten on the love seat. At least she wasn't drooling in anticipation of a kitten-snack. Returning my attention to Gabe, I knew damn well that he was playing with me. "Then you were acting like an old woman. That better? I can take care of myself, you know." Mostly I could. I'm not sure what would have happened if the cavalry hadn't shown up when they did yesterday. Tristan had been out cold on my kitchen floor, but for how long? Hate can be a potent motivator, and that man hated me.

Gabe snorted.

Suspicious, I demanded, "What does that mean? I defended myself yesterday."

His gaze softened. Uncrossing his arms, he reached out and touched my face. "Yeah. Not bad for a dating expert."

His hand was warm. "Really?" Damn! I wanted to bite my tongue. I was not a little girl looking for approval. I didn't need to rely on Gabe to tell me when I did good.

"It's the confusing me for your father, or an old woman, that's troubling."

I lifted my chin. "Then don't fight my battles, Gabe." I meant that. I had to fight my own battles.

"No dice, Sugar."

I snapped my head back. "What?" Not expecting a flat-out refusal, I took careful stock of him. The clenched jaw and slight bulge in his temples told me he was still angry. His hand on my face indicated that he was not mad at me.

"You heard me."

Damn. I was too tired and sore for a showdown. My feelings too raw. I swear to God, one day I was going to stupidly blurt them out to Gabe. "I heard you. Now you hear me—I do not need you to play hero for me!"

He arched a brow. "Did I play hero for you yesterday?"

"Yes."

"No."

I glared at him. "Is this opposite day? My kids play this game and I hate it!" One of them gets up in the morning and declares it opposite day so that they mean the opposite of everything they say. They compliment each other all day long.

"Let's call it *truth* day."

My frustration rose, swift and dangerous. "Fine, you want the truth?" *Shut up!* My brain screamed, but the steam of my frustration hissed over it. Slamming both my hands down on my hips, I ignored the achy burn in my throat. "I'll tell you the truth! I'm sick of guessing with you. Sick of guessing where you are, what you are doing and who the hell you're doing it with! And since you've declared this truth day, why don't you tell me the truth about your new career in scriptwriting. Any plans to move to Hollywood, Gabe?"

He winced. "That had to hurt your throat."

I sucked in a breath and damned if it didn't hurt. But I wasn't going to back off now. "Looks like the truth day thing isn't stacking up the way you planned."

He dropped his hand from my face and took a step closer.

Suddenly, I could smell his Irish Spring soap mixed with his anger. "Is it my turn, Sam? Or did you want to expand on your truths?"

Out of sheer stubborn bravado, I said, "No." But what I really wanted to do was take it all back. All of it. God, why couldn't I ever be smart with Gabe? Sophisticated? Maybe enjoy having a younger boyfriend without the foolish girl-fantasies? It took every last ounce of courage I had to hold my ground.

"Fine. You want to know where I am? Pick up the phone and call. You want to know who I'm with? Ask me. You want to know who I'm doing? Look in the mirror, 'cause you're it, Babe." His voice dropped and he leaned in. "You don't like me fighting your battles, too damn bad. As long as I'm breathing, there's no power on earth that'll stop me. Now you want to run that Hollywood shit by me again?"

I blinked, feeling the heat of his body only inches from mine. "Uh—" I frantically tried to think it out.

He uncoiled, putting his hands on my shoulders and leaning his head down until his forehead touched mine. "Sam, I lost my wife and baby in a hellish few minutes. Forever. After that, I went dead inside. That hero label from that bank robbery? What bullshit. I didn't care. Putting myself in front of a bullet was nothing to me, except that I knew dying would cause my mother, brothers and sister pain. Retiring from the Los Angeles Police Department was a relief. At least I could get away from L.A. Start over here. I figured I'd live out my life alone. Then I met you."

I shivered, in spite of his forehead resting against mine and his hands on my shoulder. The pain that Gabe lived with bled through his words. I'd have done anything for him to ease that. Even risk my own heart. I reached up both my hands to bring his mouth down to mine.

Instantly, Gabe reacted. One hand locked behind my head, and the other went around my back to land on my butt and yank me hard into his hips. His mouth seared mine. Both of us were breathing hard into a kiss that had turned primitive.

"Mom! Ali has the kitten!"

I unsealed my mouth from Gabe and looked around in a fog of lust. Blinking, I saw Joel, TJ and Grandpa all standing inside the opened front door, each holding a plastic bag of groceries. Cripes, some mother I was. I didn't even hear them come in!

Then Joel's words penetrated. Stepping out of Gabe's arms, I looked over to see Ali standing by the love seat holding the kitten in her mouth by the scruff of her neck. Her spindly legs stuck out at odd angles, and her eyes were huge in her head. She was spitting mad, too. Panic shot through me. "Ali! Don't you eat her!"

Ali dropped her head slightly, her ears going flat against her skull.

"Come here, Ali," I held out my hand. It was shaking.

Ali slunk over to me and set the kitten in my hand.

Relief flooded through me. I didn't want to keep the kitten, but I didn't want her to turn into dog food either. I wanted someone to materialize and take her home with them. I needed a magic solution.

"Come on, boys." Grandpa headed for the kitchen. "Help me set out the sandwich fixings. Adam and the others will be here soon. Sam, you sit down and rest."

"Uh, the door was open."

I turned around. Adam Miller stood there with Mindy and Dom. I was most surprised to see Dom, but I went to Adam first and hugged him.

"Samantha, I don't know how to thank you."

I started to answer but was interrupted by another voice, "So it's true then? You, Adam Miller, hired Samantha

Shaw to find your murdered wife's killer?" Leslie Lee, a.k.a. Lee Page, stuck a microphone attached to a black tape recorder between me and Adam.

Outrage poured through me. Lee Page had nothing to do with Tristan's insane killing, but she had been out to cannibalize Heart Mates and me to get her front-page story. She hadn't cared what Tristan's motives were as long as it got her recognition. The truth was not a priority for Lee Page. I stepped over to block Adam from her news-reporter claws. "Get out of here!"

She fixed a serious look on her perky face. "I'm only doing my job. I'm here to give you the opportunity to set the record straight. Give me the exclusive, Samantha, and I promise you the front page."

Adam started sneezing behind me. I turned to look at him and saw that everyone had left the kitchen to watch the confrontation. Gabe stood next to TJ, whispering something to him, but apparently deciding to let me fight my own battle.

This time.

Adam sneezed again, then set off into a string of sneezes. The kitten in my arms stood up on her spindly legs and hissed.

"Mom!" Joel yelled, "Ali's got a beer!"

I looked over in time to see that Ali had snagged Vance's half-drunk beer off the table and turned toward me to make her escape. I reacted quickly, turning and shoving the kitten at the reporter. Then I whirled back around to grab Ali's collar as she tried to snake by me.

Ali stopped cold and sat down. "Good girl," I told her, taking the bottle of beer and petting her. "I swear, Ali, I'll let you have some beer just as soon as it's safe."

I realized that poor Adam was still sneezing. Looking over, I opened my mouth to suggest that Mindy take him home when a loud, outraged shriek interrupted me. "Eek! It peed on me!"

Looking over at Lee Page holding the kitten away from her soaking-wet green silk blouse, I burst out laughing. Everyone around me laughed.

Joel rushed over and took the kitten.

Holding her silk blouse away from her body, Lee Page said, "Well, Samantha? Are you going to give me the exclusive to this story?"

I stopped laughing and looked at her. "I believe the kitten gave you my answer."

She stormed out of the house.

Joel gathered up the animals and secured them in another part of the house so Adam's allergies would calm down.

Gabe's arm came around my shoulder. I looked up at him. "Is this what you want, Gabe? This kind of chaos?"

He modeled his sinful grin. "Hell, Babe, I'm just grateful that you're not the one smelling like cat pee this time."

Please turn the page for a sneak peek at
Samantha Shaw's next adventure,
NINJA SOCCER MOMS,
coming in May 2004
from Kensington Books!

I drove my 1957 Thunderbird across town to the Stater Bros. shopping center. Chad Tuggle had his independent insurance office squished between the Stater Bros. grocery store and Rapid Dry Cleaners. As I got out of my car, I looked down at my short black skirt that covered most of my thighs. Over my silk black camisole I had on a man's white shirt tied at the waist. My calf-high black suede boots added a little fun to the outfit.

It had been a long time since I'd seen Chad. I was going on what Janie told me about him. Before I could think myself out of it, I walked up to the glass-fronted suite and pulled open the door.

Sophie, Chad's part-time secretary, was not at her small desk facing the door, so she had to be off today. Chad's big cherry wood desk took up the right half of the office. It was a three-sided unit, like a rectangle with one end left open. The big desk faced out to see people coming in the door. Chad's computer sat on the small part of the desk lined up against a partition wall that separated the front and back of the office suite. Then against the far right wall was a credenza that had fancy office machines on the left side. The right side of the credenza had a bunch of soccer trophies. The three huge gold cups on fat bases took center stage—the championship trophies.

I didn't recognize the set of stone bookends that had been cut and painted to resemble soccer balls. Those must be new, probably a gift from his latest championship team.

The wall over the credenza had pictures of Chad with his teams, winning and appreciation plaques and framed newspaper articles. The championship-winning hero coach was not necessarily a humble coach.

And where was the not-so-humble coach?

"Sam—that you? I didn't know anyone was out here. What brings you by?"

The loud voice yanked me from my thoughts. I'd forgotten about Chad's tendency to talk loud. The years of yelling directions to kids in a soccer game over screaming, insane parents had left its mark. He came out from behind the divider wall carrying an *Everybody Loves the Coach* mug. Obviously Chad had been in the back getting some coffee in the little kitchenette behind the partition. "Chad, how are you? I just stopped by to chat about insurance if you're not busy."

"I'm never too busy for you, Sam. Come sit down and we'll catch up. Then we'll talk insurance."

Chad walked around his desk with an easy, athletic grace. He wore dark gray slacks, a light blue short-sleeved button-down shirt and tie. His forearms were muscled and tanned. Lots of time outdoors. Instead of fighting premature balding, he cut what hair he had into a buzz. With his light green eyes, he didn't need hair. Hovering on the back end of his thirties, he kept himself in good shape.

Chad set down his coffee cup on his desk blotter then said, "Hey, how about some coffee? I just made it."

Sitting in the barrel chair facing the desk, I slid my purse to the ground and crossed my legs. My black skirt slid up. "Uh, not right now, thanks." I flashed him a smile, only to find him staring at my thighs.

Finally, his gaze climbed to my face. "So, Sam, how's business at the dating service?"

"Well," I took a deep breath and pulled the tied ends of my white blouse down. "It takes time to build a client base. Word of mouth is helping us grow. In fact, I'm looking at getting a new computer program for book-keeping."

"Really? What program do you use now?"

He was making this too easy. "Peach Tree."

"Yeah, that's good, but I like using the Excel work-sheet. Here let me show you." He turned in his chair and called up a computer program.

I leaned across his desk, getting a whiff of coffee and strong spearmint. Did he have a lifetime supply of Altoids in his desk drawer? I had to fight a twitching smile at the mental picture of Chad popping Altoids for that minty-fresh breath all bellowing coaches needed.

Or was it cheating coaches?

He turned his head. "Can you see from there? Come around and you can see better."

I got up and looked down at my purse. The disk was in there. But first I had to get him to pull up the soccer program and think of a way to get him to leave for a few minutes. Up to now it had been easier than I expected. Luck like that wouldn't hold for long. Leaving my purse on the floor, I walked around the desk and leaned over Chad's right shoulder.

"See, here's the program." He opened files and de-scribed the functions.

I only half listened while my mind spun. How could I get him to open the soccer books? *Think!* "Chad, can you keep accounts for two businesses on there? I mean like say your insurance business, then another enterprise of some sort?"

He leaned back to look at me, accidentally brushing his face against my breasts.

Resisting the urge to jump back, I forced myself to smile at him. I don't remember Chad ever being this aggressively carnal. Guess I didn't measure up to his cop-a-feel standards back in my team mom days.

"Sure, I use the same program to keep the SCOLE books."

Bingo! "You do? Could I see that?"

He closed the files for his insurance records and opened the one for SCOLE while chatting away. "You know Sam, it might be fun for the two of us to go out to dinner sometime. Or maybe have drinks at Don Jose's. Hey, after dinner I could show you my new digital camera. We could do some test shots and I'll show you how it works . . . for your dating service. Or we could use my new camcorder. I even know how to download videos to the computer."

And I bet you'd bring your spearmint Altoids or whatever was seeping out from his desk. "I thought you were dating—" I couldn't think of her name. I could picture her—the soccer mom slut. Every team had one. The mom that came to every practice in short shorts and tank tops and schmoozed with the coach while the other moms sat in a lawn-chair circle and chatted. This one had succeeded in getting the coach away from his wife. What was her name? She had a belly-button ring, which was too daring even for me. "Dara." That was her name.

His neck turned red. "Sure we date, but it's not exclusive or anything. Janie told some pretty ugly lies about Dara and me. Ah, here's the files for SCOLE." They opened up on the screen.

Lies, my ass. But I had a job to do here. And I was going to need money to promote Heart Mates and pay my bills. Then there was Blaine's salary. Plus, I really wanted to help Janie get a little revenge. "Yes, I see. You're very good at this stuff. Did you take classes? Go to college?"

His shoulders puffed up. "I taught myself. I can teach you how to do this, Sam."

Liar, liar, pants on fire. I knew for a fact that Janie took night classes to learn about bookkeeping and this program when she had been the treasurer. She taught Chad. "That's awfully nice of you, Chad." I leaned closer, brushing against his shoulder to study the files while I tried to think of how to get him out of the office for a few minutes. Or at least in the back. I saw his cup of coffee sitting on his blotter. "You know, maybe I will have something to drink."

He tilted his head back. "Coffee?"

There was a doughnut shop across the parking lot. "Actually, I'd love some hot chocolate." Would he be dumb enough to run to the doughnut shop and get me hot chocolate?

"I have hot chocolate in the back. Won't take a minute to nuke some water and make it for you." He reached toward the keyboard.

I laid my hand on his bare forearm.

His gaze snapped up to mine.

"Could I look at this while you make the hot chocolate?" Would that give me enough time?

"Sure. Look all you want and I'll explain how to use the software when I come back." He got up from the chair.

There wasn't much room inside the three-sided desk. I backed up to the credenza. Chad brushed so close to me that his spicy cologne mixed with my passion fruit lotion.

"It sure is nice to see you again, Sam. We've missed you in the soccer circles." His gaze dropped down to my breasts. "You're looking good these days. Real good."

I wanted to throw a drool cloth over my bust. It was a struggle to arrange my face into a simpering expression. "Uh, yeah, you too, Chad."

His grin radiated self-assurance as he reached up to touch my hair. "So is it true, do blondes really have more fun?"

I hear better lines at my dating service. "They get more thirsty," I said pointedly, to get him to leave.

He turned and headed around the desk.

Relief spread through me, but I had no time to enjoy it. Once Chad disappeared around the partition, I raced to my purse, dug out the disk and went back to the computer. I would make a copy of the SCOLE books and then leave before Chad got back out with the hot chocolate. I'd claim I got a call on my cell phone . . . or another excuse. Jamming the disk into the proper-sized hole, I guided the mouse through the clicks to save the file to the 'A' drive.

The computer groaned and hissed. A little rectangle graph popped up, slowly filling with blue as it saved to the disk.

The blue stretched to the quarter mark. "Come on," I begged. From the back, I heard a short slam, like a microwave door, then beeps as Chad set the timer to heat water for the hot chocolate.

The graph hit the halfway mark. I squirmed on the chair. "Faster."

"Hey Sam, did I tell you that Mark made JV on the

soccer team at school?" Chad's loud voice carried over the room divider.

Three-quarters done. The microwave beeped and I heard the microwave door pulled open. *Answer him!* "That's terrific, Chad. Mark's a great kid and a talented soccer player." Almost there. The blue stripe hovered only a millimeter away from the finish line.

Clinks and other sounds came from the back, followed by Chad's voice. "I really think he'll get a college scholarship. I've hired him a private soccer coach."

The blue line filled up the rectangle. *Done!* I yanked the disk out and heard more movement from the back. Was Chad coming out? Damn, no time to get to my purse. I whirled around to the credenza and the slim disk flew out of my fingers. It clattered against the glass front of a team picture then landed on the credenza behind the fax machine.

Heat burned up my face and prickled under my arms. I heard Chad moving around, so he must still be doing something in the kitchen. I had seconds. I leaned over a machine to reach behind the fax and get the disk.

Just as my fingers closed around the disk I heard the whirring of a machine starting up.

Freezing, I thought, *What the hell was that?* But I had no time to worry about it. I shoved the disk into the built in bra of my black camisole. I had to get out of here.

But that noise kept going. A grinding. . . . Suddenly I realized I was being pulled down.

The paper shredder! Ohmigod, the tied shirttails of my white top were caught in the shredder! The machine was eating my shirt! Full-blown panic blossomed into fight-or-flight. I grabbed the knot in my shirt and yanked.

The shredder wouldn't let go. It was set flush into the credenza and kept pulling me forward. Cripes, now what?

Wait, there had to be a cut-off switch. I leaned forward, looking around the face of the machine. I couldn't find a switch. And worse, the plastic disk in my bra was slipping.

The grinding noise began to sputter in anger. The knot! The shredder was sucking in the tied lump, fraction by fraction, separating it and consuming it. I had to get out of the shirt or the machine was going to yank me down into its grinding blades.

"Sam! What . . ."

I turned my head to see Chad materialize next to me, holding a can of whipped cream and looking confused. "It attacked me!"

His face cleared. "Hold on," he said, then crouched down and put a hand on my leg to move me over. He opened a cupboard door and reached inside.

The machine stopped.

I let out a huge breath in relief and did a little test tug on my shirt.

The silent shredder held on tight. I could see tears running up from the mangled knot like runs in a pair of pantyhose. The disk slipped a fraction more in my bra. I blinked and hysterical laughter tickled my throat. Oh yeah, some slick private investigator I was—exposed by a paper shredder!